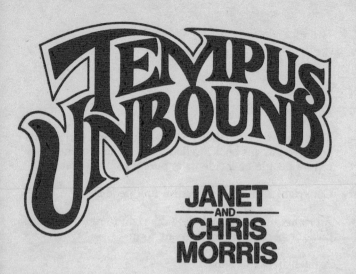

TEMPUS UNBOUND

JANET
AND
CHRIS
MORRIS

D1559771

TEMPUS UNBOUND

Copyright © 1989 by Paradise Productions

A Baen Books Original

Baen Publishing Enterprises
260 Fifth Avenue
New York, N.Y. 10001

ISBN: 0-671-69852-4

Cover art by Gary Ruddell

First printing, December 1989

Distributed by
SIMON & SCHUSTER
1230 Avenue of the Americas
New York, N.Y. 10020

Printed in the United States of America

HORSE FROM HELL

The door to the stable slid back and a great light and heat enveloped him. From that light came an adversary such as Tempus had only met in dreams.

The thing that reared up out of the light and bore down upon him was a demon horse, or a demon in the shape of a horse. This horse was scaled and it had raking talons where its fetlocks should be. It had snakes for mane and snakes for tail, and its tongue was long and forked.

It had blazing eyes and was headed straight for him.

Another heartbeat, another stride, and it was reaching out with its jaws wide and its snake-mane striking and its forked tongue questing.

He jumped for its neck, and caught hold of the snakes in its mane. It bellowed fury but couldn't stay its great, galloping strides. He ran one pace with it, then jumped for its back as its front legs hit the ground.

The snakes were biting him, this he knew, but the poison of the snakes was so profuse in his blood that not even Enlil could forfend it. It was all Tempus could do to keep his seat, bareback, on the scaled horse from hell as it careened into the barn.

And then the seed of destruction exploded in the barn where he'd thrown it, taking everything, including Tempus, with it. . . .

Chapter 1:

MAD GODS AND LEMURIANS

Up from the island's shore, where the quays were, a sheer wall protected the city's heart. One day when the sun was settling into an especially soft bed of purple cloud and setting the city's walls ablaze with particularly beautiful rays of persimmon and citrine and rose, a stranger rode a dappled horse up to the gates and pounded upon one huge bronze hinge with the butt of his spear.

"Who goes there?" demanded the sentry; actually, he said, "What goes thither?" but the stranger's ears were very old and sharp with god-given knowledge, and he made the translation nearly without thought.

"Tempus the Black," the stranger replied. "The Riddler, Favorite of the Storm God, Supreme Commander, Commander of Sacred Bands, Avatar of Enlil, the Hero." None of this was exactly true, and none false, but it fit the custom of the type of country in which he found himself, and its circumlocutions might help him evade certain other, nastier questions.

But the guard whose plated helmet reflected sunlight as he peered over the wall was not satisfied. He was well-trained; he held back the signal to open the gates.

"Where from, Lord Tempus?" Spoken in the sentry's native tongue, the phrase became, *Lord of Time*.

Which was, Tempus supposed, more true than most things said about him. "Late of the City at the Edge of Time," Tempus replied, his patience, never long, snapping so that his voice rattled like gravel on a battleplain as chariot wheels race over it. "A place without a lesser name, at the end of all questions."

The soldier's helmet dipped, as if he craned his neck for a better look at the man on the horse below. Another helmeted man joined him; the two put their heads together.

Tempus was just deciding to rein his horse around and ride back the way he'd come when the newcomer's voice rang out: "And where to, Lord Tempus?"

"What place is this?" the Riddler called back, parrying one question with another. Under him, his Tros horse danced restlessly: there were mares behind those walls, at least. And probably soft beds, rich food, warm shelter. The storm that had brought him to the island's edge was close behind. He could feel its wet breath upon his neck. Soon enough, those on the walls would see its thunderheads swallow the stars.

By the time the storm broke, he must know if he would tarry here awhile or let the storm carry him onward.

"Lemuria," answered the second man on the ramparts. On the heels of his words, distant thunder pealed.

But Tempus had heard him. He ran a hand down his horse's neck as it snorted in response to the thunder. Sweat was breaking out on its shoulder. Time to decide.

The sun was settling behind the walls of Lemuria, backlighting the two men on its ramparts, turning the pair of polished helmets into diadems of fire.

Another clap of thunder pealed and the very air shuddered. Past time to decide. "Lemuria before the fall, or after?" Tempus called to the men above, more as a word of warning to the gods than because he thought these soldiers knew the answer.

They didn't. They conferred between themselves, looking past Tempus, back the way he and the storm had come. Then the first soldier made a sign; the winch of the gatepost began to whine. The second leaned over the wall's crenel and called softly, "Lord Tempus, welcome to Year's End. I'll meet you inside."

The welcome was what decided Tempus. Without it, he might yet have let the storm carry him on, to another place, another time—whatever alternative the god had in his heart.

But a welcome from Lemuria was nothing to take lightly. Driven before the storm that had deposited him on this shore, Tempus awaited no further sign. A welcome from Lemuria, a refuge from an endless trek through timeless clouds: Perhaps the Storm God Enlil was not angry at Tempus any longer. And the god had nothing against the Tros horse, after all.

They had been long in the wind, long in the rain, with a prince of the City in tow for a time not worth remembering, or forgetting. When they had shed the prince, they had shed all earthly ties. Or so it seemed then.

Riding through the timber gates of Lemuria, Tempus tried not to wonder why it was here that the Storm God had blown them.

In his head was silence where the god's voice used to be. And in that silence, his own mind suggested that anyplace real was better than the nowhere of the god's clouds. Lemuria at any time was surely better than the Land of Dreams, where his sister reigned as queen of Meridian, and his own verisimilitude might be threatened.

The man who had served the Storm God for centuries without sleep or respite had shed all encumbrances, all ties, but those of his basic humanity. His mind said it was this root thirst for life which had rebounded him back into it, and not the god's will at all.

The clouds of Enlil were racing down his back as the gates closed behind him. His Tros horse pawed the ground and shivered at the screech of machinery and the thunder of a cruel and insatiable god.

If Enlil had put man on this earth and hunger in

man's heart to sate the god's lusts, then had the stormclouds of heaven responded to Tempus's loneliness by bringing him here, or to Enlil's quest for vicarious thrills?

Were all gods voyeurs, or only his tutelary god? Was this the Lemuria of antiquity, or that of times to come?

Once you'd ridden the stormclouds of heaven from the edge of time, anything was possible.

Anything, that was, except the god having no hand in his coming here. He stroked the horse until it calmed, sitting quietly astride it, looking neither right nor left, until the soldier from the ramparts descended to meet him there, as they'd agreed.

This was the watch captain, Tempus was nearly certain, when the man came up with a horseman's eye upon the Tros and a clipboard in his hand.

"Lord Tempus, please accept our hospitality," said the watch captain formally. "Year's End custom dictates your welcome." The soldier's voice said he wasn't pleased with that particular custom; Tempus heard wariness and suspicion, recognition of the sort of man being welcomed—the sort of man who came into an unfamiliar city with a full panoply of weapons, armed and armored in eclectic and expensive style.

The watch captain's gear was equally strange to Tempus's eye. His helmet, seen close at hand, was devoid of crest or nosepiece, bereft of decoration as was his dark, mottled tunic, cinched with a weaponsbelt and worn over leggings tucked into cavalry boots.

"Hospitality accepted, soldier, for however long it's extended. Life to you, as we say in my country." But no more of the formula would pass his lips, not here, not now. Lemuria of wondrous knowledge, was this? "Just tell me what kind of welcome you mean."

From his tunic, the watch captain took a sheaf of papers, sorted through them, made a mark on his clipboard, and handed Tempus an envelope. "All you'll need for tonight's in there: lodging coupon, map of the city, suggested itinerary, calendar of events, guest cards.

You're the seventh stranger, in before sundown. Strangers arriving at Year's End are our special guests—talismans of luck and fate, welcome anywhere and everywhere. We ask only that you seven dine together at the ninth bell, up at Pinnacle House, as guests of the Evening Star, our chief counsellor. You'll do this?"

"A guest honors his hosts' customs," Tempus replied. "Where's a good place to stable my horse?"

And so it began, as the god would have it, on New Year's Eve in Lemuria. The Tros horse was content with his stall, the straw was fresh and the sweet feed was a mix that Tempus could have subsisted on himself if all else failed. The water in the horse's stall was clear and pure and replenished itself with a soft gurgle whenever the horse took a drink or Tempus filled a sea sponge to bathe the trail and cloud dirt from the dapple's coat.

When he'd done with the horse's bath, he rubbed the stallion down with clean straw and lugged his tack outside to a trunk before the stall. It was empty. He locked it and took the key. Lights had come on in the stable by then, soft glowing globes that neither flickered nor smoked, though there was a whole line of them spaced between the box stalls.

He'd seen no grooms, no stableboys, but there were other horses in the stable.

He saw few souls on the streets, either coming here or going now, as he left, headed toward the inn in front. This inn was called the Day's End, and he'd chosen it at random, not consulting the list in his pocket, just looking for a likely stable.

Crossing its deserted threshold, he told himself that the folk hereabouts were all indoors preparing for their celebration of New Year, however it was done in Lemuria.

Behind the front desk was a maiden, under another of the globes of light which did not flicker. Lighted globes of any sort were rare globes of power in places

he'd stayed before; sorcerers' tools in upcountry strong-
holds. Here, they were everywhere.

The maiden was still growing into womanhood, chastely
dressed, covered to the neck. Her hair was as short as a
boy's. She took his guest chit without hesitation, calling
him "Lord Tempus," as the sentry had, with a smile to
soften the sound of it.

The sound of it reminded him of how arduous a path
had led him here: in this tongue, so ancient, Lord of
Time had a meaning deeper than that he'd intended
when he'd chosen it, so long ago, in a simpler land he
could never find again unless the god so decreed.

The maiden said, "Lord Tempus, if there's anything
you need, just give us a call." She handed him a different card, with holes punched in a pattern on it. "Your
key."

He took it without comment.

She was looking at him still, in that way people have
that tells you they have more to say.

So he prompted, "Yes?"

And she said, "We have a safe here, but none in your
room, if you'd like to leave your valuables or . . ."

"Or?"

"Your . . . ah . . . weapons?"

"I wouldn't like that," he said, and headed for the
stairs to find the room that matched the number on his
card.

This was as strange a place as he'd ever been, and yet
there was no need to attribute more than truth to the
legends of Lemuria in order to explain the strangeness.
Lemuria, it had long been said, was pssesse dof great
wisdom, wondrous knowledge, undreamed comfort for
the body and the soul. Perhaps the god was granting
him a respite, a reprieve from wading through mankind's follies, up to his neck in fools and blood.

But perhaps not. Enlil was the Trickster. And the
storm was nigh.

He opened the shutters on his window once he'd
found his room and learned the trick of using the card

to open the door by shoving it quickly in and out of a slot below the doorknob.

The shutters were easier: they opened like any shutters in any place he'd ever been, and they let in the massing storm to blow around the room and moisten the featherbed, the side table, the fruit and flowers on the desk.

"Enlil?" He called the god's name softly; it rumbled in his chest. Only distant thunder answered.

He stood before the window in the wet wind, looking up at the sky as the stars disappeared. For the first time in far too long he was abroad in the world of men with only himself and his horse to succor and protect. It was a release beyond measure that this was so, and a smile quirked his normally tight-drawn lips.

When he turned away from the window and bolted the shutters against the rising gale, the mirror above the desk was fogged with moisture.

In it, he looked unscarred by time. With his image softened by the mist, he might have again been the intense young philosopher who'd sinned against heaven and hell and been sent, accursed, wandering in the world forever. His yarrow-honey hair had grown as long as it had been then; he'd clubbed it back. His high brow was yet unlined and the eyes in his head stared back at him, long and full of the god, who'd lent Tempus his very face—or stolen his likeness and put it upon a thousand temples, once their bond was forged.

Enlil had put into him the strength and speed of immortality, and taken in trade his sleep and his heart. Once, Tempus had thought the Storm God to be his only safety from the evils of hell and a wizard's curse. He'd supplicated Enlil upon his knees, and the god had struck a bargain with His supplicant, a young man full of hubris and rage.

If the god had thought, back then, to teach him humility, the god had erred. Tempus had taken on Enlil's attributes, and the god had found in Tempus a fractious ally.

If the sorcerers he'd known had had their way, he'd have been powdered bone, longsince. But he'd shed the curse put on him by an archmage, despite all wizardry could do against him. Now only the god, whom he'd made an ally to withstand the curse, remained. But the god had enemies in the Underworld and, out of habit, the god's enemies were his.

He'd played heaven and hell against each other for centuries, on battlefield after battlefield, and never suffered more than he could personally bear— or less.

As he left for the dinner he'd agreed to attend, he wondered whether it might not be better to leave his weapons, as the maiden had suggested, to accommodate convention. Or so as not to tempt fate.

But Tempus did not disarm. He went to the dinner as he'd come to Lemuria: in full panoply, leather and weaponsbelt, lacking only shield, spear, and leopard mantle, which he'd left with his horse in the stable.

When a man is a newcomer to a strange country, it serves no purpose to pretend otherwise.

Or so he thought until he reached Pinnacle House and met his dinner companions.

Chapter 2:

AS GUEST OF THE EVENING STAR

Pinnacle House was ashimmer. A thousand candles burned in man-high chandeliers; mirrors played tricks upon the eye. Indoor plants stretched skyward, where balconies crisscrossed high above a tall man's head. Banners wafted there, brightly colored flags and tattered standards, barely more than streamers from forgotten wars.

The flags of Pinnacle House hid the ceiling with their red and green and blue and white and yellow silk. There were dogs in the house as big as ponies, with square muzzles and alert brown eyes. The dogs roamed loose and though dogs in a home were not sacreligious, as dogs were in a temple, Tempus was from a tradition that held dogs to be unclean.

He would have dispatched them on the spot if those who greeted him at the door had not heeled the beasts, who beat their tails and pricked their ears at him and whined.

The glowing globes were here too, he noticed, though their steady light was dwarfed by the candles everywhere.

A servitor in a black tunic with a white undershirt led him from the antechamber where the dogs still sat on marble tiles like statuary, through a greater atrium where the storm blew whistling and hidden chimes chattered in the wind, into a dining room with a blazing hearth.

Three women and a man stood by the head-high mantlepiece in heavy, ornate clothing too warm for the room. Each held a crystal goblet. One of the women was laughing.

The pleasant sound of the woman's laugh continued for a moment after the buzz of conversation had stopped. Then she too fell silent.

The eyes of the four rested on him as the servitor suggested, "This way, my lord," and led him toward them.

"Lord Tempus, Favorite of the Storm God, Commander of—"

"Tempus will do," he interrupted, and the servitor bowed with an annoyed flourish and stepped out of his way.

The woman with the pleasant laugh was tall and athletic under her black velvet, which hugged her torso and showed a flash of creamy breast. "Lord Tempus, I'm your host this evening, Pinnacle House's Evening Star." She held out a hand and he took it, for the first time in ages uncertain as to what he was supposed to do.

But she squeezed his fingers firmly and he squeezed back, then let her pull away. "Call me Chiara. Let me introduce you to my friends, and then we'll find the others at the bar."

She gestured to the first of the other women. He hadn't noticed anything about the others since Chiara, the Evening Star, had taken his hand and squeezed it.

A witch can do that to you with a touch. A sorceress can cause all but her person to fade to insignificance. But he was not wary of Chiara's magic, if magic it was. She had an ageless face of triangular beauty, a regal nose, a surprisingly sensual mouth that gave disturbing color to a pale face. Her eyes were luminous brown, like the eyes of the great dogs in the front hall, and as steady on him.

She was saying, "Tiye, Queen of the Upper and the Lower Lands," as she pointed to a smaller, dark-skinned woman in a heavily embroidered sheath and cloak.

He bowed from the waist before the tiny woman. The title meant nothing to him.

"And Faun, daughter of the Sun, Shepherd of Sandia." This third woman was nearly as tall as Chiara. Her skirt and laced bodice were of softest skins, sueded and bleached bone white. She murmured a greeting, and his name on her lips softened the sound; her accent had a lilt he could almost place.

When Tempus looked away from Faun's pale blue eyes, Chiara was again holding out her hand to him.

"And this, my friend Tempus, is Zimri-Lim, King of Mari, a great warrior like yourself."

Tempus would have touched hands with the swarthy, stocky man in robes, but the other saluted him first.

He answered back by touching his fist to his heart, as the other man had greeted him, though it was not the greeting of men of the armies in any place he'd been. Still, the difference between men and women was being stated. The recognition of a warrior could not be ignored.

Zimri-Lim said, "Commander, it's good to have you with us. I thought I'd find no one to swap stories with among these barbarians." And he took a sip of pale liquid from the crystal goblet he held, thin as a sword's point and clear as pure water.

Tempus had no more knowledge of Mari than he did of Sandia, or the Upper and Lower Lands, but he knew that they'd discussed him before his arrival: he'd not let the servitor finish reciting the string of titles he'd given at the outer gate, yet this king called him "Commander."

And then they all did: "Yes, Commander, tell us of your journey here, and of where you've been before," said tiny Tiye imperiously.

"Tell us what the weather's like outside," Faun proposed instead with a narrowing of her blue eyes. "Is it

going to storm, do you think? Did you come out of the
rain from the south?"

"Tell us later," Zimri-Lim decreed. "We've all night
for stories. I'm hungry." He turned to the woman who
was called the Evening Star, chief counsellor of Lemuria,
and said, "Chiara, our friend the commander hasn't met
the others."

"I was about to suggest that. Lord Tempus, if you'll
come with me . . . ?"

He took the arm that the woman held out to him,
feeling suddenly large and ungainly, telling himself that
this was a dinner for strangers and none of these knew
more than he about the protocols for the evening.

Or about this place, with its globes of light and its
great mirrors and its gargantuan hearth. When Chiara
led him through a door and down three steps, what he
saw nearly took his breath away.

Pinnacle House was high on Lemuria's cliff face, but
he hadn't expected a wall of glass to be all that kept out
the wind and the sea. No place he'd ever visited had
the skill to fashion such a wall, or to be unconcerned
that the storm's rage might shatter it.

Before that wall were three men, drinking from smaller
glasses, each dressed in a variation of the tight tunic
and leggings he'd seen on the watch captain. One was
of Tempus' own stature, and his face was turned away
as he stared out at the drop to the sea. The second had
marksman's eyes and they fixed upon Tempus with a
coldly analytical stare. The third smiled, straightened
his gray-clad shoulders, and came forth with an outstretched hand to give Tempus the same greeting that
Chiara had.

"I'm Rath," said the friendly guest as they clasped
hands. "You must be Tempus. We've been hearing
about you. Now that you're here, we can begin."

Before Tempus could ask what they'd been hearing
and from whom, this man, who had a disarming way
about him and a youthful air belied by his weathered
face, turned to his companion with the steady stare and

said, "Mano, greet the commander and finish your drink. Time to eat."

The man with the marksman's eyes never took them from Tempus's face as he tossed off the ruddy liquid in his short glass in one swallow and held the glass out to one side.

From a dark corner, a servant scurried to take the emptied tumbler.

"Life to you, Riddler, and all that goes with it," said Mano, and wiped his lips with the back of his hand. This one was a professional soldier of some sort, Tempus was certain by his bearing, by the way his head sat upon his neck, and by the nuances of carriage and attitude that a lifetime of watching one's back instills in a man. He had a barrel chest and large head, graying hair, and a strange weaponsbelt slung on his hip. And he knew the formula of mercenary greeting that men used in the lands Tempus had so recently left.

Yet it had sounded strange to him, partly because of the accent, which he could not place, partly because Mano had not completed the phrase in the customary fashion.

The third man still stared out the window. Tempus waited no longer for him to turn around. He knew who the man was now; the tilt of the head might have been enough, if they'd been alone. His presence explained why the others had heard tell of Tempus, if not what.

Among so many strangers, perhaps he should have recognized this familiar form sooner. Yet of all those present, the one man whose name Tempus knew was the one he knew least well.

At least the others were human—so far as he could tell. Tempus said quietly, "And you, Ash? No greeting for an old acquaintance?"

The immortal lord of dreams did not look at Tempus, but continued to stare out the window. The others moved away, talking among themselves concertedly, as Chiara called them to the table.

Only when the chatter diminished did the tall man

with gray-starred hair say over his shoulder, "I hoped I'd find you here." —

And Tempus, without moving one step closer said, "You mean you didn't contrive it? This?" His eyes swept the room again, so strange and quiet in its strength and power.

"This meeting? No. Why should I? In Lemuria? Are you here looking for her too?"

Tempus's skin grew tight all over his body. His throat dried up and his spittle turned acid. He took a deep breath and exhaled it before he said, "She's gone, then? From Meridian?"

Tempus didn't need to ask what 'she' the other man was referring to: before him stood Askelon of Meridian, lord of dreams, entelechy of the seventh sphere, one-time husband of Tempus' nemesis, Cime.

Cime. Cime was gone from Meridian, abroad in the world. Cime was Tempus' sister, by some's reckoning; foster or not, the bond was there. She was his beloved, from which all curses and all ruination had sprung when they were young. She was his most hated rival, a killer of men who meddled with magic. She'd been tempered in a crucible of destruction beyond anything Tempus had undergone. And now she was gone from the land of dreams. "Does she have her rods?" he wanted to know.

Her weapons. Two rods of power, diamond rods she wore in her hair that he was sure had been lost to her. But then, he'd been sure that Ash and she had come to terms.

"Or their equivalent, yes." The dream lord shrugged his shoulders. The movement rippled his cloak as if he were a dog shedding water. Now he did turn. "I'm not asking you to do anything about this, I want to make that clear. I merely thought that you should know."

"And our meeting here? You still insist it's coincidence, not your contrivance?" If Ash had brought him here, this place was more dangerous than he'd suspected. If Ash had convened this meeting, the entire

Lemuria he'd been wandering might be a figment, an unreality, Meridian dressed up for a masquerade ball.

"Not the way you mean," said the man whose likeness overlooked a sea and whose domain was not of this earth, or any other, except once in a thousand years. Askelon had gray eyes that matched his gray-starred hair and a sadness to him that always made Tempus want to put him out of his misery.

Cime had almost managed that once. Tempus had failed at every try.

"Then how is it we meet here?" he asked the dream lord, unafraid of anything Ash could do to him personally: Tempus couldn't sleep; Askelon's domain was dream. And yet, even reminding himself of that, a chill went through him. He could walk away now, leave the dinner, leave Lemuria, saddle his Tros horse and ride back into the storm.

The Storm God loved him, after all. The god would take him up in those maelstrom arms and put him down some other place, horse and all, safe and sound. This might be the last moment for a long while that he could escape what fate had in store.

"Then how?" he asked Ash again.

The dream lord came one step toward him.

Tempus put out a forestalling hand.

Ash stopped and nodded gravely. "All right. I know you're angry. What's done cannot be undone. Let's sit and break bread together and see if we can answer your question."

"Now, Ash."

"I swear I didn't contrive to get you here. Your god and your heart did that. I can reach this place, however, and there are many right now which I cannot. Meridian is not in a phase state that makes it easy to be in your world. So if you came here and I came here, one might suppose that your god facilitated this meeting."

"Or one might suppose that time, being different for Meridian and the world, was amenable to your manipulation."

"You didn't have to go anywhere near a place I could reach you. But you did. And now you know she's out there, somewhere. What you do, or don't do, about Cime is up to you."

"You're not asking me to bring her back to you? Because I won't." Tempus crossed his arms.

"Heavens forfend. I don't want her back, unless there's no other option for the benefit of all. Which I doubt. I renounce all claim, on this spot, in this moment. I just thought . . ." Ash shrugged again and the familiar gesture made Tempus's thoughts ripple with memories as if a deck of cards were being shuffled before his eyes.

"You thought what, dreammonger?" Tempus growled, the hairs on his neck standing on end.

Outside, the first bolt of lightning was loosed from heaven. Behind Ash, the cliffs and the sea were daybright for an instant. Then darkness returned.

"I just thought you deserved a warning. This *is* Lemuria on Year's End night, after all. The universe can change here forever, in an instant. Every soul who wanders in here is here for the casting of a lot, the forging of a fate, the making of a decision which will rebound throughout eternity. Surely, as ignorant as you are of the arcane, even you know that."

"I . . . suspected as much. So what? Enlil brought me here, so far as I knew. That was before I saw your ugly face." Now it was Tempus's turn to leave.

He started for the door through which he'd come.

Chiara appeared to bar his path, a startling, radiant and imperious presence. "Lord Tempus? Askelon? Dinner is served."

"I'm not . . . " Tempus began.

Chiara interrupted, and her hand came down upon his arm. "Of course you're hungry, and we've been dawdling. You must accept my apologies. It's terribly bad luck to have an unhappy guest on this special evening. And we have so many matters to discuss.

Come, we can't have the Council short its quorum."
Smiling sweetly, she waved him ahead of her.

Ash was on his heels. "See?" whispered the dream
lord as he came abreast.

"Quorum?" Tempus wanted to know. "Council?"

"Every guest pays for his supper one way or another
in this world, Riddler," the dream lord whispered nas-
tily. "Surely you hadn't forgotten that?"

The woman was still hovering ahead of him, herding
them deftly into her dining room.

He wanted to demand whether she knew whom it
was she had here, in the person of the dream lord. But
then, he could have asked the same about himself. And
no doubt, of these others, if he'd been familiar with
their histories.

Lemuria: before the fall, or after. Suddenly he knew
it didn't matter at all, that Lemuria was everyplace it
had ever been, contiguously present, simply out of
phase with the rest of reality.

Ash had admitted that much.

So Tempus wasn't in the world at all. Not yet. And as
he sat to that table with those cultured folks who could
look the dream lord calmly in the eye and not flinch,
Tempus wanted desperately to be in the world, at any
cost. He owed the Tros horse that much, even if he
didn't owe it to himself.

Then the Evening Star sat him on her right hand and
began flirting with him so overtly that he was uncomfortable, worried that the god would notice, and have
His appetite for carnality whetted by that means.

Once the god got started, this dinner party could
become something quite different in the blink of an
eye.

So he looked away and saw Faun, the blue-eyed
beauty from Sandia, in her pale gown of softest skins.
And he said to the god in his head, "If you must,
choose this one."

And no more. One didn't ravish one's host, of this he

was quite certain. Not when one's host was the Evening Star of Lemuria. Even if one's host was asking for it.

Not if you shared a body with the Storm God, you didn't.

The Evening Star said, picking up a goblet as thin as the shell of an egg, "A toast to our Year guests, one and all: may you find the answers you seek before morning."

Tempus drank, and clinked glasses, but did not repeat the toast. He wasn't sure he wanted answers. Before he'd encountered Ash here, he wasn't even sure he had questions.

Chapter 3:

THE CASTING OF A LOT

After dinner, Chiara served yet another wine, little cakes with "Ice cream, coffee with or without brandy, and cigars in the sitting room, gentlemen, if you please."

If food and drink had mattered to Tempus beyond the warmth and energy they provided, the meal would have been one he'd have classed as a wonder on its own. The frozen sweet cream and cakes made the women groan and giggle, and the men drank heavily of wines the like of which Tempus had never encountered.

And he drank too, as he seldom did, because Ash drank and taunted him over his crystal goblet. Tempus's god liked wine and all strong spirits. Tempus didn't, because reflex and thought were slowed, and thus the god had an easier time wresting control from him.

This night, Tempus matched Askelon glass for glass. He told himself that, with the dream lord across from him and Faun at Askelon's side, control was not the issue. That was in the hands of the Evening Star, in any case. She was conducting a ritual; this was clear to Tempus.

But he'd never encountered women so comfortable with power, unless those women were hereditary queens or witches. Each time a course was served, the Evening

Star would lean toward him infinitesimally, making sure he saw her indicate which of the array of disparate tableware she wanted him to use.

In the same way she guided his tentative hand to the utensils on either side of and above his plate, she guided the conversation away from anything substantive.

They talked of the food, of the drink, of Lemuria, of the weather—of anything but the purpose of this ad hoc council, of casting lots or forging fates.

When Faun asked Askelon to interpret a dream for her, the Evening Star chided her gently, "Not now, dear. Not yet. No one works at my table. We've the whole night for serious talk. Now, we need only savor the world's bounty and appreciate our good fortune—"

"And the god's favor," Tempus said then, deliberately pouring a thin stream of golden wine from his goblet onto the white tablecloth.

"And the gods' favor," Faun giggled, picking a piece of bread from her plate, dipping it in a little oil, and dropping the bread atop the wine.

The Evening Star's forehead rippled and smoothed as she suppressed a frown. She and Askelon exchanged glances.

The sacrifice was complete, however, and Tempus wasn't sure then or after if the god had made him do it.

Still, a consecration was not out of order, even here, when so much of the earth's harvest was displayed.

Each course was familiar to some guest, as if the chef had been preparing for days. Tempus learned that hearts of palm in honey delighted Tiye; that lamb's eyes were a delicacy to Zimri-Lim. Mano spoke heartfelt praise of black fish eggs on white, buttered bread. Rath pronounced the raw flank of cow, ground fine, the best he'd ever had. Faun loved the rare and poisonous-looking mushrooms that gave Tempus pause. Askelon took blue-mottled plover's eggs in his hands and cracked them open with unconcealed delight. And the Evening Star nibbled orchids sauced with a jelly made from rose hips, watching all with a wistful, approving smile.

When Chiara led the way to the sitting room, Tempus was relieved to be out of her orbit, if briefly. The pairing of the guests was overt by then: Faun and Askelon left the table together; Zimri-Lim, the king, had Tiye, the queen of a different place, upon his arm; and the marksman, Mano, followed with the man called Rath, the two talking jocularly in slurred tones of the quality of the meal and especially the drink.

Tempus went last. He was more than a little drunk and in a strange place with no one to guard his back, it was common sense to honor custom. Thus he was exposed for all to see when he froze on the sitting room's threshold before the black pillars dotted with blinking lights and the windows into other worlds and all manner of sorcery that made him grab the swordhilt upon his hip.

"The comfort of a familiar weapon, Riddler?" Ash couldn't resist saying. "This," he pointed to his temple, "is the only weapon with any power here."

The guests were settling on long, multicolored divans. "Commander?" Faun said. "Come sit and tell us why Ash calls you 'Riddler.'"

He still had not gone an iota further into that room. Here, too, were walls of glass. Chiara was drawing the curtains over one. She called to him from there to take a seat.

He flushed and moved awkwardly into the room. How long had it been since he'd been embarrassed, by anyone or anything? He couldn't remember when he'd last cared what appearance he might make, or what someone thought. It must be the drink, he decided.

But the flush stayed with him, as if it heated his blood, and then he knew that the Storm God was well and truly roused. He could feel the anger massing in him that was as vast as the world and as inexorable as the urge of time to move forward.

He closed his eyes and wished he hadn't drunk. What difference if Askelon was here? The dream lord had lost Cime, therefore the dream lord had nothing he wanted any longer. And if Ash was here as a guest, then that meant, surely, that he was as much a supplicant of fate as any of them.

Except Chiara. Did she know she taunted the god, coming to sit with him on the narrow couch for two, her hip brushing his? Customs differed, he told himself. No matter how he felt, he wouldn't be here if he shouldn't be.

If fate's purpose were no deeper than to bring the Evening Star and the Storm God together on New Year's Eve, then only the god and the chief counsellor of Lemuria could judge the import of that.

For his part, with the drink running in his veins and the room growing warmer with every breath he took, Tempus would as soon have taken Faun by the hand and gone out into the storm to cool his flesh with her.

But there would be much talk and time before any such chance came his way. And there was Ash, who once again stood between him and something he wanted.

If there were truly fates to be changed this night in Lemuria, Tempus would volunteer to change Askelon's without a qualm, should the opportunity present itself. Even, perhaps, if it did not.

The Evening Star leaned back beside him, all perfume and warmth. He was beginning to sweat. He couldn't imagine where the heat came from, or how they put up with it.

But no one else seemed hot as they took yet more drink from servants and the men, all but him, lit long wrapped leaves that stank and burned his eyes.

Even Faun took out a smoke, a smaller, whiter one, and set it afire with some sort of flint she flicked with her thumb.

The room's flickering lights and white windows wherein things moved in bright daylight had Tempus's attention. He could see siege engines in one window, and massive, silent explosions. In another, a wild wind blew and trees and great buildings bent before it under a sky with too many stars. In a third, the sea was full of dead and floating fish. In a fourth, a whole populace fled an enemy army of many chariots and a city flamed behind. In a fifth was Meridian, he knew it at first glance and looked away from its seductive majesty. In a sixth window, a dust storm raged over a half-buried city with white and crumbling walls.

And in the seventh he saw the hills and the rocky shore where he was born, and, in the distance, the very rock sanctuary where he'd given his soul to the god he still served.

Distantly, he heard the other guests chatting around him. He knew that someone spoke his name. But he sat looking into the windows onto the past—his past—and onto the others' pasts—his future if he lived so long— and into Meridian's ageless present, and the sweat on his face and neck dried stiff and cold there.

"Every soul who wanders in here is here for the casting of a lot, the forging of a fate, the making of a decision which will rebound throughout eternity," Askelon had told him. *"We can't have the Council short its quorum,"* Chiara had scolded him. And: *"May you find the answers you seek before morning."*

So he said, ignoring the talk around him, in a voice loud enough to silence one and all: "What is this place and what's going on here?"

Everyone stared at him and then, slowly, all refocused on Chiara.

Mano said softly, "Can he really not know?"

And Rath answered, "An ancient, remember. Different time frame."

"Right," said Mano.

But by then Chiara had shifted on the narrow couch to face him. "Lord Tempus, folk call you the Riddler. Ash tells us a god is with us when you are. Lemuria's honored by the attendance, at Year's End and New Year's start, of yourself, your god, and our other special guest, the entelechy of dreams. We come together to choose a path, each of us, for the year. For some, the path will be a longer journey, all the choice they need to make. For King Zimri-Lim and Queen Tiye, it's a glimpse of their futures and a chance to change them if they return home with the right knowledge. For Sandia's Shepherd," she nodded her head slightly to Faun, "it's a chance to change the present by finding a key in the past. For Mano, and I think for Rath, it's the present that has brought them—the present where they struggle to make futures right. For Ash, it's a dispensation from those he serves, a chance to make an error right. And for you . . ."

She paused and Tempus could hear his own breathing. " . . . perhaps you and your god will know. You want the world, and here it is. Choose a debarkation point from here, Lord Tempus, and that place will be outside your door tomorrow morning. Tonight, you may be the answer I've sought, who knows?" She smiled and it was not a smile like any Tempus had ever seen: it was proud and devoid of humor; it was an invitation and an invocation.

Inside his head, the god rustled wordlessly. And he knew then that he'd been wrong: it would not be inappropriate to ravish this host. Or at least, neither she nor Enlil thought so. Anger overswept him so that he nearly rose to leave. He was more than a stud, to get godlings on this mare or that.

Crap, we'll see who chooses how this night is spent, Pillager, he thought. But the god did not argue, or even reply. If this woman was the sorceress she seemed, he would not let the god have His way with her. Not with Tempus's body. But he knew in his heart that Lemuria's wonders weren't sorcery. At least not the kind he was accustomed to dealing with by fire and force.

He had to do something in the silence that followed. Everyone was watching his reaction. And he was drunk enough, and rebellious enough, to make his feelings clear. In a blur of movement, he pulled a throwing star from his weaponsbelt and cast it toward the window onto the world of his birth.

It shattered and sparks flew.

No one moved. No one acted as though anything unusual had happened. Faun reached forward to a table by her knee and picked up some dried stalks. She tapped them against her palm until the exposed ends were level and the other ends hidden in her fist.

She was humming softly as she did so.

The window was now a gaping, shattered vessel. Inside it was blackness.

Chiara said, "It's clear you have no intention of returning to your own past to change anything you've done. Therefore, we are—if rather abruptly—begun upon the sequence. Tempus, called the Riddler, judges the past he represents whole and unalterable."

Ash caught his eye and shook his head pityingly, as if Tempus had lost his last, best hope.

He wanted to say he hadn't understood; then he didn't. He wouldn't change anything. He regretted nothing, he told himself. There was too much he couldn't anticipate, let alone comprehend, about this ceremony for him to meddle with the lives of those he'd touched, fates already written, times gone by.

Tiye, the tiny queen, was whispering into Zimri-Lim's ear. Then she looked at Tempus and her eyes were too bright not to be veiled with unshed tears.

"This is the Storm God's child, Set's boy, Shamash's instrument in the world. Must we live with his decision, we who had no part in it?"

"He is the eldest child," said Askelon.

"What about you?" said King Zimri-Lim to Askelon.

"Unfortunately, I'm not a mortal sprung of woman. Under any reading of the law, Tempus would have to go first."

"Then what of us?" said Zimri-Lim, putting his arm around Queen Tiye.

Askelon shrugged. "Find the answer in your dreams, if you wish."

"Chiara?" Tiye asked tremulously. "Is there no hope for my mad son and my poor country, because of this barbarian? And for my new friend, Zimri-Lim? Must his country be lost to history, because the beginning is wrong?"

"There's fully a millenium between you two," Chiara said soothingly. "Things can be changed and wisdom can be gained from every moment of every day. Don't seek to tie yourselves to one another's fates. And remember, none has yet drawn the lots."

"We can still do that?" Zimri-Lim wanted to know. "Even when the Adad of the Storm has given such a sign?"

"We'll do it all. We always do," said Chiara, and again she shifted in her seat next to Tempus.

And rose up, saying, "All of you are here because of urgent need. On the shoulders of most rests the fate of your people. Some are rulers of record, some are merely guardians of fated moments. All of you have prayed and dreamed and fought and forced this opportunity out of time itself. Lemuria is at Year's End. New Year's sun will rise on final choices. Make them with the wisdom you brought here and the wisdom you gain here."

She walked over to Faun, Shepherd of Sandia, and took the stalks from the other woman's hand. "Lots are for luck. Lots are for fate. Draw your lot, all but the Riddler, who has forfeited his turn and thus goes last."

Again, Tempus caught Ash shaking his head at him.

This was the god's game, Tempus now knew. He didn't care what place he walked into tomorrow morning, as long as it was a place in the world, and not Lemuria. Or Meridian.

"One lot apiece, one chance to undo an error or secure a fate." Chiara moved around the room, holding the lots. All eyes followed her.

When she stood in front of the black pillars with the lights and the glowing windows, she said, "Let's start with the youngest. Faun, be careful not to look into your world, or at the stalks as you take one from my hand."

The woman in skins did as she was told and returned to her seat beside Ash, who ran his arm along the couch's back behind her head, and then squeezed her shoulder with his hand.

"Mano, come and take a lot, but do not choose what to do with it," Chiara said then.

The man with the marksman's stare was at Chiara's side in three strides. He took a lot and returned to his seat. It was not particularly short.

Then Chiara called Rath, cautioning him the same.

And then she faced the remainder of the guests. "Come now, Tiye, and take a lot."

She went, did the tiny woman, and chose a stalk. It was not a great stalk, and her face fell when she looked at the length of it.

Then Zimri-Lim went up without urging to choose his, which was longer than Tiye's had been.

"Askelon?" prompted Chiara.

The dream lord went to the woman and put his hand over hers, which held two stalks. When he took his hand away, he held a long stalk.

"Tempus," said Ash, "come get the stalk your god has chosen for you."

When he got up, he was slightly dizzy. When he reached Chiara, her face was full of excitement. Her nostrils were fluttering.

The stalk was as short as Tiye's or shorter. He didn't know what it meant, or care. The god knew, but the god wasn't telling. Enlil had one thing in mind and so did Chiara. His body knew very well what was going to happen here tonight. He didn't need a yarrow stalk or a window into the future.

The woman who was the Evening Star put her hand on his knee and left it there after she'd joined him on the small couch.

"Faun and Mano have the longest stalks, I believe," said Chiara. "Rath, measure yours with Mano's."

The two men did, and Mano's was somewhat longer.

"We hope," Chiara said, "for a clear decision, and thus we have one: Sandia makes its choice first, in the person of its Shepherd."

"I . . . may I defer to the results of Mano and Rath?"

"I wish I could help you, child. What is it you want from Lemuria?"

"Warmth," said the Shepherd. "Meat. Living seas. It's the doings of Rath's time, and Mano's, that—"

"Ssh," said Chiara. "Lemuria can give one change, only. What will it be?"

"Living seas," said the woman as she came to her feet, her fists balled, face pale.

The two men called Mano and Rath were whispering together. Only when Faun brought her lot to Chiara did they stop.

The Evening Star took the stalk and ran it through her fingers—once, twice. Then she nodded. "Freely given, freely received. Come with me."

The two women walked to the pillars where the windows were. Before the one that opened onto a sea afloat with dying fish they paused and Chiara touched glowing buttons with her fingers.

Their bodies obscured the details and Tempus looked away in time to see the two men in leggings talking together again in low voices.

At the same instant, Ash leaned forward and said, "Are you beginning to understand, Riddler? All of these are here to wipe away their guilt, just like you."

"What will it be, Ash? Now or later? You're one guilt I can wipe away without benefit of magic windows."

"Now, Tempus. You'll find you have a choice to make here, just like all the rest."

"To leave you gutted on the couch? I think the god would approve . . ."

Mano came to sit beside him. "Tempus . . . Lord Tempus . . . I'd like to talk to you about this choice you're making."

" 'Tempus' is sufficient. Talk, fighter."

The man's face didn't show his surprise, but his body tensed. "Rath and I think we know where the problem matrix started. We've been working on getting here to fix it for a long time. If you're really not partisan, we could use a little help . . . for the benefit of mankind and all."

"Excuse me," said Rath, joining his friend. There was no place to sit close enough for private conversation except the table, on which Rath perched. "Commander . . . sir, we're willing to bet you'll find what you're looking for, if you'll throw in with us. We've done a lot of reverse engineering on this. God knows we've had the time."

"Which god?" Tempus asked curiously, aware that he wasn't hearing the context of this proposal.

"Which time?" Askelon said, as his shadow fell over them.

"Look," Rath craned his neck to peer up at the dream lord. "I'm having a hard enough time crediting any of this as more than a psychological affect of the matrix fields. Could you sit down and behave like a good fellow? Please. We're trying to cut a deal, here."

The language usage was strange to Tempus's ears. It must have been to Askelon's, for he switched tongues and spat a brutal-sounding breath of short, terse vocalizations.

Mano answered back in a series of monosyllables, then said to Tempus, "We're from your future, Commander. We're sure you're in our timeline. We've been exploring error chains and we think you can help us. Will you?"

Askelon obviously didn't like the idea, so Tempus said, "I might. What do you offer?"

"A trip to see your sister, for starters. Then a way out of there, if you like, to our time or anyplace we've got coordinates for," Mano said quickly.

"Trust nothing," Tempus warned, "that Ash has told you about—"

"She's coming," Rath warned, and stood as if to shield the other two from Chiara's notice—or Ash's interference—with his body.

The two women were indeed returning.

Askelon put his hand firmly on Rath's shoulder and pushed the other man aside. "Tempus, you mustn't.

You have no idea what the results of collusion might be, or what results these two seek in the first place . . . "

"Sit down, Ash," said Tempus. "I'm not a child. I'll see when the time comes."

Faun's face was pale. The window before which she and Chiara had stood was opaque now, showing nothing whatsoever.

She sat beside Ash and her hands were trembling. Blue veins showed on them. "It's done," she said shakily. "For better or worse. I hope it won't be worse. So many gave so much for me to come here."

She leaned back and against the dream lord's arm.

Tempus was liking this whole situation less and less.

"Mano?" said Chiara. "Are you ready?"

"Not quite. I can ask a question, yes?"

"Of course, if you must. But then make your choice."

"If Lemurian technology can impact biospheres, then why aren't you caretaking the entire system?"

"More than once a year, you mean? Humans create their futures every day of every year; only you can alter your worlds. We merely offer an annual opportunity. Otherwise, there would be chaos. Now, your choice?"

"There's chaos anyway," said Mano, getting up from beside Tempus. "We're looking for a key to unlock certain technologies, you must realize. I want to use my lot to bring back, into my time, whatever knowledge Lemuria has that can help us stabilize our . . . ah . . . conflict."

Chiara closed her eyes and then opened them. "You'll send others back here, next year, with such a request."

"It's my choice, isn't it?"

"It is that," she said, and motioned him to the pillars where the windows were. They paused before the window in which the great city under the sky of bright stars was being destroyed. Their bodies came together before the window and Tempus could see no more.

He was going to ask Faun what she'd seen when she and Chiara were up there together, but Rath was trying to get his attention:

"If we're right, Commander, the person you're looking for is in the time frame that led to the problems we're here to solve."

"And what time frame is that?" Askelon asked from the other couch.

"My native one," Rath replied.

"Then you deal with it," Askelon suggested.

Tempus had had enough. He said to Askelon, "Stay out of this." He said to Rath, "Do the best you can on your own, for now."

And then he stood up. "Chiara, I'm not making any determination here but that of the god's. You and I both know what that is, and it needs no witnesses. When you're done with this, come find me."

He turned to leave the room, dropping his stalk on the couch as he did so.

He saw Ash get up to follow him, and he saw Rath pick up his discarded stalk.

He merely didn't care about the latter. So far as the former was concerned, there was a long night ahead. In it, many problems could be solved, including that of the dream lord.

When Ash hurried out the door after him, Tempus was waiting beside it. "Looking for me?"

"Tempus, don't do this. You're laying yourself open to results you—"

"Would you like me to go back in there, pick up that stalk, and use it to bar you and Meridian from ever affecting anything in my world again?"

Askelon blanched. "You wouldn't."

"I might. I'd like to spend some time with your friend Faun. I think I need her to explain to me what's going on here. If she says the right things, perhaps I won't after all."

"Don't you get tired of being the god's pawn?"

"Don't you get tired of being less even than that?"

Askelon wheeled and returned to the sitting room. Tempus, alone outside, began exploring the deserted halls of Pinnacle House, looking for a way out into the storm.

He didn't find it. In fact, he found nothing familiar, not a servant or even a big, square-muzzled dog, until he found Faun, wandering the hall and clutching herself.

"The dream lord said to make you come back," she said, shivering.

Looking at the girl from a world with dying oceans, clutching her skins to her waist, he was no longer sure of what he wanted from her. But the god was. Enlil was awake and alert to any opportunity.

With all the control Tempus could muster, he said, "And how do you think you're going to manage that?"

She tossed her blonde head. "However I must." Blue eyes met his and the contact was like the kiss of lightning.

"Can you find a way out into the night?"

Faun frowned and took a step back.

Could she feel the god in him coming forward? Could she hear the difference in his voice? Was that what she saw that made her bold and defiant, timid and deferential, all at once?

His ears roared with a thunder that might or might not have been external. His body tingled and pulsed along its length as the god sought to put Himself into Tempus's muscle and bone. It was like being stretched, and like being compressed. It was like being crowded into the corner of a very small room.

He hardly heard her voice when Faun said, "I think I saw a balcony over this way . . ." and led him there, the pale skins on her hips swaying with her every stride.

Did she know what she did, switching her hips before the Lord Enlil? Why did he care so much? He wanted this one, himself.

But not this way. So while their shared body followed the woman through doors that opened to her touch, out onto the balcony she'd promised, into the wind and the gusts of driven rain coming in spurts from heaven, Tempus said to Enlil, *This one is mine, Pillager. Freely given. Not your sort.*

In his head, the god spoke as before his eyes, lightning flashed, turning the skin-clad girl before him bone white. *Not My sort, mortal? They're all My sort. And yours, for you are Mine to do with as I please.*

Back off, Lord Storm, and the other, your choice, we'll have without remonstrance from me.

Before his eyes, which were both blurry and ultra-sharp from sharing his vision with Enlil, the Shepherd of Sandia crossed to the balcony's rail and leaned on it. The wet wind sprayed her, soaking her hair, whipping her skins around her legs. And she leaned forward into the storm, her arms folded on the railing, her legs widespread, as if she didn't know the Storm God and the man who was his avatar discussed her fate behind her. Or as if she did.

The god urged Tempus forward. *A bargain, is it, mortal son? When have you bargained with Me and gained? Our flesh is one. The prize awaits, a gift from a foreign land, for the taking.*

Tempus wanted, with what was left of his reason, to argue with the god. But the wind was high and the spray of heaven was on his face, in his eyes.

And the Shepherd of Sandia still leaned over the balcony, unmoving, her high rump offered like a ceremonial gift.

Rape was the god's choice, never his. He went up behind Faun until his swordbelt touched her buttocks, and leaned forward so that both his hands curled on the rail beside her folded arms. He leaned forward further and spoke hoarsely in her ear, "Do you know what you're doing?"

She didn't move, and yet she pressed back against him. Then she turned her head just slightly. The rain had soaked her face; drops ran from her lips. "We need you for the ceremony," she said, her eyes never leaving the stormy horizon.

If she'd admitted lust, perhaps the god would have slunk back from Tempus's skin to await Chiara, His chosen sparring partner.

Faun shifted her weight and her buttocks no longer

pressed against him. His right hand left the rail and closed on her breast.

For a moment longer, she ignored him. Then her head dropped and his free hand found its way under her skirt. Caught between him and the unyielding balustrade, there was no way for her to escape him.

Never mind that she didn't try: here was strife enough for the god, passion enough for them both, and a woman who leaned into the wind and the rain while he took her against the railing, as if she strained to mate with the very storm itself.

When he took his hands from her neck and her breast and stepped back, she smoothed her skins down over her rump and leaned there for long moments before she faced him and said, "Now you'll come back with me?" Her chest was heaving. Her wet lips were parted.

"Why should I?"

"Because I'm bringing the seed of the god into Sandia, and because I ask it."

Her cheek was scraped but her head was high. He waited for the god's response, but there was none. This was not the sort of woman they were accustomed to— but then, he'd sensed that.

The rain blew her skins against her legs and rivulets ran down them. As he watched and said nothing, she began to shiver once again.

"And you, too," she added into the silence, "are welcome in my country . . . "

"Despite this?"

"Or because of it. We could use a storm god." She smiled and he didn't understand the smile.

"Ash will not be pleased," he said with a grin he couldn't suppress as he motioned her to follow him in out of the gale. Still the god was silent. No urge to throw the Shepherd over the balcony overcame him. No demand to humble the arrogance in her rose up in him to blind and deafen him.

The god might be all–knowing, but women who offered themselves as this one had were beyond their shared experience.

He kept waiting for a reaction he could count as familiar, all the way back to the sitting room. He didn't find anything in Faun that displeased him now, as he usually did once the god had used him to touch a human female.

"Where is Sandia?" he asked tentatively, just before they rejoined the others.

"That's a silly question from one so wise. Out my bedroom's door in the morning, is where. Come home with me and you'll not be bored, or unappreciated. We've great problems, but spirits to match. Bring your god or come alone, now or any time."

"And what would I be there?"

He put his arm across the threshold, leaning on the doorjamb so that she couldn't step by him into the room.

"Commander, whatever you are wherever you are . . . Survival's the thing, isn't it? If I brought you home from Lemuria, that would be a change, for certain."

"For better or worse?" Ask a silly question . . .

"There's only better; if I told you worse had already come to worst, then you'd—"

Ash's shadow fell on them. The dream lord looked from the sodden woman to Tempus, who had the storm in his hair as well, and scowled.

"You're too late," he told them both. "Rath has already cast your lot, Tempus. Fool. And you, Shepherd, what's best for your country is surely not this travesty of humankind."

Tempus still had his arm across the doorway. Ash pushed at it. Tempus grabbed the dream lord's wrist.

Only a twist and it would break in his hand. But under his palm was the Heart of Askelon, a cuff of antiquity which burned his flesh so that he could hear the sizzle and smell the serum as it charred.

He let go, and a patch of his flesh came away, left on the cuff's gem. Ignoring the pain, he stepped back, "Don't let me hold up your leavetaking . . ."

Faun in her turn stepped aside. Once past them, Askelon said to her, "Coming, Shepherd?"

"The night's not over," she said. "I must stay awhile."

"Then find me in a dream," said the lord of Meridian and started down the hall.

Tempus saw the uncertainty on the woman's face and nearly spoke to it when Ash called back, "Don't wait too long, Faun. Your godling's going to be busy for some time, reaping what his ignorance has sown."

"Go with him, if you wish," Tempus told her flatly. "I can't take you in tow the whole night."

It was for her own good, especially if what Ash had said was true.

She blinked away hurt; then her chin rose. "Anytime, Commander," she reminded him.

Then she left to follow the dream lord down the hall.

Alone, he stepped into the sitting room. Only Rath and Mano were still inside with Chiara and the room was tingling with conflict.

On the black pillars beyond them, every window was opaque. The two men sat in nearly identical positions, elbows on knees, looking between their feet at the carpeted floor.

Chiara noticed him first, and came toward him with relief on her face. But not even her greeting chased the worry and the fury there.

She said, "Tempus, it's good to have you back. Our friends here have exhausted Lemuria's patience, and perhaps your own: they've used your lot to their advantage, and called it a proxy. How say you?"

Ash had been truly furious about what Rath had done. So Tempus said, with a quick glance at the men who now looked up at him wordlessly, "We agreed on that. It's not your place to judge, Chiara. The god is ready for you now."

Blunt words, cruel, and purposely wounding, said in front of these incomprehensible men. Speaking thus was foolish and risky as well: Tempus had no idea what Rath's casting of his proxy lot portended.

But he was angry with everyone and everything now—
with the god, who could not let well enough alone and
meant to have the Evening Star of Lemuria for his own.
So far as the god was concerned, Chiara was the main
course; Faun had been only a snack.

Tempus was angry with himself, for not understanding better what was happening here, and for not wanting to show his ignorance. And most of all, he wanted
to flout Ash's judgment and do whatever would make
the dream lord unhappiest.

What he'd said made the two men in leggings jump
up from their seats and slap each other's hands and
crow. "Thanks, Lord Tempus," said Mano. "If you want
to talk, come to my room. Otherwise, see you in the
morning. I've got to get some rest."

And Rath added, snagging a full bottle of wine as the
two men headed for the door, "I knew we could count
on you. We won't let you down."

All of this meant less than nothing to Tempus. By
morning, he'd have dragged from Chiara, privately, all
he needed to know about Lemurian rituals.

Or so he told himself when he took her in hand,
saying, "Now let's get you serviced, since that's what
you and the god have in mind."

Her eyes, when they met his, were too wide. Behind
her head, he noticed that not only the windows in the
pillars, but the colored lights as well, had all turned
dull and as dead as stone.

Chapter 4:

CUSTOM OF THE COUNTRY

Not one of the hundred pillows in Chiara's bedroom was still on the bed when the god finally had had enough of the woman who was Lemuria's Evening Star. She was lying belly down on marble tiles in a slick of oil and wine and surrounded by candles he was quenching, one by one, with his fingers.

His shortsword was in the middle of the mess, hair from her body and her head on his blade.

He hadn't done a protracted ritual for the god in a very long time, and Lemuria's was as ancient and primal as Enlil's name.

There'd been moments when fear glazed her round, brown eyes, and moments when he was sure the god was over-estimating what Tempus's human flesh could give and hers could accept.

Still, he'd never killed a woman unintentionally, and though she might hurt when passion fled, now she was merely intoxicated, malleable, sated and unresisting in the middle of the floor.

Once he'd snuffed the last candle, she reached out for a pillow and put it under her chin so that she could watch him more easily.

The big bed might have been easier on her, but she and the god had done things by the book. Still on her

39

belly with the pillow under her head, she said, "You'll
really go with Rath and Mano into their horrid world
tomorrow?"

"You tell me." He was looking for his leathers among
her pillows.

"Stay here. With me. We could recast the lot. You
could be free of the god, forever, here. Stay, and you'll
learn of pleasures you never dreamed . . ."

"I'm a fighter, a soldier, a simple mercenary who had
the bad luck to fall in with an insatiable god. It's been
so long, I wouldn't know how to do anything else."

"You could be the first not to succumb to Lemuria's
legerdemain. Don't cast a lot, and you're safe here until
you do. We have strife, all the strife of many lands. You
can help all of humankind—"

"You must have mistaken me for a politician or a
would-be king. I'm not the one to chart any soul's
future. Not after what I did with mine."

"What do you want, then?"

And Faun's words came back to him: "Survival, that's
the thing."

"I'm offering that. Tempus, you're the gift of heaven
to me. I haven't felt like this for—"

"Don't tell me how long. I have a profound aversion
to aged crones in perfect bodies."

She threw a pillow at him. Under it was his jerkin.
He went to get it.

She grabbed his leg. "Take me seriously."

"I took you as seriously as I'm able. For more than
that, you'll need a deity incarnate."

"So you're refusing me?"

"Dogs' bellies, woman, what do you think we've been
doing here? You've had your ritual performed, punctili-
ously. Any other woman I've known would be uncon-
scious, or crying in a corner, or begging me to leave.
What is it you think you haven't had yet?"

"I'm offering Lemuria, all its power, if you'll not go
wandering into places you don't belong."

"Are you so sure I don't?"

"You haven't the slightest idea what awaits you in the world of Rath's society. You'll be destroyed there."

"I've heard that before. One of those men said a certain person I've been looking for might be there—a person from my own birthplace. If that's so, I need to know."

"Ash says that you'll wreak unparalleled havoc if you let those two trick you into serving their purposes."

Ash. "Ash says whatever will get him his desired result. Which in this case is probably not anything I'd agree with if I knew the specifics." He pulled his jerkin over his head, cinched on his weaponsbelt, and stooped to get the shortsword from the tiles.

"Again, Lord Tempus, renounce the proxy. Use your lot to spend time in Lemuria, learning what you will. You can find a lost soul from here without risk to you or anyone else."

He took the sword in his hand, stabbed a white lace pillow with it, then took the pillow and used it to wipe the hair and oil from the sword.

"Chiara, you don't understand. I've finally shaken loose from all but the god's hold on me. I've lived too long to do nothing, day after day. Therefore, a sortie into the unknown is welcome. This place is too quiet for my taste."

Now she sat up and encircled her knees with her arms. "Me, you mean. I'm what you don't like."

"I don't like doing the god's bidding, if that's what you mean. But you're mistaken in taking it personally. I'm merely not in the mood for the company of women."

And that was true, he told himself. Faun had been an opportunity to assert himself, a digression from the god's plan, and no more. He needed mortal women like he needed a rash or an infestation of fleas. He'd finally freed his heart from men and women both; the taint of the curse that had struck him loveless, lifelong, was a habit too strong to break.

Going where he cared nothing about anyone would suit him well enough. And the urge to move on was nearly overwhelming, now that the god's ritual was done.

The Evening Star got to her feet. Covered with oil, she was as magnificent as any temple statue. He said, because her face said too much and, in all this talk, he'd said too little: "If you like, teach me how to return here when I choose it, not because Enlil decrees it. When I'm done exploring, I'll come this way . . . " From here, he could go anywhere. Sandia, even.

"It's not so simple," said the Evening Star, biting her lip. Yet her expression brightened. "Still, we shall try."

And so began his tutoring into the ways of Lemuria, which lasted until nearly sunup. And which taught him one thing he hadn't expected: the Evening Star had more to give than the god had taken, and tricks of seduction no rampaging Storm God had ever learned.

She also had a chamber in which she could call up hot and cold rain and steam and dry heat with a touch.

Although he learned more than he wanted of Lemuria while he was with her, the thing he most remembered was sitting in that dry, hot place with Chiara while she told him what it was like to care for worlds she'd never see.

When she embraced him on her threshold, the sun was rising and he didn't realize why she said, "Be careful, bold Tempus. Everything I told you, remember. And watch out for those you met here."

When he put his hand upon the doorknob, he winced as his skinned palm touched the metal, although the wound hadn't hurt him before now.

But he turned the knob, and stepped resolutely through the door that opened to his tug before he really looked at what awaited on the other side.

The door blew out of his hand on a strong gust and slammed shut behind him, but he hardly noticed.

In all his travels, in his wildest encounters with sorcerers and demons from deeper hells, he'd never imagined such a sight as the place before his eyes.

Confronted with such strangeness, he wished he'd

thought to bring his horse. But he hadn't thought. The Tros and all his gear were back in Lemuria, behind a door he couldn't open when he turned and tried.

And Askelon was swirling there, part of the gust that had ripped the door from his grasp, or at least the cause of it. The dream lord was semitransparent, floating in midair. The towers of the city behind him showed through his flesh.

Ash said, "Your meddling is becoming dangerous, Riddler. Fail here and die here, for all our sakes. For you can die here, if you try hard enough. In this godless place, not even Enlil can save you. But don't come to me to protect you from this evil—not if you don't leave well enough alone."

And Ash was gone in his personal whirlwind, leaving Tempus to wonder if what the entelechy of dreams had said was true.

He squinted in the air that stung his eyes, trying to make sense of the jumble like rotting cliffs before him. And he called tentatively to the god inside his head. "Enlil?"

There was no answer.

He tried again. Only silence.

Enlil often failed to answer him these days. It didn't mean that Askelon was right; it didn't that Enlil was not here with him.

And if all that were true, so what? To die a natural death in a strange land was something the very threat of which had been denied him for centuries.

If Ash were worried enough to spend so much energy on such a theatrical manifestation, then there was something here worth sniffing out, more than met his tearing eyes.

He crouched down where he was. This place stank. It was loud and its ground was slagged, as if the whole area had been razed in a great battle. He looked up at the sky. It was brown, as if a volcano were active nearby.

A volcano might account for the roaring in his ears.

But only one thing would account for Askelon's behavior: Cime was here, somewhere. That was clearly what Ash meant by telling Tempus to leave well enough alone.

But where would she be?

And where were the two he'd met, Rath and Mano, who'd said they'd see each other in the morning?

Was this morning, here?

Again he looked at the sky. He couldn't tell. The overcast was too heavy.

Somewhere, something screamed.

Chapter 5:

LANGUAGE BARRIER

He'd smelled the sea and headed for it blindly, not knowing what else to do. Everywhere was noise. Everywhere was the foul miasma that made his eyes tear. Everywhere was slag, broken and jumbled. His legs ached from stumbling over its unyielding, uneven surface. He was beginning to wonder if Askelon had somehow tricked him into a waking dream of hell.

But his heart knew better. He marked the place he left with a cairn of rubble, so he could find the door to Lemuria again.

He'd stared at it a long time before he moved on, knowing he could try to open it right now, go back to Chiara if he succeeded. But that was what they wanted— what Chiara wanted, what Askelon wanted.

It had never been what Tempus wanted. He tried to ignore his disquiet that the door, when he'd tried to open it after it had slammed, would not budge.

At the right time it would. When he was done here, it would. He told himself that the god would let it open, once he'd done what He'd come here to do. He had the precious knowledge he'd wrested from Chiara— Lemuria's secrets—to pry it open, if worse came to worse.

But he couldn't remember those now. The god had

45

Cime in his mind, and the god was adamant. He'd squinted at the door then, just before he turned away. It was marked with glowing letters—a sure sign of sorcery afoot.

Enlil hated sorcery only marginally more than Tempus did. Or than his sister, Cime, did.

If the door was barred to Tempus by magic, then the unknown sorcerers of this place were intent on confrontation.

From confrontation, Tempus never backed away.

This accursed town stank of magic. Not only the door into Lemuria was hung with spells: glowing incantations danced before his eyes wherever he looked. Unreadable exhortations pulsed red, orange, yellow and white. Warding signs hovered over buildings they protected, over doors boarded up and scrawled upon, doors with heavy iron grates, doors hanging askew on their hinges, doors opening into the ground and doors reached by rusting stairs high on buildings' sides.

The sky grew browner as he sojourned deeper into the slum that stank of enchantment. Even the sea smelled wrong, forgotten, rotten and foul, but the sea wind was still better than the choking air from inland.

He'd been in slums before. He knew the worst of them, he'd thought. Until now. No slum Tempus had ever seen was so vast; no slum had cobbles half-buried in slag and open holes to Hell that steamed in full view, covered only by pierced shields even he would hesitate to lift.

He came to a wide road like a frozen stream. The thoroughfare was a racing course for demon chariots, he found out when he was half across and a herd of them charged him, roaring and screaming as they came.

He broke and ran: it wasn't fear, he told himself, just common sense. But his throat was dry and his heart pounded. He'd never breathed air so poor, not even on the highest peak of Wizardwall.

Not until he'd come to the far side of the racetrack did he notice other men, and these were unkempt and filthy. Some slept against the buildings; some hunched over a fire in a rusty iron drum. None gave him a second glance and he kept going, toward the sea.

Here were alleys, as in any slum, but the very height of the crumbling buildings daunted him. Between those buildings, weeds sprouted, wrecked chariots sat where they'd been left. Men slept in some.

He smelled food and vomit and beer, and looked up. This was a bar, like any bar in any land, but a mages' bar: you could tell by the glowing swirls and curlicues that danced in its windows. Too, a likeness of a dog was there, and the dog was being caressed by women as it hoarded its beer.

He would have moved on by, but three, then four, sorcerers came out of the bar, staggering and smelling of strong spirits and the sickly odor of death garlands.

One wore a blouse of red silk and a collar of gold around his neck; his face was as black as night. Another, with him, had shaved the sides of his scalp and what hair was on it curled yellow, red, and purple, straight up; this one was conjuring incantations from a silver box.

The sound was meant to mesmerize or wake the dead: it had a pulse like a heartbeat and to that pulse the third and fourth enchanter danced on the broken street in some sort of overt ritual.

It was the dancing pair who saw him first. One was as tall as Tempus, and twice as wide, and this one smiled a wide smile, exposing a gold tooth with a gem in it, and pointed at him, uttering a spell. His partner wore a chain around his waist of formidable dimensions.

Tempus didn't understand their words; the spell fell haplessly aside. He moved toward them, where all four spoke together and looked his way.

In normal circumstance, a crowd like this would break apart if you forced the issue, stand back and let you pass. But a crowd of foreign sorcerers in silk and gems, who summoned chants to deafen and pointed jewel-encrusted hands at you overtly—this was a different matter.

The gold-toothed one stood right in his path, uttering another spell, or a taunt, in short, hostile monosyllables. The other three spread out, and that was when Tempus drew his sword.

He saw the silk blouse out of the corner of his eye as its owner tried to slip behind him. His left hand took a throwing star from his belt and cast it as the blouse slid out of view.

The silk-bloused man behind him screamed in surprise and pain. Tempus heard the thud as the man went to his knees, wailing. By then, the gold-toothed one had produced a short club; the chain was off his partner's waist and in his tea-colored hands.

Well, Enlil, Tempus tested. *A share of this?* Then there was no time to think about the god: all three men came at him together, the one with the chain a trifle ahead of the others.

With the speed of battle on him, it was no great feat for Tempus to throw up his left arm and let the chain snap around it, though he could feel the shock of impact crack the bone above his wrist. Nonetheless, he pulled sharply inward with that hand, and the unexpected movement brought the attacker stumbling forward, neck exposed where a downward stroke from Tempus's sword neatly severed nerves and cut deep between the third and fourth vertebrae. The sorcerer dropped like a stone, falling on his silver box.

Even as Tempus straightened to deal with the gold-toothed one, who had a short club and an uncertain expression on his face, he could appreciate the relative silence.

The shaven-headed one was screaming hoarsely, though he hadn't been touched. If ignorance was protecting Tempus from the spell-casting, then he was pleased enough with that. But not ignorance or the god could protect his flesh from the knife the shaven-headed man now held.

The one with the short club pointed it at him and fire spat thunderously from its tip, but Tempus was already moving toward the one with the knife, using all his god-given speed to take the offensive.

The fire-spitting club clapped like thunder and jumped in its wielder's hand a second time. This time, something of its spell seared Tempus's neck. He felt a sting and a pinch and the warm trickle of his blood.

A point for magic, then. If the wound were poisoned, and the magic strong enough, he was dead on his feet, or captured if that was what this enemy had in mind.

Before any poison dropped him, he must finish these off. It was the only thing in his mind that mattered. The god, now—or his own blood lust—was fully in control.

With a left arm broken above the wrist, his only chance was in the power of his attack. The chain, still wrapped around his broken arm, hid the damage, but not for long. He shook a length of the chain down into his hand and, gritting his teeth at the pain, flailed the loose links at the gold-toothed man with the sorcerer's wand. The club-like wand flew out of a shattered hand and the man fled.

Fled. Good. There remained only the knife-wielding, shaven-headed attacker still moving toward him, so slowly to Tempus's eyes, in combat-distended time.

The shortsword he'd carried into this place was the god's own gift to him. Its tip reflected the sorcerous light from the bar as he closed with the knife man, an unexpected forward lunge that brought the blade into the soft belly.

He didn't notice the knife falling from a frozen hand. Tempus watched the eyes of his enemy as they widened while, at belly-level, he brought the shortsword up a hand's breadth and down again, until it grated on pelvic bone.

When he pulled his sword out of the crumpling man, he realized that there were onlookers in the bar's doorway.

Tempus faced them, wiping his sword on his leathers, letting his body's readiness say what his tongue could not.

A stout man in an apron was in the forefront. He met Tempus's eyes for a moment, mouth agape. Then he closed it and backed up, pushing the others behind him farther inside.

The bar's door closed tight. Tempus stepped over the shaven-headed enchanter, lying in the widening circle of his blood, very carefully: sorcerer's blood could bite like acid, ravage like poison. Mustn't get any on himself.

When he was clear, he leaned against the brick wall for a moment, chest heaving.

The pain that the battle had deferred would be on him soon enough. With infinite care he unwound the chain from his arm, dropped it, and examined the misshapen limb turning blue as he watched.

At least bone wasn't poking through. The wound on his neck was burning as ragged edges of severed flesh tried to seal. And his hip hurt from something: a misstep, perhaps. He limped off, his back aprickle, down the alley he wouldn't have chanced before, hoping the god would heal him before any friends of the sorcerers picked up his track.

He didn't know how long he walked, then trotted, among the narrow streets. People stared at him openly as he passed. Well, he was spattered with blood and moving fast, still full of the god's speed.

Tempus had forgotten about the seashore. He'd lost track of it, in any case. All he could smell here was oil and smoke and foul, rotting food.

He passed stalls where victuals were spilling out onto the sidewalk and realized he was hungry. He stabbed a tuber with his sword and kept going. Someone yelled, and a white-clad boy came running out, but didn't follow. He ate the tuber on the run.

How long he wandered, Tempus didn't know. Until the brown light faded; until Lemurian-type globes on poles began to glow. He stayed off the racing tracks as best he could, crossed them when he dared.

And finally, when he was beginning to stagger, he found a meadow guarded by great statues and dotted with trees. There, at least, he could see who came and what massed against him. The god's speed was not meant for human flesh to endure, hour after hour. He was as exhausted as he'd ever been, and his arm was a blaze of agony.

He found a tree he liked, on a knoll, and there he stood, his back against it, chest heaving.

Some walked by and gave him only the quickest glance, the most covert notice: one soldier, lightly armed, leaning against a tree in the dusky air was nothing remarkable in this place. That was something.

The local peacekeepers must be spread thin, with all the malevolent enchanters roaming loose. Still, anywhere he'd ever fought, or been charged with maintaining order, he'd established a police presence to do the job.

Why had no one come by, during the battle with the four wizards, to take a hand? And then it struck him: in this thoroughly accursed place, could the sorcerers be the law of the land? If so, that would explain his sister's presence here.

Cime slew enchanters, where and when she could. A slum full of them would keep her busy for quite a while.

Where there were slums, there were landed gentry. Palaces. Estates. Merchant quarters. He was heading toward them, by the manicured look of the meadow.

Here was quiet of a sort; better air; a respite from the stench and noise. The welcome feel of tree bark at his back lulled him. He slid down the trunk to sit in the grass, carefully arranging his left arm with his right.

Sleep never came to him, but the god's healing made him dizzy; he had all he could do to splint the arm on his belt knife, using strips of jerkin, to make sure it healed straight and strong.

A whinny nearly brought him to his feet when the night was full-blown. Too many stars twinkled above him; they were all in the wrong places. He remembered that from Lemuria, and reason quenched any hopes that the whinny might have been his Tros horse.

But a horse it was, no matter he was still in the land of demon chariots . . .

When the horse was close enough that he could smell it, he called to it.

Hoofbeats answered. Soon enough it came out of the dark, bearing a rider in a helmet that had no faceplate, but only a chinguard.

This rider was a soldier, and Tempus got wearily to his feet, relieved, to greet the cavalryman when he dismounted.

But the rider did not dismount. He shined a strange torch at Tempus and spoke in that brusque tongue. This time, the god's ear was turned to the words. Though they made no sense yet, he recognized words he'd heard before.

And he knew the man wanted him to approach the horse.

Which, despite his wounds, he was glad to do.

The horse's shoulder was soothing to his touch. It was no horse such as he'd ever seen: its rump was huge and its neck short, nearly crestless. Someone had cut off all its mane. It snorted at him and he ran his hand from its withers to its bridle as he looked up at the mounted man, who continued speaking.

The tone of these words was increasingly loud and hostile. He heard more words he'd heard before: "Fuckin-A, Asshole. Back off, Slime." And some that he had not: "I'm not going to tell you again. Get away from my horse. Drop those weapons and assume the position."

When the soldier paused, Tempus touched his chest, repeated the first part, which he was sure was a standard salutation because he'd heard the sorcerers use it: "Fuckin-A, Asshole." And spoke his own name, slowly: "Tempus," adding his titles, and using the other's name, "Slime."

In response, the soldier named Slime took his feet from foot-holders on his saddle and dismounted.

Eye to eye, the two faced each other. The cavalryman reached for his weaponsbelt.

This was clearly no friendly greeting. Tempus saw the club there, but didn't try to stop the man.

The cavalryman said something else unintelligible, and Tempus shook his head. Out came manacles of a delicate sort, and the club.

Tempus put his good hand on the club when the cavalryman pointed it at him, and pulled.

The cavalryman staggered back, waving his manacles as he struggled for balance, and Tempus took that opportunity to swing up into the horse's saddle, using his right hand only, trying not to bump his splinted left arm.

He landed half astride the horse, his belly on the saddle, and grunted with pain as he pulled himself over and erect.

Thus he saw the enchanter's club which spat fire come out of a sheath on the cavalryman's belt just in time to knee the horse into a run. Only then did he realize he was facing yet another magic-bearing foe. This was no ordinary soldier, but one of his sorcerous enemies. A belated realization that this town was ruled by magic made him cautious too late.

The club spoke thunder and spat fire and smoke: once, twice. Shouts accompanied it.

The galloping horse under him shuddered, then bolted. Tempus was content to let it run. It knew the terrain; he did not.

He leaned down, hugging its neck, breathing hard. In the wind and the dark, he could have been riding any horse on the heels of any battle that had gone badly.

He knew the horse would return to its stable if left to its own devices, and that its stable would likely be a bastion of sorcery, of enchanter cavalry.

He simply didn't know where else to go. Meeting the

enemy head on might be foolish, but so was fleeing blindly through an unknown land where he did not speak the language.

As the horse ran, he pled with the god to give him a sign, help him find understanding, guide his path.

He could count on the fingers of one hand the number of times he'd pled with Enlil in the past.

And the god, finally, answered.

Or least the horse stopped dead, rearing and snorting, at the sight of a demon chariot with blazing eyes of light blocking their path, smack in the middle of one of the slag-covered roads.

Chapter 6:

REUNION

The horse's neck was white with froth. Tempus sluiced it with his hand as the blowing beast danced in place, throwing its head so that foam from its mouth sprayed him like a rainshower.

Out of the demon chariot stepped one man, and then a second. Tempus was not about to wait for another thunder club to spit at him.

The horse under him reared, walking about on its hind legs: it, too, did not want to be struck by the thunderwand. But it had panicked. He had to get it down on all fours where it could run; hitting it between the ears would bring it down, but it would be too dizzied to heed him. As he was urging the horse to pay attention to him, and not the chariot of wizards, one of the men called his name.

For a moment, he wasn't sure he'd heard it. Then, again, a voice called, "Tempus, for god's sake, get off that horse and come with us. While you still can."

The language was the Proto-Akkadian they'd been speaking in Lemuria.

The voice was that of Rath, or Mano, at first he wasn't sure which.

But he brought the horse down as best he could: he

had to shift the reins to his splinted arm in order to hit
its skull with his fist.

Then he threw a leg over, slipped to the ground, and
slapped the beast smartly on the rump. None of this
was the horse's fault. He watched it go for a moment,
wondering what he'd have seen if he'd let it carry him
to its barn.

Then he paid attention to the men urging him into
the demons' chariot, which was covered like an enclosed wagon.

One was approaching. "Tempus, come on, man.
Hurry. We're all in enough trouble as it is . . . "

"You heard, then, about the wizards who attacked
me?" Tempus said as he went to meet Mano halfway.

"Heard—I guess . . . Your arm. What happened?"

Holding the door to the demon wagon was Rath, who
admonished, "Later. Get him in here. If we get caught
out like this, with him, it's all our asses."

Rath's words made sense enough, and the emotion
under them rang true to Tempus.

Still, folding himself into the demon wagon was daunting. It had a front and rear bench; a baleful, lighted eye
in its ceiling, and as strange an array of glowing glyphs
and knobs as any he'd seen in Lemuria.

When he was almost inside, Rath slid onto the front
bench and Mano shoved Tempus impatiently from
behind.

He twisted to face the importunity. Mano straightened up, raised both hands, and backed a pace. "I'm
sorry. Truly sorry. This is for your benefit, Commander.
Please, we worked so hard to get you here; don't let it
be for nothing."

From the front bench, Rath spat a string of short
syllables. Tempus recognized only "fuck" and "ass," but
he realized now that the language he'd heard them
speaking in Lemuria was native to this place.

Neither of these men had ever said anything to make
him assume they weren't from here, but then he hadn't

known what "here" was like. He almost balked at entering the demon wagon.

But Mano's face was not the face of an enchanter; it was the face of a beleaguered subordinate trying to do a difficult job against heavy odds, and short on luck. Tempus had seen that face a hundred times.

To it, he listened. He scrambled awkwardly into the rear of the wagon, guarding his splinted arm, which was beginning now to itch and pulse as his god-given healing progressed.

Mano got in beside him, saying, "Slide over some," and shut the door.

Then the light went out, a roar like a huge cat came and went, and the purring of a panther followed it: the demon cart was moving. He looked straight ahead, and saw that Rath was guiding the cart with the wheel he sat behind.

He looked to one side, and saw trees and the occasional building fall behind. He looked to the other and saw Mano, sitting sideways on the bench, regarding him.

"What about your arm?" Mano wanted to know.

"It will heal in the god's time."

"Your neck?"

He'd almost forgotten that. "Dried blood, mostly. Don't concern yourself. I'd thought to see you both sooner."

"Sorry, Commander," Rath said wryly from the front seat. "We were unavoidably detained."

"By wizards? This place is a pit," Tempus said. "You didn't tell me how thick the magic was."

"By *what?*" Mano wanted to know.

"Yeah, you bet," Rath said. "Look, sir, we've got to get you oriented, get you a language session, if Mano will oblige . . . ?"

"Ah . . . " Mano cracked his knuckles. This was, Tempus judged, a point of argument as yet unresolved between them.

"Mano?" Rath prodded. "This was your damned idea. You like how it's working? I told you this would—"

"I'll take care of the language problem, if Tempus—if the Commander will allow me to instruct him?"

Tempus inclined his head. "And maps, and a lesson in the customs and laws of this place. And some idea where it is you think my sister is—all are not only welcome, but necessary."

"Oh boy," said Rath from the front seat. "You got it, hotshot. Mano, he's your baby. It's your show. Yes to whatever, right?"

These men used language strangely, but Tempus gathered that Mano was in control of intelligence, and Rath's specialty was something else. And they argued between themselves, with him as pawn, as to who was in overall charge.

"I said, yes," Mano muttered. "Let's go to my place now, then."

"That's a relief," Rath said, and turned the wheel in his hands so that the cart veered sharply to the right, throwing Tempus's bad arm against the door. He grunted.

"Hurts, yes?" Mano said.

"Hurts yes," he replied. And looked the fighter straight in the eye. "At your bidding, I'm here. You must say what you want, and who these sorcerers serve, before we go further. If you are on the side of magic, I cannot—"

"Believe me, Commander, I'm not. Neither is Rath. And we need you beyond my power to express. Just let me go at my own pace. We've a lot to tell, a lot to show. First, you must let me teach you the local language, very quickly, in a strange way. Trust my good faith and all things will become clear."

Rath, in the front seat, snorted like a doubtful horse.

"I'll trust my instinct, where you're concerned," said Tempus. It was the best he could do in this demon cart, headed now through a throng of other bright-eyed demon carts, up a canyon faced with huge, sheer-sided buildings, all with lights abounding.

"Good enough. Beggars can't be choosers," Rath said quietly. "We'll take what we can get. Right, Mano?"

"You bet," said the other.

"Cime is here?" Tempus heard himself ask as he craned his neck to see the buildings whose tops scratched the very sky.

"Oh she's here, all right," said Mano. "And up to her venerable neck in something that's brought me as far back in time as it's brought you forward."

"In time?" Tempus wanted to know. "All things are the same distance from Lemuria."

"Never mind, Mano. Not yet. Give him some English first. I'm barely managing all this idiomatic transposition."

"We'll rest and I'll teach you at my home, which is safe. You can heal there. Your friend Cime'll be easy to find when you're ready."

"I'm ready now," Tempus said, though he knew he wasn't.

This place was horrible beyond words: everywhere were signs of sorcery. Whole birds and rabbits hung in windows. Weird robes decorated frozen people under lights, warnings to the unbelieving or the unconvinced that sorcery held this place in thrall.

"You'll feel better in the morning, after you've had some sleep."

"I don't sleep," Tempus told them.

"Terrific. Well, we can match that, with a little help from a bottle or two," Rath said. "We'll be pulling into that building there." He pointed at one. "Just sit quietly until we tell you to get out. Then we'll be getting into a closet that lifts on a winch to the upper floors, so don't be nervous. And don't say anything, if you can manage it."

"I understand," Tempus said. "Secrecy. We don't want them to know our whereabouts."

"Them?" Mano echoed.

"The sorcerers who will come looking to avenge their dead."

"Oh boy," said Rath again as the demon chariot began a descent into a deeper hell filled with others of its kind.

When they'd found it a place in the cave under the building, they got out and led him to the promised closet. Mano touched a boss on a panel, which lit. Rath put his fingers to his lips as a wide-eyed woman in furs and a staring man in a wool robe joined them before the doors closed.

The two newcomers turned and faced the closing door without comment until it opened and they got out. Tempus would have followed; his stomach was churning; his ears had blocked when the closet winched upward.

"Not yet," Rath cautioned. Mano touched the panel of bosses once more and the door closed. The closet continued to rise.

Tempus was considering the possibility that he'd fallen in with a contingent of warring sorcerers, and what he'd do if he became sure that he had.

If these two hadn't known his sister's name, hadn't been welcome in Lemuria, he'd have eviscerated them here and now for the pure pleasure of ridding the world of two possible wizards.

But they had and they were, so he did not. There was plenty of time, if treachery was afoot, to deal with it.

In so strange a land, men who knew the lay of it had value. For the nonce.

When the door of the closet opened again, revealed was a rich antechamber, fine furnishings, more softly glowing lights in sconces. And an inner door to which Mano had the key.

"Primitive, but comfortable enough," said Mano, with a sly grin and a snide edge to his voice.

"Cut the crap," said Rath. "Don't push your luck. "As if heeding his own words, he stepped aside, motioned Tempus to proceed him, and went through the door last.

And Tempus for the first time relaxed, having someone at his back who was concerned for the party's safety.

The familiarity of that maneuver—entering a strange place with a point man in front and a rear guard behind—reminded him of what he'd liked about these two. And that reminded him that Askelon had been distraught that he should join them.

Therefore, they must be worthy allies, despite appearances.

The appearances were all of fielded sorcery, which Mano said were, "Reasonable and unmysterious. When you have language, I'll explain."

They sat him in a big soft chair and demanded to see to his arm. He told them that the god was seeing to it, which they didn't believe until they'd cut away the leather, and were making a splint of his beltknife.

Mano's unconcealed amazement at Tempus's arm's progress matched Rath's wonder at the quality of the god-given knife.

"If you took this to Sotheby's, Commander, you'd be rich as a king."

"Riches are for women," said Tempus. He needed to make it clear that he couldn't be bribed.

Mano hooted and came with hot tea. "Drink this." He tasted it first, watching Tempus over the mug's rim, to show it held no harm, before he put the mug into Tempus's hand.

As Tempus drank, Mano said, "If you'll take this and hold it in your hands, and these and put them over your ears, and look into this window," he indicated a small box attached by a wire to a spidery hat he held, "then, with the god's help, the language of this place and time will be clear to you in no longer than it takes for your tea to cool."

"It's not magic," Rath was quick to add. "It's technology."

Tempus had heard them use that phrase before, an odd construction of syllables they'd applied at Chiara's to the wisdom of Lemuria.

"It's a teaching aid," Mano said, "a knowledge giver. If you don't like its story, you can crush it underfoot in an instant."

The fighter's eyes were imploring; his upper body was so tense that Tempus knew this was very important to him.

And perhaps, if language could be thusly taught, to them all.

"Give it here." Tempus held out his hand.

"Let me help," Mano offered.

The settling of the muffs onto his ears was painless; the holding of the box in his lap caused no ectoplasmic snakes to issue forth from it to entwine him; no acid ate his palms; no miasma of any sort rose from it.

"Push this to learn; this to stop learning." Two nipples protruded from the box.

When he hesitated to push one, Rath reached down and pushed one for him.

A voice like the god's voice in his head told him to "Look at the screen." In his lap, a little oblong began to glow.

On one side was his native tongue in script, on the other a foreign language. As fast as the god, the knowledge came into him, and he knew it wasn't from reading what words he saw, but rather from what he was hearing and something he was feeling inside his skull, as if a wind were stirring there.

But he let it happen, because he was daunted here, out of his depth, because his instinct said that he needed to know what the box had to teach, and because he wouldn't show fear in front of these men.

When it was done, so far as he could tell, he still had his soul. And his god. The noise of the teaching had roused Enlil, and over that outpouring of context and content the god had raged: *Think you that simple learning will make you in My image, petitioner? Ask Me for wisdom, and you shall know more than these fools can ever teach!*

So, wordlessly he'd humbled himself once more before

Enlil, and the god showed him what these men dared not: that they needed him to fight a tide of magic here that Cime alone could never stem.

Moreover, that these two were not contemporaries, nor of one mind about what should be done and how. And that the old rules still obtained: only greedy, godless men were deaf to wisdom, and in their hands knowledge and power forever equalled only folly.

Folly abounded here. The one called Mano had come back to visit his ancestors to root it out, so Enlil claimed.

And the god was never wrong.

Leave them, Enlil told him. *Reconnoiter on your own.*

But the god was a trickster, and jealous to boot. And Tempus was sore and hungry and unready to brave the horrid streets alone just then.

When the dawn broke, it would be another matter. By then he would have heard all the two men had to say, and found a way to go about these streets unremarked while he searched for Cime.

But with or without these two, search for her he would. And find her, no matter how bloody the trail.

He and Enlil were both agreed on that.

Chapter 7:

SHOW AND TELL

"Say what you want now, Mano." Tempus searched for the English words and they came easier to his mind than to his lips. A map of the city of New York was spread before them on a round table. The map was dizzyingly complex, yet the simplest task before him this evening had been finding his place on it. "And who these sorcerers here serve. Whatever you know about the enemy, tell me. Then how you think to thwart them."

"He still talks like an import," Rath criticized.

"So what?" Mano answered his compatriot first. "We can say he's from Venezuela, if we have to." Then he rubbed a stubbled jaw and answered Tempus, "What you're asking's not simple, Commander."

"Why not, Mano?" Rath interrupted. "He wants mission definition, threat assessment. So would I, in his place. So *do* I, and I've been going along with you on faith so long that I can't write even the most basic report anymore. I mean, how do I say that on September the fifth I made a swing through Atlantis, transferred some technology back with me that I promised not to declare, and smuggled in an alien to beat all aliens . . . ?"

"You *don't* say, friend, because that was our agreement. You need my help with this more than I need yours, yes?" Mano stood up and so did Rath.

The two were eye to eye. "It's about time you laid it out, *friend*. All I want to do is stop these cult murders, or whatever they are, before they end up on the front page of The New York Times."

From this, Tempus inferred that Rath was responsible to local authorities for the outcome of this sortie, and that Mano, as he'd implied, was a visitor like Tempus, responsible only to his own conscience here and now.

Also, seeing the two so close to open conflict, his initial impressions, back in Lemuria, were strengthened: Mano was a professional fighter—the alertness in every muscle declared it; the way he balanced himself to counter any move by Rath affirmed it; the restless energy in his lean, large frame and the constant, slight movement of his eyes, back and forth to Tempus to make sure no threat came unexpectedly from that quarter, confirmed it beyond doubt.

Next to Mano, Rath seemed soft, nearly boneless, and yet the intensity of the local official's demeanor could not be mistaken. And that too swung the balance in Mano's favor if push came to shove between them: Rath was the defender of this place, with too much passion and too much at stake.

Rath's face worked; his brow shone; his dark-stubbled upper lip glittered and his chest rose and fell under a knitted chiton that was beginning to sop the sweat. Yet Rath's clear light eyes were steady: he would protect his turf, even from his ally. And he'd been pushed as far as he would go with no explanation. His round chin jutted.

Mano was the first to break the stalemate. His own angular, blue-stubbled jaw relaxed; his lips quirked; his weight came off the balls of his feet and he murmured something in a language that was not English nor any other Tempus knew as his eyes hit the floor and he brushed the side of his nose with a knuckle. "You got it.

Let's have a beer and we'll crash and burn everybody's questions."

Tempus knew that men speaking untruths often touched their noses or otherwise hid their lips when they did.

Perhaps Rath did not know the signs. Or perhaps he did, and still was content to hear what he might: men this committed and this controlled would not risk utter fabrications; some truth would out, though not all; confidence must be built for joint endeavor. From long in the field, any good leader learned that what was withheld could be as instructive as what was told.

The beer loosened Mano's tongue, so it seemed. Tempus drank water that bubbled and tickled his nose and smacked of fruit, because Rath said, when Tempus wouldn't take beer, that plain water here wasn't fit to drink.

Bad water was nothing new in the world; many streams could kill you, turn your bowels to jelly, yet Rath spoke as if the fact pained him, as if he were personally guilty for the water's foulness.

Strange land; strange pain; strange bedfellows. And a stranger, compacted tongue that was still bemusing Tempus as he spoke it: this learning was not like the god's, and his ears and the place behind his eyes tingled each time someone spoke and his new knowledge came into play.

So he wasn't sure how much of Mano's speech he understood. He watched closely because of that, reading every lineament in the fighter's face and every shift of bodyweight and twitch of muscle. From these, he deduced that everything said was true, though chosen carefully not to afright or dishearten.

"First things first," Mano had begun when his beer was only scud in his glass. "Tempus asked what we want to do, what the best result—or the mission definition—is. I got some of what I need from Lemuria, admittedly. Maybe I could have done all of this without you, Rath—but not without Tempus, because his

ladyfriend, Cime, is part of the matrix from which the
problem stems. Remove Cime from play—get her out
of this time frame, back to someplace she's comfortable,
or you are, Commander—someplace not in America,
or in this century, but in any distant past—and that
disturbance will probably be enough to let us penetrate
the enemy and destroy him."

"By force of arms?" Tempus asked.

"Probably," Mano said and ducked his head.

"What's she got to do with fundamentalist crazies and
doomsday weapons?" Rath demanded.

"Rath, you keep underestimating your situation. I've
told you before, you've got an actual black magic cult
that's spreading, that's going to utilize everything from
suicidal Muslims to voodoo practitioners to Christian
martyrs. You think you've got problems now, wait a
hundred years."

"Come on, Mano, I told you, that shit won't play
anymore."

But Mano said to Tempus, "Commander, you're more
capable of dealing with this problem than Rath is; he's
just a glorified beat cop cum public servant in a bureau-
cratically impotent nexus."

"What?" Tempus said.

"Rath doesn't believe in magic," Mano explained flatly.

Tempus shifted to regard Rath, who was pulling on
his damp, knitted chiton. Rath summoned a weak and
sour smile. "Well, it's the twentieth century, fellas.
Come on, Commander—I didn't even believe in Atlan
—in Lemuria, until Mano took me there. I've been
doin' damn fine, just keepin' my mouth shut and my
eyes open and my Delta Ten in its holster."

"But the signs of sorcery are all around you here.
Any fool can smell it."

"Not if that fool don't know what it smells like. Look,
Tempus," Rath sat forward. "I'd still like to wake up and
find out that all this is just a dream—Mano, here, with
his time travel black bag; you with your skirt and your
Metropolitan Museum weapons; that Lemurian dinner

party with those walkin' mummies and the girl in skins and what's-his-name from the Land of Nod: Askelon."

Tempus blinked and said, "If you wish the dream lord's interference upon us, you're more of a fool than I'll drink with." He stood up, urgency and fury mixing in him; his hand went instinctively to his sword; his eyes searched the room for signs of Askelon's transportational whirlwinds.

"Easy, Tempus," Mano said as if talking to a skittish horse. "Rath's a barbarian in your terms; his people don't understand the power of dreams; they think no more of dreams than of lies—or of gods. Consequently, this . . . sorcerous . . . enemy's capable of using its power against these people without the checks and balances that the dream lord and the gods represent."

"Godless and dream-deaf?" He'd felt that. He'd just refused to credit it. His god rustled inside him and actually growled in his inner ear. His hackles rose. "Then how do we oppose this sorcery, if there are no gods working here, and no one heeds his dreams?"

"It's you and me, fella, and the god you rode in with." Mano showed white, perfect teeth and then his mouth drew so tight his lips nearly disappeared. He picked up his glass, drained it of scud, and set it down, hard, on a table made from a slab of rock with a school of fossilized fish whose bones were embedded there for eternity.

"You call this a briefing?" Rath demanded, exasperation making him spit.

"You asked for it. Don't complain if you don't like what you hear. Your ignorant society's allowed this mess to get so bad—will allow it—that I had to come here. You have no idea what it cost in lives and lifetimes of wasted effort, and in coin you're just too damned primitive to understand. These people that Tempus calls sorcerers are using the matrix—what you'd call field potentials if your science had any real grasp of what Maxwell's equations are about—to manipulate reality. They're breaking through dimensional gates and interacting with forces that don't belong in the same phase with human beings. And they're using power sources that punch nasty holes in spacetime. You think living in a world where that's the way war is conducted is some kind of fun? Where I'm from we've got worse than doomsday weapons: we've got expectation vectors which stack the odds against what I like to think of as the good guys."

"I don't get this," Rath said.

"You get bodycounts from your increasingly mean streets, don't you? You get spikes from your government agencies about engineering anomalies and information leaks that couldn't happen, don't you? You get ideological wars fought by crazies that think human mutilation's part of the arsenal, don't you? You get cold explosions and what you think are UFO abduction reports, don't you? You live long enough, all that's going to seem like run of the mill, everyday police work."

"Ah, shit, don't tell me I'm mixed up with a UFO nut . . ."

"I'm telling you what you asked me to tell you: if we don't shut down these . . .sorcerers, for lack of a better word . . . before they wrench reality into something you can only barely relate to, the nice, logical world you think you're living in is going to disappear and be replaced with something a lot like Tempus's worst nightmares."

"I don't sleep," Tempus reminded Mano.

"Lucky for you; nobody's messing with your brain while you do. But the rest of us do," Mano said. "Rath does. Rath, keep in mind, as long as you're using Aristotelian logic, and going from a base of agnostic phenomenology, you're going to lose this fight, and my society pays the price. As long as you don't believe in good but you do believe in evil, which is how your surviving religions have been coopted by the other side, you're going into this battle unarmed."

"Well, that leaves me out, because I don't believe in god, or abstract battles between some capital-G good and capital-E evil, and I don't know anybody who does—not the way you mean. And like I said," Rath was nearly yelling, "I can't make a report out of any of this. I'd be on semi-permanent R&R in Bellevue."

Tempus asked, as much to give Rath a chance to calm down as because he needed to hear it again: "They don't serve the gods, these folk? They go up against evil on their own?"

"Their gods are weakened with disbelief. They, themselves perceive those gods as impotent against evil; they credit evil with more power than their gods, and thus their gods, such as they are, are powerless against evil." Mano shook his head. "It warps hell out of the . . . how can I say it . . . out of Fate, if you like, when one side's using the energy sea for a power source and the other one projects fear into a dimension where you get what you expect."

"How can I help?" Tempus said uneasily, one ear cocked to the god in his head, who was silent but for the odd and occasional growling he'd been hearing intermittently.

"By getting to Cime, by getting me in there with you, where we can take out the group she's infiltrating."

"Jesus, I thought you'd never get to anything I could understand," Rath said. "We're going to arrest the cult leaders? Great!" Rath reached behind him and came out with a thunderclub, which he put on the table.

Tempus, on his feet, drew his sword.

Mano held up a hand. "Don't sweat the hardware, Commander. I'll explain it in a minute. As a matter of fact, Rath is going to take you down to the Twenty-Third Precinct's police range and tune you up on kinetic kill weapons."

"My ass I will."

"That's right: it's your ass, and you will. He needs to know what's simple physics, and what's not, before we go in there."

"In where?" both Tempus and Rath said at the same time.

"Into the locus where the woman in question is."

"You know where she is? Then the hell with target practice—he's not licensed, anyway. I'll get some backup and we'll go roust the bastards. Any drugs there, or illegal weapons, something to hang an arrest on?"

"We're not going to arrest these people. We're going to kill them," said Mano flatly.

"The hell you say!" Rath, too, stood. "Over my dead body, in this city, are you—"

"That may be the result," Mano said, and he too rose up. "Tempus, are you ready?"

"Since you first spoke her name," he admitted.

"Just for Rath's benefit, we don't start trouble unless they do. Until they do. If we can enlist her aid, we'll be able to clean out the whole nest of them."

"She's not started killing them yet?" Tempus wanted to know, following Mano as the man motioned he should, into a bedroom, with Rath trailing behind.

"Not that we've noticed. Maybe Rath will say different."

Mano was pulling clothes from a closet, glancing from the tunics and leggings and pantaloons to Tempus, and back again.

Rath said, "Lots of people get killed here all the time. How am I supposed to know if some woman's been—"

"She sucks out their souls, through their eyes, mostly," Tempus explained.

"Oh. Well," said Rath, rubbing the back of his neck, an odd expression on his face. "I'm not sure we've any soul-sucked stiffs down at the morgue. What exactly does that look like?"

Tempus started to tell him, but Mano held up a hand for silence. "Put these on, Tempus. We're close enough that they should fit. If you want your regular gear, which I would in your place, keep it under wraps—that is, under these clothes."

Tempus did as he was asked. While he did, the men argued over propriety, and about training him with "guns," which were thunderclubs, he now knew.

He could have left them, shaken them any time. But

Mano knew where Cime was, or thought he did. And Mano was making more sense to him than anything else about this place.

Which was not much, but enough. The god still growled wordlessly in his head, as the god had never done before.

That bothered Tempus more than anything he'd heard tonight, almost as much as Rath was bothered by Tempus's sandals: "Sandals? He'll never cut it, looking like that."

"He will. It's uptown society, not working-stiff uniform. Anyway, your footgear will hobble him. It's been a torture to me; I wouldn't make my worst enemy wear those shoes. And we're not twins; his feet are bigger."

This was their way of decompressing, Tempus knew. But still, the loose clothing felt strange around his legs and arms, as if it might trip him or tangle him up. But under it he had his weaponsbelt. Even if the shortsword protruded somewhat, the long coat covered it well enough.

The god was still uncommunicative, albeit snarling, when they reached the demon cart in the cave. Two other demon carts—"cars," he reminded himself—had pulled up beside it so closely that its doors could not be fully opened.

Rath said, "I'll pull out. I don't want him chipping my paint."

Mano took that opportunity to pull Tempus aside, saying, "Come over here. I need to make sure you and I have an understanding."

"Speak," said Tempus, instinctively stepping into shadows where Rath might not see them clearly enough to guess what was said.

"I want your word, Commander, that you'll stick with me on this, all the way to the end, whatever happens with your ladyfriend, or your sister, or whatever she is. I wasn't kidding: I really need your help. I guess I want some declaration of allegiance . . ."

Tempus's lips drew back and he stared past Mano,

into an ugly corner where mold covered great worms of tubing and huge struts. "Shoulder to shoulder? To the death, with honor? In such a place as this?" His words were hardly more than a whisper, hoarse and heavy with memories. Why had he not expected this? Rebellious for a moment, he almost refused to take this one more man under his protection, one more time. "I'll bury you when the time comes, with honors due. You have my word. You need only tell me the custom of your country." And he clapped Mano on the back.

The startled look on the other man's face came and went; some honest realization followed. And then Mano clapped his own right hand on Tempus's, which still lay on the foreign fighter's left shoulder. "I'd say I'd do the same for you, sir, but I guess we both know it's not likely to go that way. I'll see you back to your own time, or to Lemuria, no matter what it takes, before I go home."

Their hands parted. Mano, having told Tempus he had no intention of dying here, blinked and flicked his thumb in the direction of the car, which was just beginning to light and roar. "Let's get going."

Together they headed for the demon car, which Tempus knew from what he'd learned had nothing of demonic nature about it. As Rath began backing it out of its close quarters, the eyes on its tail blazed red.

Suddenly its roar became an explosion so loud and fierce that Tempus was thrown back from the concussive force. A fireball blossomed red and yellow, green -white and dirty, consuming the closest cars on either side in secondary explosions. He shielded his face with his coated arm from the blossom of flame and flying gobbets.

When he looked again, he could see only flames; a naptha fireball threw no more heat.

He was sprawled on the oily slag where the shock had thrown him, staring at the destruction. Mano was pulling him up. "Come on! Let's go. They know where we are."

Tempus irritably pulled his arm from the other's grasp. He was no child, no green young fighter to be taught the tactics of infiltration, of fighting sorcerers, or eluding enemies house to house.

But he followed Mano anyway. He'd given his word, and Rath was no longer among the living.

In his head, the god was no longer growling. To Enlil, he said so vehemently that his lips moved, "Lord Storm, the next time you wish to warn me of this enemy, be more specific."

Mano was running up the slag incline to the street. He swung around and said, "What?"

But Tempus waved him on. The words had been in the native tongue he and his god shared, and nothing an outsider need understand.

He hoped Rath had a heaven to go to, and said a prayer in case he did not, consecrating the soul of Rath to the god of war, and suggesting that the Slaughter Priest find him if he wandered, and lead him into the Storm God's part of heaven.

Dying in a demon car in Tempus's stead surely entitled him to that.

The explosion danced before his eyes for many moments after they'd run from the cave while others were running into it. Before such a craven and unglorious death by nonattributable fireball, not even Enlil could help him stand.

He remembered Ash telling him he could die here.

He should have known that Askelon would not bother to lie to him. The truth was more than wounding enough.

He spent a breath or two cursing Askelon, who'd let Cime come to such a pass, to such a place. If this place was a demesne of evil, then Askelon should sojourn here as well, to face what he had wrought.

When they were out on the street, Mano held his hand out from his body, palm down, at waist level: slow down, the motion had meant for untold years to such as they. And then three times he moved that same hand down and up: Go cautiously; stay single file.

This Tempus was glad to do, and walk in the stinking air on the harshly lit paves of slag called concrete, until Mano motioned him to his side.

They stood on a corner where two roadways intersected. Mano gestured to a pole with glowing red eyes. "Got to wait for the light to change."

He would have known that, if he'd thought about it. But the god was restless in his head, as if Enlil paced back and forth, and the god's anger was rolling over him in waves of hatred for this place and everything about it, which was more accursed than anywhere either of them had ever been.

Chapter 8:

THE AMERICAN WAY

The city streets and the buildings on those streets were ablaze with pulsing lights that pushed back the night. Mano hailed a passing yellow car, and it turned out to be a taxi.

He could read the words now; the only problem was, they only made sense after he did. A taxi was a car for hire, like a lorry. Its driver had a nut-brown face and, despite Tempus's language lessons, nothing the man said made sense.

Between the bench in back and that in front was a blockade of cheap glass; in it was a slot to pass the money through. A box kept track of the fare with lighted numbers that rose alarmingly, since Tempus had no local coinage.

He asked Mano if Mano did. Mano chuckled and told him "Don't sweat it."

This meant yes, and Tempus went back to listening to the god vent his fury upon the unbelievers of this land.

Enlil was shaken; Tempus had never heard him thus. The god said, *Leave these infidels to their hell and I will not think ill of thee, mortal servant. Your sister is a slut, We both know that. And none here deserves Me, or you.*

Tempus silently reminded the god when he'd said that about foreign lands before, places where the Storm God had other names. *We brought the fear of You into those unbelieving hearts. We can do it here, O God.* At least long enough to get Cime out alive.

But Enlil's distress frightened Tempus as nothing had since he and the god joined forces. They'd battled hostile deities with less compunction. Was it that Enlil had only Tempus, a sole believer, here?

Or was it that magic was, as Mano said, so completely in control that this land and its future was all but lost? Who knew what the god could see? Not Tempus.

Doest thou love me, Pillager? Is that what this is about? After all these years, has Thy heart softened unto me, so that You don't want to lose a worthless servant, as You so often remind me that I am?

It's not wise to bait your god, not in a place where gods are scarce as worthy men, growled Enlil in his head. And then, with a sudden thrill across his flesh like a breeze from a pure and unpolluted sea, all pain left Tempus. His arm stopped itching and aching. His legs felt young and strong, not rubbery and near to cramps. His hip relaxed and the place on his neck where the firespitting gun had struck him no longer counted off his pulse.

The god did love him, then. What a place to find it out. He didn't tease Enlil or comment further. He merely enjoyed the pleasure that absence of pain could be.

If they were truly to accomplish such a feat as removing Cime from this living hell, then man and god needed all the succor they could muster.

The resentment in him, so deep and long accruing, of Enlil's demands and tests and visitations began to ease.

He could feel the god looking out his eyes, spreading into his hands and feet, into his loins and heart, into every inch of him as Lord Storm looked upon the godless and the soulless who walked among them.

For the first time, he could tell an enchanter at a glance. He could see as one of his soldiers once had boasted, the color round a man that told the state of his soul.

And he could see those who had no nimbus whatsoever about them: the walking dead, or soon to be dead; those who'd given everything they had and now were just animals abroad in human clothes.

The rage of Enlil only increased as the city streamed by the taxi's windows. By the time Mano paid through the slot and opened up the door, Tempus was not sure what of him was man, and what was god.

Out onto the sidewalk of concrete they stepped, and here the very slag was swept and clean. Topiary trees in pots dotted a grand entryway. A man in a gold-trimmed coat and hat looked them up and down, then accepted a pass-through paper Mano held out, and bowed his head, disapproval on his face.

So had they come into this place of pulsing lights, and so had the god decided that sorcery was indicated by the colored birds of light and scintillating fish of light, despite Tempus's knowledge of electricity and English words. Fish and Fowl was the place's name, and the music in it would have roused demons if demons had not already been roused to make it.

Through a crowd of drunken folk, and folk dancing entranced within a circle of light, and women who were obviously whore, and men the same, they threaded their way, to another door marked MEN and in there, Mano ever looking back to see he was not lost.

The god wanted to raze this place immediately: mass lightning, bring thunder, blast the evil from the earth.

Tempus was not ready to start razing New York City. He told the god to wait, to pick and choose, to save both their strengths.

Mano and Tempus's god-given sight were proved true and right by the number of sorcerers they saw: outside had been men puffing on glass pipes until their eyes rolled in their heads and the gibberish of possession spewed from their mouths; here were men vomiting in troughs and men who got on their knees to other men within metal stalls.

"Bathroom," Mano explained, though no baths were in evidence. When Tempus touched his arm and indicated a travesty going on behind a swinging door from which the smell of feces wafted, Mano shook his head and quirked his lips: "Customs of the country, yes?"

"Affront against nature," the god gritted through Tempus's lips.

That voice brought Mano's head around. "Whoa, big fella. We're not here to put the fear of god in everyone we see."

"Why not?" Tempus said.

Mano seemed to think about that. "Too many of 'em," he said, closing his pants with the metal teeth like gears sewn there. "Save it for the big fish."

"For big fish, we need big harpoons," replied Tempus, thumping so loudly upon the stall door where the two men were that someone coughed and choked and someone swore. "Hurry, in there," he called in his best battlefield voice, "or I'll come in and hurry you."

This place should be empty for what he wanted to say and what the god wanted to do: Enlil would materialize weapons to fight magicians here and now, if Tempus asked.

There was a flurry and a pair of young men, barely more than boys, came tumbling out of the stall, tripping over one another to get by him and cursing all the way.

"Upon your heads, so be it," he warned the boys who cursed where Enlil could hear. In response, one of them called him something he'd never been, since his mother had been dead before he was of manly age. Something in his voice, or in his face, or in his size, sent them white-faced out the final door, looking backwards all the while and letting in a brief clarion of music and laughter riding on noxious smoke and passion's acrid stink.

"All right, we've emptied the place." Mano sat on a wash basin. It creaked but held him. "What is it?"

"They know we're here. We may have problems. Want better weapons?"

"Than what? A shortsword? Yeah, I bet you do." Mano misunderstood. "Well, the gun—you remember guns—went with Rath. Anyway, you don't know how to use that sort of thing."

"The god will give us weapons if we wish a manifestation."

"Ah . . . let the god decide if we need a 'manifestation.' I'd love to have supernal backup, don't get me wrong. But we're going to see if she'll just . . . come with you, have a little talk, relive old times—"

"She will not welcome reliving—"

"Figure of speech. She'll let us know how to proceed. Or you can have your . . . manifestation. Agreed?"

"Agreed, but it's you who needs the better weapons."

A boyish grin cracked Mano's facade for an instant; he cocked his head and inclined it. "Nice to know you're thinking about me, but I'm okay. Brought stuff from home. Little surprise if we need it."

"What you had did no good against the demon car deciding to explode."

"No, no, it didn't decide. Somebody decided for it: explosives; remember your learning tape . . . No magic except in how they got past the alarms. At least, I don't think so."

This last was in response to Tempus's disbelieving arch of eyebrow.

"Okay, magic, then. Well, we knew they weren't going to play fair, that's why I went all that way to get somebody like you. So we don't play fair either. I'm just your righthand man on this, is how to think about it."

That brought Tempus up straight, away from the door. This one knew more than he pretended, and was asking more than Tempus could give, now with death so probable in this endeavor that even Enlil was concerned.

"I've had righthand men and buried them, I told you."
Then he reached into the idiom and said, "Look, cow-
poke, I don't want to marry you. We'll just have one
dance. Got that?"

"Damn, that's a good tape," Mano said. "And okay,
you got it, I told you before. Your way's the way it
plays. But you misunderstood. I'm not asking for anything more than we agreed upon in the garage. I didn't
know there could be any—"

"There can, but not in this way, in this place, with
such as you. Souls who get too fond of me die young."

"You did misunderstand." Mano was sober now, looking past Tempus to the empty stall. " 'Righthand man'
is just a phrase from this culture meaning . . . . assistant, aide, best boy, lieutenant. And that's *all*. Now, can
we go say hello to the lady?"

"Go. First." He motioned Mano to preceed him, out
into the throng. And through it they went, the god
ramping inside of him like a bothered bear, hot for
blood at so many who had no respect for Him.

When they were behind the place where couples
danced on squares of light, Mano again showed his pass-
through and another man opened another door for them.

Inside, the air was cleaner, the light softer and
unflickering, the people fewer.

These were gaming. Tempus knew the signs, if not
the games themselves.

And there indeed, as Mano had predicted, was Cime,
in jewels and velvet and feathers as dark as night, her
black hair bound up with two rods that glittered like
diamonds.

She was leaning over a rotating wheel, watching a
ball bounce in a trough there. A man was beside her,
with a hand on her bare back.

Mano's hand closed on Tempus's just as his found his
sword hilt under the layers of loose clothing he wore.
"Not yet," Mano reminded him.

"As we agreed," said Tempus, though the god did not
approve.

Did he want to slay her or the man with her, or all of these? For a moment Tempus wasn't sure. She'd cost him so much. She was all he'd ever loved and all he'd ever hated. They could not stand to be together, yet they suffered apart.

He almost spoke her name but the god dried it on his tongue.

There were more dangers here than Cime's proximity, Enlil thought. And Mano was urging Tempus toward the bar, where they'd be less remarkable than standing frozen where he'd seen her, staring.

Turning his back on the sight of her was one of the most difficult things he'd ever done. At the bar, Mano ordered beer for both of them and Tempus watched his own two hands, afraid to look up into the bar's mirror, afraid of what he'd see.

Was she whoring here, in among mages, as she was wont to do? Would Mano understand her reasons, or the curse, put on her millenia ago as this place counted time, that made her take any man for pay? Would he think ill of her? Or worse, underestimate her because he did? Or worst of all, dispute her honor so that Tempus was caught between them?

Knowing he might have explained, but had not when he could, what kind of sister she was to him, he hunched over the beer when it came, waiting for what must happen next.

He thought he'd have to raise his eyes, see her in the mirror with that hand on her flesh so casually, then go to her and put himself between her and the sorcerer who stroked her as the two played their game of chance.

For a sorcerer it was: that single look had made it clear. A man in black and white with jeweled studs down his starched front, blond hair, a lantern-jawed, but pretty, face.

He said to Mano, still watching his fingers, reddish in the bar's ruddy light as if blood already washed them, "I can't abide her living in with magic." It came hard through gritted teeth.

Mano's hands weren't on the bar; his beer was untouched by Tempus's.

And it wasn't he who answered.

From close behind him, Cime said in a voice that wrenched his soul, "All this way to interfere, and then cower in a corner. It couldn't be harder to face me than face what it took to get here. Turn around, you big, eternal fool."

He did, and she was so close they nearly touched. She shook her head and whispered, "Get out of here, idiot. You know not where you are, or you'd come with your whole army of bloody boys behind you."

All that was said in a dialect unknown here and now, and Mano cocked his head and elbowed Tempus.

"My friend," Tempus croaked in English, "Mano. This is Cime." And then he couldn't think of another thing to say.

But Mano could. "Dear lady, I suggest you come with us. Right now, without a fuss." His hand was inside his jacket, in an ominous and pointed display of threat.

Cime looked from Mano's face, to the hand, to Tempus and back to his dark-haired companion. "So my lord Tempus dared not come alone, after all. Interesting idea, no doubt. But I have a client, presently."

Tempus looked away. His whole body ached from suppressing the urge to grab her by the throat. What he'd do after that, even Enlil was not sure. As his eyes sought a refuge from the pain of watching her, his glance fell upon the man she'd been with, who'd noticed where she'd gone and stood with one hand on his hip and a calculating air.

"Shake my hand, boy," she told Mano when nothing at all happened for too long. "Next time, make a reservation."

A bit of coin, she meant. An old game still played out, a curse he'd once believed was lifted by the dream lord. Tempus reached into his pocket and came up with nothing: he'd brought no local money. Beneath the coat and local clothes, he had a coinpurse. In that was gold; but beside it was his sword.

Time was slow in this place. He could feel it creep by, lashing its tail, pregnant with violence, well before the god began once more to growl.

Mano was talking to Cime, he realized: "Coin you want?" He pulled out one, and tossed it. By chance or fate, it dropped down her low cut dress.

She looked askance at Mano, then at him. Watching Tempus, she reached down inside her dress, caught up the coin, and put it to her lips. "When I'm free, I'll call you, Mano."

"Stay right where you are," Mano said, "and we'll take care of that."

Out came Mano's hand. In it was something like a thunderclub in size, built without the round snout that guns here had. Yet the speed of extraction and the way Mano moved made Tempus know it was a weapon.

Tempus grabbed Cime's arm, and pulled, jerking her off her feet and using the arm he held to swing her around and pin her against him. The misery and the joy of that contact made him slow to react to what he saw.

The room lights began exploding, one by one. People began to scream. Mano was pointing his wand at this spot or that and everywhere he pointed, lights went out, metal melted, glowing red, then yellow, and white as it heated.

Chairs scraped. Things and folk fell and scrambled. Women begged for help. Men cursed and suddenly it was completely dark for an instant.

In that moment, he could see a pulsing beam crossing through motes of dust. Then, above, the ceiling started to creak and moan as if it was going to fall on them.

The bar mirror behind him fell from the wall and crashed.

And Mano grabbed him by the coat, saying, "Bring her."

He still had her pinned. He couldn't let her get her

hands free. The wands in her hair would wreak more havoc than Mano counted upon.

Now the room was lit intermittently with bursts of flame and resounding with gunfire as men shot into darkness.

Something sped past his ear: enchanters could see in the dark; so, evidently could Mano.

He let Mano guide him by a fistful of coat, while he dragged and wrestled Cime along as she cursed him.

A square of light opened before his eyes: the door which Mano held.

"Hurry. Through there."

Out here were the dancers and the drunks, a melee beyond the room marked MEN. He stepped on something as he lunged through with Cime grasped before him like a bag of spelt: a human arm, that rolled sideways under his tread.

Then Mano shut the door and backed away from it. With the snoutless thunderclub aimed at it, its edges flared, and spat sparks, and melted till they seamed.

"That door's seal won't hold if someone tries it soon," Mano said, weaving the wand over the doorknob, which turned white hot. "Out the front, the way we came."

Cime wasn't struggling hard against him, he realized. She didn't scream for help or do more than curse halfheartedly.

Something in him, perhaps the god, understood why that was: proximity of flesh to flesh, when it was theirs, had a way of confusing everything.

Even the god was distracted by her rump against his groin. Without more than a moment's hesitation, he brought her in under his arm, sharing the coat he wore, as if she were cold, or stuporous, or lost in love.

Through the deafening music and the unknowing crowd of revelers they bumped and serpentined, until they found the front door and the street outside.

Only then did he realize how hard she was breathing, or how she was trembling. Or how much of her was touching him, all down his side.

There he could hear her, could see her in the street-light. He brushed a loose lock from her forehead with his free hand as Mano was hailing a taxi.

Cime said, "Why did you do this, fool? You need more enemies? You need a close look at eternal death?"

"You can't win this on your own," he heard himself say. "You don't understand what's happening here."

"And you do?" she scoffed, and jabbed her shoulder into him as if to shake him off.

He pulled her harder against him. "Why did you come with me, then?"

She laughed and the sound chilled him. "Your friend gave me a deposit, then killed the one before him in line."

He almost pushed her away. Then he recognized the ploy, the intentional hurt, and said, "If I cut out your tongue and sent it to the dream lord, we'd both have what we want of you, Ash and I."

"Tempus, bring her," Mano called urgently. The big man was holding open a taxi's door.

He almost refused. He had Cime under his arm, and the god awake and attentive in his mind. He could find the door to Lemuria and be gone with her. It was safer than getting into a demon car that might explode. He stared into it and saw a driver with a yellow face and slanting, hooded eyes.

But he'd given his word to Mano, and Cime was still holding the other man's coin.

He said, "We'll straighten this out," to her: a warning, a promise; too little, too late. He could never say the right thing to her.

A second peal of mocking laughter from her lips proved that. "You mean your friend will. You'll wring your hands and pace and closet with your god, as you always do, and come up empty-handed in the end."

He grabbed her by the hair then, exasperated, knowing what he must do. With his free hand, he pulled the diamond rods from her hair and it came tumbling down

around her shoulders as he let her go with a push
toward the waiting car.

Mano lunged to catch her, swearing.

"She'll get right in, docile as a lamb," Tempus
predicted.

And she did.

He held up the rods by way of explanation as Mano
got in beside her and told Tempus, "Go around the
other side."

When both doors had slammed and the cab pulled
away, no one had come chasing them.

Perhaps no one had yet come out from the back
room; perhaps, with all the noise, the carnage there
had yet to be discovered.

Or perhaps the sorcerers' den was too illicit, even
here, to risk exposure even in destruction.

He didn't know. He didn't care. Cime was between
him and his self-proclaimed righthand man. The accursed city was speeding by, the street on which they'd
found her already out of sight.

Cime was sullen now, refusing to look at him. She
leaned away from his touch, toward Mano. He saw her
hand brush the other's knee.

He closed his eyes tight, cautioned the god to let him
choose his own path and stop counseling immediate
gratification. The pressure inside him was making it
hard for him to think.

"Mano," he said, "what was that you did in there?"

"I told you, I brought something from home. And I
told you not to worry."

"They'll come after me. They think they need me,"
Cime announced. "They think I'm one of them. But
those were good kills, fighter, even if they all rise up
from the dead, it makes my heart glad to see them fry."
She squeezed Mano's knee overtly now.

Mano looked at her hand there, then questioningly at
Tempus, and Tempus realized that Mano had no idea
what Cime was all about.

And so did she. "I'll have to thank you properly for

such a service," she told Mano. "It's the American way, and in this place we observe the customs of our hosts."

"Give him back the coin," Tempus heard himself growl. His hand closed on the back of her neck and it was all he could do to control himself as he squeezed.

"Somewhere along the way I must have lost it. That's my fault, not your friend's. It's an easy enough debt to discharge, if you stay out of our way."

Mano said, "Let's calm down, folks. There's plenty of time for talk when we're alone."

"Where is it you think we'll be safe, fighter, much less alone, now that you've started a battle you're not qualified to finish? Frying such as those won't kill them permanently. When they're brought back to life, which won't be long, they'll be on us like a plague."

At that, the driver turned an ear, and Mano said loudly to him, "Take the Triboro. And put on the radio."

Noise flooded the cab.

Over it Cime asked again, "Mano, where do you think you're taking me?"

"Right back where you came from—first, the house you have a key to, where they are; second . . . well, you know the rest."

"Into the den of them, just you two?"

Mano said, "And you."

She hooted like a soldier.

Tempus said, "Mano, are you sure?"

"Did we meet your expectations back there, Commander?"

Tempus couldn't find an answer. He was listening to the god suggest ways to stuff Cime's mouth and humble her before heaven. And he was worrying about the lost coin.

So he said, "We won a quick victory with the element of surprise. Cime's a prize they won't give up easily, she's right. Is this place secure?"

"Brother, this fool's a match for you: it's right in the midst of them."

"They don't know," Mano reminded them both, "that the lady wasn't taken prisoner against her will. The advantage's still ours, if we're bold enough to take it."

Tempus merely shook his head and sat back. The god was promising him weapons fit for destroying whole cities full of sorcerers, once they got to a place where there was solid ground and a manifestation could be made.

He saw Cime slide her hand up Mano's thigh and tried to ignore it. He should have known she'd behave like this. She always did.

If the god were not as foolish as he, by now they'd both be immune to her. But they were not. And now she was at risk, because of Tempus, because of Mano's eagerness to slay sorcerers when he had no idea how to do it.

The weapon he held fried bodies, not souls. How many were dead back there? However many, that number of deadly enemies would soon be wholeheartedly on their track.

And Cime was watching him out of the corner of one eye, mischief on her face, while her hand seemed innocently to brush Mano's leg again and again.

Finally Tempus growled, "Stop that."

Mano started guiltily and pushed closer to the door.

And Cime said, "Now Tempus, you be good or I'll not protect you from the wizards—not you, not your silly, bumbling god, and especially not your friend here, who's started a number of things tonight he may not be able to finish on his own."

Chapter 9:

GODSPEAK

The weapons of Enlil manifested themselves soon after Tempus's discovery of a garden behind the house Cime had taken beyond the city's limits. He'd been totally forgetful of the promise of armaments, just determined to get away from her before he strangled her or slit Mano's throat.

She would forever throw herself upon any man of his she could find. That Mano had given her a coin made things worse: the outcome was assured. She would discharge that debt, if she had to rape the fighter to do it.

And Mano was uncomfortable beyond what he deserved, caught between the two. Rather than explain too much, and expose his pride to Mano's consolation, sacrifice, or, worse, pity, he left them alone, hoping that Cime would get it over with, and Mano learn what he must from her.

The garden was dark and walled, and flowering thornbushes grew there, emitting a dusky smell like a clean woman on a fertile day.

The too-starry sky was clearer overhead than it had been in the city. He could hear the sea, somewhere, or something that sounded like the sea.

The god liked this place better; its rich earth was only slightly tainted; grass here grew thick, though it

had a limey smell to it; there were iron benches wrought
in painstaking patterns of leaves and branches. The
house behind, though small, was appointed like a pal-
ace: leave it to Cime to find a bower, a den, a web in
which she could catch her prey.

He'd seen her bedroom through an open door. It was
a shrine, hung with gossamer and mirrors framed in
gold.

He'd promised himself then to burn this place to
cinders before he left it.

The garden nearly changed his mind, so much did it
remind him of better times and cleaner lands. But
beyond a fence a dog barked, and then the god began
His work.

First the stars were blotted out by clouds racing in on
a west wind; then thunder roared, and Mano came to
the glass-windowed doors to call him inside.

He didn't look around; he could not let Cime plant
jealousy and hatred between him and his sworn righthand man. He was afraid he'd see Mano tousled, or half
dressed. He called back, "When the storm is done,
we'll have god-given weapons, better than yours against
this enemy. Stay inside until I come in, no matter what
you think you see."

By then, the lightning was working in the heavens
like pulses of enchanter's fire. The distant cloud banks
showed as bright as day, then the closer ones flared
white and gold.

Ball lightning and sheet lightning and forked lightning emblazoned the sky in a multitude, and with every
flare came thunder enough to wake the dead.

The ground under him began to spew up a loamy
smell, and along his forearms, the hairs tickled as the
storm came nigh.

Thunder was booming like a heartbeat when the rain
finally started. It washed him clean in seconds and
bounced as high as his knee in the courtyard. And
where it puddled in the garden, something began to
grow.

The ground cracked open; then mud washed down from a sprouting root. This root came writhing out of the ground like a great snake, illuminated intermittently by the flashes in the sky.

He stepped back in case somehow it were not the god's, or malevolent. In his head, Enlil was nearly absent, just deep breathing that came and went in time with the cracks of thunder and the flares of godly light.

Up the thing grew, higher and higher, and from its stalk branches began to sprout. Three bolts of lightning cut the sky in quick succession, leaving Tempus dizzy and momentarily blinded.

When he blinked away the afterglow, the questing root was a tree and on the tree were blossoms. Each was red and had a distinct mouth, open wide.

And when he reached out to touch the tree, now as high as his shoulder, a godly voice pealed, *No! Not yet, mortal fool!*

And thunder chastised him so that he clapped his hands to his ears and bowed his head in pain.

While he was thus, a bolt from heaven that seemed as wide as half the sky forked down, and forked again, and fretted like a living thing above the garden wall.

Then it found the tree, and darted groundward like a snake striking with its tongue.

The lightning met the tree and the tree sizzled. He could have sworn he heard it scream. There was a flash that turned everything white but the tree, black in the midst of that whiteness.

This sent him staggering back until his body struck the house's wall and he was content to lean there, his face turned away from what the god had wrought.

He thought he'd seen souls, in that last blast of lightning. He'd surely seen Enlil himself, striding down the lightning path, a greater image of Tempus himself with all his weapons drawn and a death-grin upon his lips.

Then he saw nothing but afterimage, and blades of grass drowning in the rain, and heard nothing but thunder, as if the chariots of all the gods raced across the heavens.

Until he heard an echoing blast, a final concussion that stopped the rain and stilled the wind as if they'd never been.

He looked through the night, blinking the rain from his lashes, shaking it from his hair. The tree was still there, as tall as he now, and gnarled. And on it were pods where blossoms had been, and a few blossoms yet remained.

He knew what he was looking at, but he was as exhausted as the god from those labors.

By Thy leave, he told Enlil, and drew his sword to hack a branch with two pods and a blossom from the tree.

It dropped into his hand before his sword could bite the wood, if wood it was.

The weight of the branch was surprising; and it was hot, like a human limb, and yielding.

He saw sap like blood running from the severed end, but carried it into the house in any case.

Then he put it on a glass table before three white couches and sat on one, regardless of the mess he made, storm-drenched, muddy and covered with bits of leaf and grass.

Elbow on his knee, chin on one fist, he stared at the branch with its two pods and a flower. Then he stirred the branch with his sword. Sap still dripped from it, but the flow was easing, the sap drying on the table. Good. The poison there would be handy in this battle.

Carefully, he lifted one pod with his sword's point: it burst open, and a crystalline seed fell from it. He did the same with the second, carefully.

Then he stared at the new weapons that the god had given him to fight sorcerers, and waited for Mano and Cime to come join him.

When they did, he'd have to explain all this. Or hide it beforehand.

He thought for a long while, waiting for them to

come. When he'd decided that these weapons need not be shared, they still had not come into the room. By the time he'd wrapped the two seeds in their pods and put the pods in his beltpurse, they still had not appeared.

When, finally, he got the sap cleaned up and carefully—so carefully—piled upon a leaf, which he folded over it into an envelope that he could secret in his coat, they walked in upon him.

But by then there was just the blossom on the branch, and it told nothing more than that the tree was outside.

"So, still taking drugs, are we?" Cime sniffed. She was disheveled; her lips were full of her pulse and she walked with wide strides. "We can't have you doped up, not here." She picked up the flowering branch and said, "Your god, no doubt, seeing to your needs?"

She walked to the glass doors that led to the garden and paused there, a hand tight on the jamb, when she saw what Enlil had wrought.

The branch fell from her hands. "A whole tree of *that?*" she murmured.

Tempus stood up. "Perhaps the god thinks it will be a longer battle than you do," he said.

"Give me my rods, thief," she demanded. "Now that you have all of this, you can't say you need them."

"I'll trade them to you for services rendered."

"Getting bolder, are we? Learning to take what we want? I'll believe it when I see it," she sniffed.

"What's up?" Mano wanted to know. At the same time, he motioned Tempus closer. Very quietly, he said, "You and I have got to talk . . . about . . . her. Nothing happened, Commander, I promise."

He tried to keep his voice even, but it sank deep in his chest. "Promise nothing, where she's concerned. We'll talk of that later. Now, I must teach you about the god's weapons."

"Teach him somewhere else." Cime stepped back from the door to the garden, locked it with a bolt, and came to stand between them. "I invited neither of you. You must have someplace to stay. Go there, both of

you. Leave me to fight this battle you've started but
can't win on your own. And take the tools of your god
with you, uproot His disgusting tree from my earth,
before all is lost because He's planted such a sign where
any wizard can see it."

"I can't go back where I came from until this is
done," Mano told her. "They found my place here, and
killed one of our party there already."

"Then you went out looking for revenge. And now
you come to me, the both, tails between your legs and
that's all—no manhood whatsoever, seeking to hide
behind a woman's skirts?"

"If you want those rods, Cime, cease the baiting,"
Tempus advised. "Mano, stay away from the tree until
I've explained it. Now that you see why I was hesitant
to bring this sharp-tongued harpy among us, you'll
trust my judgment better. I need some time with her
alone."

"Oh don't bother, Tempus. Anything you've got to
say, your boyfriend can hear. Anything you're going to
do won't be something a young and tender flower like
him can't see."

"I'll take a shower," Mano offered softly, and backed
away, despite Cime's taunts, to disappear down the
hall.

"Well," she rounded on him, hands on her velvet-clad
hips, "you have me alone. What good can that possibly
do you, with your god in residence and little more to
offer?"

"We must infiltrate this clutch of sorcerers of yours,
and you're going to help us," he told her bluntly.
"Otherwise, you'll not get your rods back. Without
them, you'll need me for protection."

"And that's a terrifying thought. Why are you doing
this? Can't you find meddling more your speed? I roamed
millenia to get shut of you and your maudlin warring,
all your guilt and your maddened god."

He wouldn't tell her how he'd come here. He wouldn't
tell her about Lemuria, or Ash. But he would tell her

what she needed to know. He got her rods out from under his coat and tapped them in the palm of his hand.

She came to attention, naked fear on her face that he'd snap them in two or crush them underfoot. Without them, she'd be at the mercy of the evil here, naked and defenseless.

"You're going to do as I say," he told her. "This time. And you're going to be resourceful, respectful, polite and indefatigable in my behalf. When this is done here, you're coming back with me."

"Why? I like it here. Women are freer and men are no longer lords of all they survey merely because they have scrota."

"Because you know that's not true, and you know you don't belong here. You and I are going to right the wrongs you've helped create here, then settle our own differences, once and for all."

"Ah, the god has made you a full fledged deity on your own, then, that you can deliver all you promise. This should be amusing."

He said, "Into your chamber, woman. Now. We need privacy for what I want to say."

Tossing her head, she led him there, wondering aloud that he had the courage for it.

He wasn't sure he did. He mustn't hurt her. He couldn't touch her, not the way he was feeling. And yet he had to get past words with her, to remind them both how all this had come about.

Chapter 10:

SEEDS OF DESTRUCTION

"Truce," Tempus offered lamely in Cime's bedchamber once he'd closed the door behind them.

She was sitting on her bed, running long fingers through a white fur spread worked with bits of shiny shell and beads. Instead of mocking him outright, she hung her head. "Come sit with me." She patted the place beside her.

He went, despite himself. The god wanted to go to her, split her, force surrender.

So he must be very careful not to lose his head.

They'd sat like this before, and tried all this before. It never worked. She wanted her rods back, that was all: she'd find a way to get them. She always did.

When he sat down, she tugged at his coat. "Who gave you the raincoat? Mano? Apt, at any rate. But take it off, it's soaked. And so are you."

He knew he shouldn't, but he did.

This close, she was a headier drug than even the heat of battle when the god was high in him.

Her wide, pale eyes had thick dark lashes. Only the slightest tracery of smile lines gave any hint of how long she'd lived.

Or how little both of them had learned. His arms were still tangled in long and unaccustomed sleeves

99

when she leaned forward, up on her knees, and kissed him on the lips, fingers twining in his hair.

All time stopped, all reason fled. Would the heavens truly open up and swallow them for this transgression? Was there no solution for what was wrong with them?

He felt her hand slide down his back and heard the god warning she'd steal her rods back while he languished under her spell as if he were the woman here.

So he caught her hand, closed his mouth to her questing tongue, and pushed her back.

Her eyes were almost swallowed by her pupils then. Her chest heaved. She said, "Fool once, fool forever. What is it now? Your god won't loose your collar for even a little while?"

"Cime . . ." There was nothing he could say, yet everything must be said. "I can't let you stay here. I can't bide the thought of us going on this way, living in damnation, eternally apart."

"Shed the god, Tempus. Take up your fate in your hands. Act like the man you once were."

His fingers were deep in the flesh of her wrists. Much more of this, and the god would have his way with her. And then what?

"I came here by way of a place that offers a chance to fix an error, anytime and anyplace. From there we could go back to when things went awry, perhaps get a message to our foolish, younger selves."

"Get a message through your thick head, would do as well. Askelon swears he knows for certain that your father was cuckolded by his second wife, my mother. Thus there's no blood relationship between us, and the archmage who cursed us for what we did was lying when he called us siblings. Thus all the curse is false, just jealousy in magic clothes, and breakable, but for your guilt. That's why I left Ash, or didn't he tell you: he's known forever, and used us both, and never said a word."

Now the god was sure to have her. Curse or not, true or not, the fire in her lit Enlil's.

And Tempus was shaking visibly. His grip on her wrist grew weak, fighting the god's lust to snap it to see fear shine in her eyes.

He let go entirely, and sat back. "Come with me willingly when this is done. We'll see who's right. We can solve it."

"Give me my rods and take me now." She moved toward him; he moved back. "You know nothing less will sate you. Rest you. You've come so far for this . . ."

"No," he told her and the god both. "Not until I know for certain."

"And if I should die, fighting this clutch of mages? Or you should? Here, you can lose your life, without even this settled between us. I couldn't live without knowing you were . . . doing your accursed worst somewhere. Let's have this moment that all the fates conspired so long to deny us. Flout the gods one time. Maybe you'll like it. It could become a habit."

Somehow, her face was so close that her breath puffed against his cheeks. Her breasts burned the air between them.

"No, I said." He rolled off the bed, away from her and, breathing hard himself, stood looking down at Cime, all invitation and temptation atop her furs. "You've got my man's coin—what of that? First me, then him? I can't tolerate your whoring."

"Seems to me," she said, shifting so that her legs were parted and she leaned on one elbow, showing him how and why she'd brought so many sorcerers to their deserved ends, "that you had something to do with that."

Now he and the god were one in fury. "You blame all things on me, and I'll give you reason to curse me as you've never cursed man or god before."

Then he couldn't withstand the taunts and invitations, and reached for her with the god's strength and Enlil rising in him.

Fear froze her face as her head hit her pillow, and the sight of it put ice in his veins. With all his strength, he made his hands let go of her, pulled himself off of her, and walked very slowly to the farthest part of the room.

Only when he turned to tell her, "See to Mano or give him back his coin," did he realize she'd picked his pocket.

She was sitting on the bed, legs curled under her, fixing her rods in her hair and smirking defiantly. "Thank you. You're nothing if not predictable. See to your god, why don't you, or cast him out?"

She sprang off the bed like a tumbler. "Now that we've our truce, let's get that damned tree of yours camouflaged, or cut it down—"

"No!"

"—before every sorcerer in the Northeast Corridor is on us. You don't know what it's like here. They have machines that fly, devices to look through walls, and weapons of untold destruction. You can't win this, I told you once. Get thee hence, Tempus, while you still have a soul to flee with."

"We'll leave together, when we do," he mumbled, feeling foolish, and clumsy, and dull of wit. Inside, Enlil berated him for losing their chance to take her. *Pillager, she's not your type*, he told the god, and then endured the answer, which made his body burn and sweat.

By then she was up beside him, on tiptoe, waving her hand before his face: ". . . show you something, perhaps then you'll understand."

She stalked to a cabinet, opened its doors, and touched something. A window like a Lemurian window came to life, sound blaring out of it. A man's effigy was there, and soon replaced by demon cars spitting fire and battling dragons, charging one another over a desert. He realized that these dragons had no feet and that English words were telling tales above their roaring just as he let the throwing star from his belt fly.

The window exploded and died, showing empty innards.

"By my mother's soul, Riddler, if you think to destroy everything you don't understand here, you'll exhaust even the god trying. That's television: pictures of events sent through the air to all comers; truth, to the extent they know it here, and news is learned this way. I thought we might see something about your escapade tonight. But never mind. We've got to hide that tree . . ."

She pushed him to the door and he went before her like a prisoner.

Out in the great room, she tugged on his arm. "I'll stir you up a potion from your blossoms; you'll feel almost like a man again when it's made."

There was no way to fend off her attacks; no way but the god's, which he was not willing to undertake.

He was blind to the luxury here now, and uncaring even if the tree should bring down sorcerers by the hundred. So he hardly noticed Mano sitting there when he said, "I've enough seeds of destruction to consign every mage you've met here to eternal hell. Let them see the tree. I'll impale all their souls upon it. We'll make potions another day."

"Nonsense," said Cime brusquely. "Mano, if not yourself, needs a touch of this." She picked up the branch with two fingers, a look on her face as if she lifted feces. Holding it well away from herself, she started down the hall. "Mano, help Tempus put something over that noxious tree his god afflicted my garden with."

Mano was watching uncertainly, still sitting on the divan. When Tempus said, "So? Let's go," he rose up and asked Cime what to use. She called out, "Take a blanket from the closet."

Mano did, and joined Tempus, who was already squatting down before the tree, counting pods.

Mano knelt beside him: "I think I know how you feel now, sir."

"Mano?"

"I mean—I've got no idea what any of this means—

the tree, your . . . friend's . . . advances—I can't figure
it. And what's this about weapons?"

"The tree," Tempus said in a low voice, "has twenty
pods on it, plus two I've got here." He tapped his belt.
"You take a pod, open it, and extract the seed of destruction therein. Once the seed has been out of the
pod, you can use the pod to wrap it in again. But if the
seed is out of the pod for . . . a hundred heartbeats, say
. . . it will destroy what's around it." He hunted for
words in English. "Not just the physical—a wall, a
door, a building—but the soul, the lifeforce, of anything caught in its fire."

"Oh, sort of anti-sorcerer grenades," said Mano, sounding relieved. "Great. How many can I have?"

"As many as you're willing to field," said Tempus. To
take upon your soul, he meant. "Up to half, at any rate."

"What about your sister? Doesn't she need some?"

"She has her rods back," he admitted.

"And you left her alone in there?" Mano started to
his feet, and toward the house. "What if she runs out on—"

"Mano, she's got your coin. She's not going anywhere."

"Tempus, I've got lots of questions, yet," Mano said.

Tempus had begun cutting pods with his shortsword.
Misunderstanding, he said, "We might have a second
budding, depending on how pleasing all this is to Enlil.
Stay away from the sap. It's poison to any flesh." Except his own. "And Cime's making a strengthening
posset from the petals of the flowers."

"No, I mean—you're sure she'll stay, without you
having the rods? And what's this coin bit?"

"She . . ." He took two seeds, rewrapped in their
pods, and handed them to Mano. "Sleep with her, or
get back the coin. Your choice."

"Uh . . . you're sure?"

"Quite sure."

"Shouldn't I hold off, either way, if that's tying her to
us?"

"She's in as much trouble now as we are, Mano, after
what we did back there."

"Then maybe you should take her and leave, Commander. I'm in over my head with you two, I admit it."

"She'd come right back to spite me, if the job was left undone. We'd never make it in open flight to the Lemurian door, in any case: they think she's been abducted; they think she's one of them. Head on's the only way with wizards. And Enlil wants them humbled; not just the enchanters, but all the folk here, will have the fear of Him in their hearts before we leave. Now, you've seen me prepare the pods. You do it."

Tempus watched his student critically. When the tree's fruit was harvested, all but the blossoms which might become pods later, they took the blanket and arranged it over the tree.

"That's not real unobtrusive," Mano said. "But sometimes gardeners try to protect trees from frost . . ." He sounded dubious.

"Ah, you think they'll find us by that means. That the tree will give us away. She gives us away. Our hearts do. These are not men as you know them, Mano. Stop thinking that you're fighting men."

"That's all I know how to do—all we've ever tried . . ."

"I know the problem. Let's go in. Talk to Cime about discharging her debt."

He would not force his righthand man, either way, beyond the making of a decision. But a decision he would have.

"What if I just let it ride?" Mano wanted to know, his brows knitted, looking at Tempus askance as they came into the house and smelled a spicy odor like hot mulled cider.

"Then it's held in abeyance. But I'll think no different of you, whatever you do. If you get your coin back, give it to me." He hadn't meant to say it. The god stole his tongue.

Mano's eyes widened. "You bet, sir. Phew, I wasn't sure there was a way out of that one."

Tempus watched him head down the hall in the

direction of the smell, where Cime was preparing the brew. For his own soul's sake, he couldn't let Mano know that a debt unpaid was a check on Cime. If the two went into that room together, what difference did that make?

She'd been with more men than Tempus had slain, and now that, too, was all his fault.

The god wanted to end her misery in ritual copulation. He told the god to content Himself with slaughter, for that was all He was going to get from Tempus. On this point, he would brook no argument.

When the two came back, both had shiny faces and hot eyes, but that might have been from the brew they carried.

It had been a very long time since Tempus had drunk of the red flower. He braced himself for its taste and what else it brought.

Cime had three mugs on a tray. She laid the tray on the glass table in the great room, saying, "There. I'm sure you won't mind if I join you after all. It's only fair, since—"

A knock came on her front door.

She turned parchment white in an instant. Her lips were blue against her skin as she called, "Just a moment."

Tempus was already up, his hand on Mano's arm, half-dragging the other down the hall.

Cime whispered. "No, no. Stay. Sit. Look comfortable. No weapons. Follow my lead."

She smoothed black velvet down over her hips and went to the door, then opened it.

"Cime," said the curly-headed man in a jacket standing there. Behind him was a red demon car, its lights shining in the door. "That's lucky. There's been trouble. We thought—That is, oh . . . you've got company." The man paused on the threshold.

"Bodyguards, dear," she said sweetly. "As you see, I'm fine. Many fared less well, I imagine. Is there a meeting?"

"Tomorrow evening, at Knollbrook. If you need better than these . . ."

"I don't, dear. It's late, or I'd invite you in for a drink. Tell your father I'm flattered that he worried about me. And send my condolences along . . ."

"Yes, all right," said the curly-headed man, who was young and curious of eye. "I'll tell him. Are you bringing guests tomorrow?"

"Plus two, dear," she said, and stepped forward far enough to give the young man a playful shove upon the chest. "Now scat, Arnaud. You should be home where it's safe . . ."

The young man promised her he'd go right home. She stayed in the doorway until the visitor got in his car and roared away.

Cime closed the door.

Mano said, "Who was that?"

Cime replied, "The local archmage's son, Arnaud."

And Tempus growled, "Drink up, Mano. We're going to need all our strength."

Chapter 11:

BLOOD OF THE FLOWER

Sorcerers drank the blood of men and animals for strength and power; Tempus tried to explain to Mano that the blood of the flower which Cime had made into a sweet posset was really the blood of the Storm God, Enlil.

Mano's face was sheened with a greasy sweat. He was still shivering from the effect that the posset had had on unaugmented human flesh. The god had shown himself to Mano, and taught a lesson or two about looking into the face of evil and pretending it was the face of man.

Cime said, "Go on, Tempus, let me tend to him. Go prune your tree and hone your blade and wait."

And Mano said, "Don't go, Commander. What I saw—" He turned tortured eyes to Tempus. "—all that was just hallucination. Has to be. Admit it was an hallucinogen you gave me."

Tempus's ears itched as the word acquired meaning by dint of the learning Mano had poured into him the way he'd poured the god into the fighter.

"Mano, these enemies of ours are the enemies of mankind, no longer part of it. When you go up against them, you go up against an animus of untold age and self-destructive nature. Remember that: evil destroys its practitioners first and foremost. All sorcerers are doomed to fail and to die eternally. Men die only once and find their way to heaven. Sorcerers are reborn into eternal torment, eternal repudiation of their humanity, eternal defilement and eternal unrest."

"So you don't believe in reincarnation?" Mano asked strangely. "Karma, the transcendence of—"

"Oh he does, but not the way you do, or the way some here do. In his world, those who lived before," Cime said, "and live again, are the undead and the unredeemable. Your god on a stick was closer to the truth."

"God on a stick?" Tempus wanted to know.

"They had a god come to earth," she told Tempus, "to make things right. But His words were twisted by evil men for self-aggrandizing purpose: more men have died in the name of their God of Love than serving your thirsty Slaughter Lord."

"Wait a minute." Mano rubbed his face with his palms. Sitting slumped forward on the great room's divan, he looked as exhausted as any man Tempus had ever seen—an unlikely avatar for his society; an even unlikelier sort to fight on Tempus's right hand.

"I don't understand you two, and I'm not sure that's my fault. You've got to realize that there's more to warfare than your age understood: population density studies show that combat—conventional warfare, in your terms—thins out warlike genetic strains. It's a natural culling that's part of evolution."

Cime tittered behind her hand. Tempus shook his head and shrugged.

"In other words," Mano, frustrated, went on, "your warrior types reproduce in a population until there're enough of them that a shooting war breaks out, at home or abroad. Then, before they can reproduce in large numbers, the warlike young males get killed off in the fighting and the population settles down for a while, until the genetic tendencies that together cause a predisposition to warmaking become endemic in a population. In other words, warmaking is hard-wired—human nature. These sorcerers are tough, and dangerous, but they're human. Humans using black magic as the platform for their cult violence. Look at human history: the Crusades, the Inquisition, Hitler, the Ku Klux Klan, the Muslim—"

"That's why your society's losing whatever war it is that's got you back here trying to eradicate the threat before it eradicates you," said Cime, standing over Mano, hands on her hips. "You haven't the slightest idea what you're fighting or how to triumph over it, or you'd be able to handle your 'hard-wired' crazies in your own time."

Mano said, "I'm sorry, ma'am. I didn't mean to upset you." He looked at Tempus. "I'm not saying they're not dangerous. I'm not even saying they're not powerful— powerful enough to demand extraordinary means to counter their threat. I'm just saying I didn't expect to find myself face to face with some ancient God of War. It's all science to us, you see: our enemies have technological advantages that I had to travel to Lemuria to try to match. God knows we can't win without those technologies—and without your help, sir, in cutting the legs out from under them here and now, before there are too many of them."

"Which god knows?" Tempus wanted to know. "This god on a stick? He sent you to us, to Enlil?" Tempus sat forward. "To use the weapons of Enlil, fighter, you must acknowledge the Storm God. Your vision showed you that."

Mano ran a hand through his hair. "This whole thing is crazy. Yeah, fine, you got it: I'm a serving member of whatever church it takes—your church of Enlil. Now, do I get some holy water to sprinkle on the sorcerers so they burst into flames?"

Tempus reached into his belt and got out the leaf he'd used to hold the tree's sap. "You get this." He'd wanted to keep it for himself. But he could get more, if the god allowed, from the tree. And he had Enlil inside him, a body regenerated by the Storm God, a sword meant for dispatching sorcerers.

Mano had only clear eyes and stern determination. He was poorly equipped for fighting sorcerers, just mortal flesh and blood, weak and filled with the emasculating dogma of civilization.

Mano took the leaf envelope Tempus held out and began to open it on his knee.

"Carefully," Tempus warned. Where had Cime got to? He looked around and didn't see her. She'd slipped away while he was busy with his righthand man. "If you get it on you, it will bring you a quick and decidedly unpleasant death."

On the table, Mano continued unfolding the leaf. "So what do I do with it?"

"Put it in a wizard's water, in a sorcerer's soup, or dip any projectile—a knife, a spearhead, an arrow tip—"

"A bullet? I'm short on spears and arrows . . ."

"A bullet, then, in a solution made from it and a handful of water. Then whom you kill will stay dead, not rise up with a grudge against you to hunt you throughout eternity, even back to your own time."

"They're hunting me from there back to here, for all I know," said Mano. "I should have told you—we're losing to these magicians: our freedom, our morality, our lives . . . what we've laughingly exalted as Western Civilization since fifth century Athens . . ."

Having confessed a failure awful in his own eyes and a secret deeper and darker than any other he kept, Mano folded up the leaf and stuffed it in his pocket, unable to look at Tempus. Then he put his palms over his eyes and sat there, head down.

Tempus got up, clapped him on his bowed back. "I assumed as much, Mano. Else Lemuria would not have hosted you. Nor would the god have brought you to me, or given you a vision of His Fearsome Majesty. Cheer up, fighter. You're in an army now that never loses a battle once it's begun to fight."

An army of three. Well, had never lost one up until now, at any rate.

"Let's find Cime, before she's into more mischief

than I dare contemplate." Winning at any cost was still winning—Tempus's wizened, ravaged soul was testament to that.

Mano looked up at Tempus almost shyly. "Thanks, sir. I thought maybe you'd . . . not want to play, once the extent of this mess was known."

"Any less, righthand man, and I'd have been disappointed. When we say 'to the death, with honor,' we mean it: no man who's ever fought with me lost sight of his soul through any lack of righteousness."

The best Tempus could offer must be enough. He'd lost men to magic; there are casualties in every war. But the depradations of magicians couldn't eternally trap the souls of Sacred Band fighters, or any other man who feared the gods more than evil, not when compatriots remained to make the appropriate sacrifices and put the case before the gods. It was this, at bottom, that made the difference between animals and men.

"The soulless ones," Tempus continued his lesson as Mano followed him out to the kitchen, "have less to lose than we. Without their horrid ways, their blood sacrifices and befouling of better folk with their excrement and their madness, they'd be piteous. To someone as old and as indefatiguable as I, they're pathetic one by one; only fearsome in their numbers, like rabid dogs or stampeding cattle: they have no volition. They've lost their humanity by giving up freedom of choice. They haven't control of even their own minds, so if their bowels are loose and their reason looser, then what's that to us? Animals they are, and as animals we dispatch them. It's mercy killing, most of the time, only real confrontation when you find an archmage or demon lord among them. Most, you'll find, are simply the wretchedest of men—those who've sold their humanity for trinkets and given up life and afterlife for eternal, waking death."

"I . . ." Mano stopped in the hall. "There are so many of them, where I'm from . . . it's hard to think of them the way you do—as an infestation of pests."

"Remember I don't die, Mano, the way your compatriots do; nor do I lie about what I know, even if it's kinder. You fight with me, you'll learn a thing or two. And if you perish, we'll find you a place in Enlil's heaven, never fear: none of mine have lost their souls forever."

And that was the last time he'd repeat that promise, he told himself, to any man.

Cime was sitting in an all-white kitchen, reading a huge sheaf of paper that was folded in the middle. "Well, here's some sign of you two, I think: one under 'Gangland Slaying on 96th Street Work of Unidentified Terrorist'—'Search of Premises Reveals Ties Abroad' —that's your apartment, I assume, Mano, that they're talking about. No going back there, so I hope you won't miss whatever you left behind."

Mano grunted as if he'd been hit with a stick.

"And you, Riddler—this sounds like you: 'Ritual Murder of Four Has Satanic Overtones.' It says here you were going about the streets in full battle dress, and waving your shortsword around. Is that so?"

"I had . . . only just arrived." He felt sheepish, suddenly, remembering the enchanters he'd encountered on the street. "If 'Satanic' means enchanters, they were that for certain. Dressed like—"

"No, no. It's *you* they think to be the devil worshipper. Those kids you killed probably were guilty of profane acts, but yours is the description they've given. Congratulations. You've become the leader of a cult." She looked up at him with a patronizing expression. "Time for you to stop giving lessons, Riddler, and start learning some. You, too, Mano, can benefit from what I'm going to show you."

"Show?" Tempus said uneasily.

"We're going for a little ride. The sun's up. It's not unlikely that I'd go out. We'll go show you the local temples, for a start."

"Temples?"

"God on a stick," she reminded him. "And many

more: a faceless Lord of Retribution; a pantheon of uninhabited statues; a place where ancestors are worshipped; a clutch of gods with many limbs to turn a wheel of rebirth. And the enemy's temples as well, while we're at it. Coming, Tempus?" She stood up, throwing down the document, so huge it could have contained the whole law code for any kingdom he'd ever visited.

"I think you and Mano have something to tend to first, Cime."

"Mano?" Cime said. "Are we ready for our test of manhood?"

"I'd . . . like to take the tour of local sights. And I think I'd like to give my coin to Tempus, to use whenever he's ready," Mano said.

"No!" said Tempus and Cime together.

But it was too late.

Mano had done what no one more familiar with Cime would ever have tried. And it would hold, for such audacity could not be argued.

Tempus, stealing a glance at Cime, said, "Thank you, Mano. For services rendered, I do accept your coin as payment."

And Cime promised, "I'm going to see that both of you regret this—eternally."

Mano chuckled, thinking he'd done well, not realizing that Cime could do exactly as she threatened, and never threatened in vain.

The demon car toward which she herded them like cattle was no less daunting than the thought of his sister's revenge. Even if what she said was true, and what Ash had told her was true, and she wasn't his sister in the strictly hereditary sense.

Chapter 12:

OFF TO SEE THE WIZARDS

When the sun was high in a hazy sky full of dust,
Cime pulled her demon car to the curb before a temple
such as Tempus had never seen.

This place had needle-sharp spires and festooned
pinnacles, with gargoyles and monsters guarding its
every jewel-toned window.

At first, Tempus was sure this was a mages' stronghold, a temple to the Lord of Evil, or at least a sorcerers' guildhall, built as it was, decorated as it was, and
sitting amidst monuments to commerce on every side.

When Cime said, "Go on, Mano, take him inside;
show him around the god's house," Tempus shuddered
and Enlil came rushing up to peer jealously out of his
eyes.

This god had rich followers, that was sure, he thought
as he got out of the car and the noise of the city boxed
his ears. Demon cars outnumbered folk here, it seemed,
and it occurred to Tempus that there was no guarantee
that the drivers of those cars were in large part mortal.
Habit made Mano see every upright, clothed beast as
human.

Tempus must not fall into the same trap. Simply
because his mind reeled at the implications of so many

117

tools of evil abroad in one place, he must keep in mind
that many, if not all, these drivers could be undead,
fiends in disguise, lesser mages or reincarnations of
polluted souls. How else to explain their numbers?

No city could sustain so many human folk—feed them
and tax them and police them; this, Tempus knew for
certain, from having cared for armies in a dozen
lands.

And Enlil was equally sure that no god would have a
temple here, alone, far from the temples of the other
gods, if that god were not hiding something.

"Where is the Avenue of Temples, Mano?" Tempus
asked as the man from the future led him up a wide
portico of steps.

"What? Oh, they don't do it that way anymore—I
mean, they don't do it that way here. Gods don't set up
shop across the street from one another, in competition
or because foot traffic might bring curious new worship-
pers in to take a look."

Still, Enlil was not eager to enter the temple of this
foreign god of the many steps. In Tempus's head, the
god was cautioning his minion not to proceed in haste.
Ahead loomed carven doors guarded by stone effigies
that never had been human.

"There's something I must ask you, Mano," Tempus
said when only a half dozen stairs remained between
him and the sanctum of this local deity.

Mano turned on the steps. "Sir?"

"These enemies of yours from the future—you really
think they'll seek you here, in their own past? How can
that be?" If long ago Tempus had been right, and one
couldn't step twice in the same river, then fighting a
battle for the future in the past became a paradox.

Mano replied, "I meant . . . they're not time-locked,
not the way we are. They're working from a multi-temporal
base that accesses all times at once." Mano screwed up
his face. "Gibberish to you, right?"

Tempus grunted agreement, content to stand a moment longer outside the sanctum of this local god who was powerless against fielded sorcery, but might not be against a rival deity invading his home. But down the steps, Cime waited, watching from her demon car, cold amusement on her face.

He couldn't turn back before her, show cowardice, bow his head in the face of the unknown and scuttle back to her like some child who, frightened, needs a suck on his mother's teat to get his courage back. He couldn't. And it was the Storm God Cime was out to hurt, to chase away, to daunt and taunt. If she could sow disaffection between Tempus and Enlil, she'd win her point.

She wanted him to cast out the one force that had long sustained him: the Storm God. Easier to cast love from his heart, and mercy from his soul, and human frailty from his limbs. Tempus had made that choice and lived that life for too long to turn back now.

"What?" he asked Mano, realizing he hadn't been listening to what the fighter said.

"I'll try to explain another way," Mano began again, still standing there on the steps. He jammed his hands into the pockets of his raincoat; a wind came up and flapped its tails around his calves as he searched for words with an intensity that made his face pale.

Tempus liked this Mano, who'd traveled so far in the service of ideals. Yet time had taught Tempus not to trust strangers to see things as he did. What was right and clear to him might be wrong and murky to this other. Only adventure would tell what their alliance might really mean.

"You see," Mano said, squinting down at Tempus from two stairs higher, two stairs closer to the god of the majestic temple. "We're trying to get time stabilized: to get the past to be one past, immutably fixed; to get the present to contain only natural events; to get the future to stop subdividing itself to accommodate retroactive changes . . . In other words, we want these

sorcerers to stop fucking around with the nature of
reality."

"What reality do you mean?"

"What I can see, feel, touch, and perceive: reality.
Days progressing forward in a pattern that's predictable. Contests between men and nations decided on
personal and societal strength, and simple science; common logic; dimensions restricted to up and down, left
and right, forward and back. No mind fucks. No weather
weapons. No raising spirits from beyond the grave or
importing reinforcements from some other dimension.
One discrete, forward moving dimension of time, no
more."

"You'll never manage that. What's unnatural to you is
natural to mages. And to gods. Restrict one, you restrict the other. Or do I have you wrong?"

"Yeah. No. I dunno." Mano rubbed his chin. "Let's
go in, Commander. Maybe you'll see what's wrong
better than I can tell you."

"You tell me as we go." There was nothing for it but
to mount the remaining steps, despite Enlil's doubts,
which had the Storm God ready to bring thunder and
lightning to his aid. Already, behind the temple with its
needle spires, thunderheads were massing.

They'd never turned away from a battle before, with
any god, Tempus chided Enlil.

And the god in his head said, *But this is the suffering
god, the young god, the god of misery and sacrifice. He
does not fight fair. Nor does He count triumph as you
or I. He's a martyr, Tempus. A martyr is something
inscrutable under heaven. He tries to bar unbelievers
from the very afterlife, and yet offers all eternal life
through misery and Him.*

That gave Tempus pause. If the god here would not
fight them, then why was Enlil frightened—or at least,
worried?

And the god said, *This god is a revolutionary under
heaven; He's a Sole God in his Heart, and recognizes*

none other but His Father. His intolerance has spread and been twisted into worse by His believers: He and His are losing the battle against the Evil of which your man speaks, because they fight it all alone, and any who are not with them are automatically the enemy.

"So, Mano," said Tempus upon hearing this. "Is this your god, here? And will He help us fight the Evil magicians overrunning his town?"

"Jesus, Tempus! I mean, that's the god's name: Jesus the Christ. He's a Redeemer. No, he's not mine. I'm not crazy enough to take on that kind of handicap: there's no way to fight any of this and win, if you fight by Queensbury Rules. Anyway, you've got to realize, in this time frame gods don't manifest the way yours do—did—do. Um, I guess I'm saying that Jesus is a state of mind, an ideal. If the religion of Christianity held anything of Jesus's teachings in it, it might be a true weapon against evil. But as it stands—stood—stands here now—too many venal priesthoods have twisted what this god said. Nowadays, its believers fear evil more than they fear their god, and thus it's worse than useless: it gives strength and succor to its enemy. If this god, Jesus, weren't all-forgiving, He'd come back and root the evil out of his church."

"All-forgiving?" Tempus was aghast.

Enlil, in his ear, said, *See, fool?*

And Tempus took two steps, caught up with Mano, and said, "Let's hurry and see this god. We can't keep Cime waiting."

In the temple, nothing was as he expected. The god was not there to greet them. No great manifestation of godhead met his eyes. No mighty wind came, or voice pealed. In fact, there was nothing of power in this place to warrant Enlil's massing of stormclouds.

There was a sadness and a resignation among the burning candles here, and a smell of oil that was welcome to Tempus's nose, and a waft of wine upon a hallowed, harried current of air that had spring planting and new growth in it.

Yet there were also the familiar and expected trappings of a mighty priesthood: magnificent carpets, carved benches, a vaulted ceiling chased with gold. Still, there was a god here after all. Tempus could feel the presence.

Enlil could feel it too.

Even Mano, who'd all but proclaimed himself godless, bowed his head.

Their footsteps echoed to the rafters and the echo brought back a sorrow with it that wracked Tempus like Enlil's mightiest storm. He nearly wept. He wanted, for an instant, to drop to his knees and grieve. This one was a Dying God, he realized. No one, not even Enlil, had bothered to tell him that.

This Dying God, he found when he whispered his supposition to Mano, had come of virgin birth and been brought back to life after men had killed him.

This nearly spilt the water from Tempus's eyes. In his heart, with Enlil near and hearing every word, he spoke to the Dying God and asked forgiveness for all he'd slain. Just in case. And Enlil didn't say one word, but only breathed in his ear as they waited for the god to answer.

The silence there was not broken but for their footsteps as they approached the altar. The god didn't speak to him. Nor did He challenge Enlil, as a Dying God normally would if the Storm God, the Pillager, walked into His place.

Soon enough, they stood eye to eye with a statue of the Dying God and Tempus's tears fell freely as he looked on the bloody image of a crucified corpse.

No wonder there was such emptiness here. He wiped his eyes roughly with the back of his hand. Teardrops fell to the floor.

There were tears on the face of the Dying God, as there always were on all Dying Gods' faces.

The sacrifice of tears duly made, Tempus started to back away.

Mano looked over his shoulder at Tempus, and started to speak. Tempus shook his head and motioned the other. This was the god on a stick that Cime had spoken of. If all the travesties laid at His feet were true—what Cime said and what Mano said—no wonder this god wept.

Dying Gods were sent down to give men hope, to teach that death was a gate and that something lay beyond it.

To use such a Lamb to do murder in the world of men was bad enough. To use Him to do evil in His name was abhorrent beyond Tempus's ability to forgive or understand.

When Mano and he were near the doors, a priest came swishing toward them in severe long robes.

Mano would have stopped to talk, but Tempus grabbed his arm. "Off to see the wizards, now. We've seen what we must see here."

Tempus nearly slammed the door upon the priest, so eager was he to be out of that place where suffering was exalted and meekness in the face of evil promised an eternal reward.

"What did you see in there?" Mano wanted to know. "You were crying. I mean . . . I saw the tears. Sir."

"Sacrifice as befit the deity. Blood for the wargod; tears for the Dying God. Thus it's ever been. Simply making sure that we don't overstep our mandate."

Enlil was rattling his thunderclouds now, full of bright display and godly hubris, running up and down the sky and brandishing his weapons over the temple of the lonely god that came down to walk with man and died of it.

To shut him up, Tempus asked Enlil how Dying Gods were chosen: was it lots, like Lemuria? Was there any chance that Enlil might get His turn, and walk among the living till he died there?

Only if you, mortal ass, in your ignorance and your foolish pride, decide to die as foolishly as you have

*lived. For My sake, and that of the souls here worth
saving, fight evil and triumph. Leave the dying and the
self-sacrificing to men. And think not to make Me in
your image, Riddler, as these humans have done with
their Savior. I'll not die for your sins without a fight,
especially not at the hands of rampant evil. So dry your
tears, mortal, before I mistake thee for a woman, and
gird on your courage that I have given thee, and get
you into battle against the sorcerers, remembering that
they are no better than men and no match for thee,
with My wits about you.*

And the god was suddenly gone from him: the silence
that reechoed in Tempus's head, combined with the
peal of thunder that shook the very stairs as he and
Mano hurried down them in a sudden cloudburst that
wiped away the tracks of Tempus's tears, proclaimed
Enlil's absence. The flaccidness of Tempus's limbs, come
suddenly upon him, affirmed it beyond doubt.

He leaned on the handle of the demon car's doors
and closed his eyes, dizzied, standing there while the
rain whipped him and his strength fled.

The Storm God was a jealous god, a mean and vindic-
tive lord to serve, and fond of teaching lessons. Before
Tempus's legs went entirely out from under him and he
fell to his knees where Cime could see, he raised his
head to the dark and stormy heavens, crying out silently, *Come back to me, Pillager. Inhabit me, Lord
Storm. Pour Your Strength into me, God of War and
Death, for without You I cannot fight these wizards on
my own.*

He hated this humbling and gaming with Enlil, as if
the god were some petulant woman. But allegiances,
when in doubt, must be made clear. The sacrifice of
tears he'd given to the Dying God had come upon him
unbidden. The forgiveness he'd asked for was demanded
by the echoes of countless petitioners.

In his heart, he felt no personal guilt. And the guilt
of his race was not his alone to bear. All this he told the

god, who deigned to return to him, though the heavens were still ripping themselves asunder above his head, their lightnings dancing over the needle spires of the Dying God's house as if to prove to Tempus who was whom and what was what, on earth as it was in heaven.

Mano, in the car now, was lowering the window and yelling at Tempus to get inside before he drowned.

Cime, from the front seat, made the car roar and said, "Don't worry, Mano. He's just being rebaptized. A necessary step before battle: all of us need to affirm what we believe, and cast out all our doubts." She resettled her rods in her hair.

When Tempus was in the car, she flicked a glance at him. "Now do you understand, dunderhead?"

"Well enough. It's up to us. There's no help here."

"Or anywhere," she agreed, urging the demon car out into the middle of the racetrack, where she nearly collided with another car whose eyes were blazing. "Beyond ourselves." Then she turned to Mano:

"Our wet friend, here, once had another name, in a time that wizards have destroyed, all but memory. Then he was Heraclitus, and he lived in a place called Ephesus—or a part of him did."

"And a part of you," Tempus said to shut her up. "The best part: you were young then, with a sweet tongue and a virgin's beauty."

"In those days, he said many things," Cime continued as if Tempus had not interrupted, "at least one of which you, Mano, might recall: 'war is all and king of all and all things come into being out of strife.' Remember that, in the battle to follow."

"A man should know whom he's fighting beside? I know all I need to know about the Riddler," Mano said in an obvious attempt to lighten the mood. "Ma'am— Cime, if you'd put your headlights on in this storm, we'll be safer."

"Safe, is it? If you wanted safe, Mano, you should have stayed where you were. Or left us when you could. Or—" She made the demon car leave the race and brought it to a halt by the curb. "—get out now, and trot home to your time and place with your cute young tail between your legs. Neither of us need to worry about a green—"

"Cime, let him be," said Tempus in a voice that closed her mouth.

That mouth he loved and hated above all others stayed shut until they came to a building that towered over a riverside. In the windows of its foundation were frozen folk in strange clothes, scarecrows of the soul.

"Get out, both of you. A valet will park us."

"Out?" Tempus said. "The wizards are here?"

"In there. I don't have—" Mano began an excuse.

"Idiots. Out. You can't go to the enchanter's party dressed like street toughs. You need evening clothes. I've a charge here. Go in, get started. I'll be right behind you." The amusement in her eyes was grim. "I'm going to enjoy every moment of this, brother. Dressing you and your god to my taste isn't something I'd ever thought to do."

Tempus and Mano got out as someone in a yellow cloak ran around to Cime's side and helped her from the demon car, holding a parasol over her head.

This close, the frozen folk in the windows turned out to be painted statues. Or at least, Tempus told himself that was what they were. Their glassy-eyed stares had no humanity in them. Their wrists had cracks as if their hands had been cut off and rejoined to their bodies.

Mano, too, had qualms. He said, "I don't like this. If she's got credit here, this place is probably—"

"—a wizard-run emporium, why yes," she said sweetly, for the man with the parasol who'd brought her to the doorway and headed for the car was not yet out of earshot. "That's fine. Everything must seem normal. The money's real enough; the clothes aren't poisonous. Come now, boys: no more whining. Let's see if we can disguise you as grown men."

*   *   *

Mano was as uncomfortable as Tempus in the restrictive suits, but for different reasons.

Mano had weapons about his person, Tempus had found out when they stripped, strapped under his arm as well as on a low-slung belt around his waist, as Tempus had. But Mano's weapons were small black boxes similar to the larger, snoutless thunderclub he'd used in the gaming house, and he didn't want anyone to know he carried them.

Likewise, they had their seeds to secret, and Tempus wasn't going into combat without his shortsword and his weaponsbelt. So the suits were difficult to fit, and the process of finding the right ones had taken ages.

Tempus's hackles had been up the whole time, what with the shop smelling of sorcery. And then there were the shoes, built in hell, which Cime insisted he must wear, and hose under them that fouled his toes.

He itched everywhere, and both he and Mano had not had time to practice drawing their weapons with all this strange clothing upon them. Both of them were out of sorts—and hungry—when Cime finally pronounced them "fit to be seen" and allowed that food might be in order.

This they ate in a dark and too-quiet place full of fawning slaves with impenetrable accents who bowed and scraped and gloated silently because the menu was not in the language of the country, but some foreign tongue that only Cime knew.

Thus weird food came and went: raw shellfish only a fool would swallow, that Cime sucked down as if it were sweetmeats; cold soup that smelled like a peasant's armpit; bread rolls empty in the center and served with butter so spoiled it was green and spotted; tiny fried bosses of tough and tasteless meat covered with sauce and served with three stunted ears of corn which Cime ate, cobs and all, while Tempus drank perfumed tea and longed for a cow to slaughter on the spot.

He said, "What of beef, or lamb, or chicken?"

She said, "You'll have your beef, dear," but when it

came it was obviously spoiled, at least a month overage and cold in the center.

He ate it, to spite Cime, and when he was done with all he could manage Mano asked him why he was off his feed.

"Leaving some for the god," he lied. "Anyway, only a fool goes into battle on a full stomach."

"Or in his new pants," Mano agreed.

She was doing all this to make him miserable, he knew. It wasn't fair to the fighter from the future, and this he told her.

She just chuckled and patted Mano's knee. "I don't have our friend's coin-debt, dear Riddler. So I don't have to worry about what's fair to him. As for what's fair to you . . . love and war, they say here. You get your war, then I get my love."

When the car was again brought, Mano wanted to know if this was, "A chance to whack 'em all—take out whoever we want, right?"

"With the weapons we're using, dear, we'll pick and choose our opportunities. Don't start more than you can handle. A little stealth, if you please."

Then she told Tempus, "I took the liberty of refining what was left of the sap. I'm going to put it in the punch, so don't drink of it. Keep your custom of clear water only. And you too, Mano: drink only water, and eat nothing, just throw away what you take to be polite. No one will notice."

She had driven the demon car to a large, straight racetrack. Here many cars were waiting to go through a starting gate where each driver took a ticket.

"Can you tell us about the players, Cime?" Mano asked.

"Yes, tell us how to distinguish the worthy kills from the rank and file."

"I thought you'd never ask," she giggled. The thought of carnage had put color in her cheeks, he noticed. Or perhaps it was cosmetic, to make her cheeks match her startlingly red lips, which in their turn matched her new dress of shining, tiny bosses all sewn together. Down slipped the car's window, and she took her ticket from the man in uniform.

Then she said, "Attend me, then. I'll not say this twice. You saw Arnaud; he's the archmage's son. His father, Victor, has great power here. He may be the strongest of them in this land. He's as far up the chain as I've gone, at any rate. His lieutenants are three." She named them. "Kill those five, and we've a start on seeing what crawls out from hiding when they're gone."

"That's it? You're sure this is the central command?" Mano wanted to know.

"No, I'm not sure, Mano. What in life are you sure of? There're others there overdue for eternal reckoning: Schmidt, a white supremicist. Rodrigues, a voodoo—" She glanced at Tempus and rephrased it: "—a practitioner of mind control and sympathetic magic, a doll-maker, a chicken killer. And there's Allegro, whose real name no one knows, who might be more than meets the eye, and specializes in drugging minions to do his bidding and the bidding of the others. There's . . ."

She caused the car to veer, and veer again. Cars bellowed and screamed at one another. Two collided and went spinning across the slick racing surface.

She said through gritted teeth, "Someone I know said once, 'steer for the accident. It won't be there when you get there!' "

All was normal now upon the track. In the dusk and the still-falling rain, the bright eyes of the cars were haloed red and amber and white through the wet glass. The car was blinking intermittently to clear its faceplate, and smears of dirt followed a single, great eyelash across the glass.

"Look, you both," Cime continued, "Just let the poison do its work; slay those I've named if it can be done without destroying our legend among them as true and foul believers. If I do what seems to you to be magic, don't fear. Just tricks I've learned from Askelon to help me make my way inside the enemy's guard."

Tempus agreed, since in front of Mano, and at this late moment, agreement of any sort was best. He needed more information to dare to suggest a counter plan. And Enlil would do what the god saw fit, on the spot, as Enlil always did.

Until then, if he could, he would have slept as Mano did, snoring softly in the back seat once Cime conjured music from the demon car's bumper full of knobs and lights.

"This chariot's yours?" he said, slipping into their own tongue.

"Nothing is anyone's here. All things belong to the mercantile state, and people pay to use them by the month. By the time you own a thing here, it's useless and you must get another. But where is anything worth having something that can be bought?"

She reached out to touch him. He caught her hand and, despite himself, brought it to his lips. Then dropped it. Her flesh was cold and clammy.

And ahead, cars were colliding with one another again.

"This place, describe it. Entrances and exits. Hiding places and escape routes. Any dangers of which I wouldn't be aware."

"In English, then," she suggested almost wistfully. And in that language, "You can't talk of security systems and the like in our tongue. Tempus, go back home, where you came from. This is a battle—"

"—I *can* win. And, no, I won't leave you. Unless you're saying you've changed your mind?"

"With these soulless carcasses ripe for the picking and this whole place so in need of a little judicious pruning of their bumper crop? Ha! Anyway, if I go back, Ash will have at me. Or you will. Here I'm formidable, unknown, a threat—a power in my own right."

It always came down to that with her. He couldn't understand her thirst for power, when all power brought was trouble: enemies, jealousy, thievery and more. So he said that.

And she replied, "Power is the only protection against such as you, and Ash, and folk like these. This world, especially, is made up of victims and victimizers. One has to be one or the other. And which, brother, do you think is the more comfortable position?"

"No peace here for simple folk?"

"No peace for anyone. This is a land of freedom: freedom to say and do as one likes; freedom to succeed or fail; freedom to starve or grow fat; freedom to despoil yourself and anyone else as long as you don't break a complex code of laws. Because of these freedoms, all have lost sight of honor: they're free of it. They're free from social responsibility, from personal pride, from national allegiance. They think freedom breeds excellence, which well it might among less lazy or better educated folk. But freedom from oppression leads to exaltation of mediocrity, when majority rules. It must, lest the freedom to think well of oneself be impugned by mere details like willful ignorance, uninformed opinion, greed and connivance for the one true goal all these understand: wealth."

"So you say they're corrupt as a society. It's not the enchanters, corrupting them?"

"Have you left your brain and your memory back in Lemuria? Since when have men lived up to their potential, just because they're free to do so? Where have you seen some populace of self-regulating souls, honoring each other and doing good whither they can? Tempus, you're too old for this fight—I've told you before. Take a wife, some young thing who'll live long enough to amuse you. Raise strong sons, like a man should. Teach them what you will. Don't put it on these fight-

ers of yours to make the might in your image of righteousness, to which no mere mortal can do better than
aspire. Or go live with your gods in a heaven where
you'll learn, finally, that even gods squabble like jackals
over a tender morsel. You'd think your own god, His
Vain and Myopic Highness of Hubris, would have taught
you at least that."

"Don't bait the god, Cime. He still thinks you're
attractive."

She nearly slapped him. As she tried, he caught her
wrist. She demanded that he let her go for all their
safety.

He could not refuse: collisions on the slippery road
were all about them.

When the racetrack came to an end, she gave her
ticket and some silver-washed coins to a man who
opened a gate for their demon car. Down a curving
narrow road they went, and into some village of magic,
dotted with lights and stinking of sorcery.

Mano woke as they were driving under a suspended
eye of green and red, and said, "Are we there?"

"Nearly, dear. How did you sleep?"

"I dreamed of . . . fighting," he said.

"That's a sensible dream," Cime approved. "And did
you win?" So lightly was it spoken that Mano might
have missed her concern.

"I don't think anybody won. It was back home, then
it was here. Inconclusive, I think. Bloody as hell, though.
And with some magic elements. We were all okay at
the end, I guess—the three of us."

"Cime and I were in the future with you in your
dream, doing battle?" Tempus, too, needed to get this
dream clear.

"Don't tell us about the magical elements," Cime
warned. "Don't give them the power of your words."

"Yeah," Mano answered Tempus. "You both were
there, for most of the dream, including the future part.
So what? A dream's just—"

"—a dream, dear. You keep thinking that. It'll be as helpful as real understanding might. But Ash speaks to me through dreams, so tell us the dreams whenever you remember them. Especially if a tall, dark lord with silver-starred hair comes waltzing into—"

"He's met Askelon, Cime."

"Was Ash in the dream, Mano?"

"No. I'm sure he wasn't."

Tempus relaxed and Cime pulled the car into a side street, saying, "Ready yourselves, gentlemen. The house down this drive is the lair of magic here."

On two posts to either side of the roadway, brass plates said in English, KNOLLBROOK.

Chapter 13:

PARTY DOWN

There were horses nearby. Tempus could smell them: the warm and welcome musk of their coats, the amoniac bite of their urine, the salty tang of their dung, the sweet waft of salt hay and wood shavings. And smelling them made his heart glad, even in the midst of all this land's oppressive strangeness.

The whole way up the long and winding cart-track to Knollbrook, he peered through the tall trees on either side for a glimpse of horses in the dusk, of flagged tails and whipping manes. With his window open and his arm hanging out of it, he strained his ears to hear their whinnies and nickers over the growl of the demon car and the hiss of gravel under its wheels.

When the graveled track curled around and Knollbrook came into view, he'd nearly decided that the horse smell had been a phantom or a figment with which the god had afflicted him to remind Tempus what mattered and what did not. For the closer they'd come to Knollbrook, the more the ephemeral smell of horse had been replaced by the twofold stink of sorcery and industrialization.

Here, before Knollbrook's great stone house with its many peaks and jogs and gables and porches, there was no sweet smell of horse whatsoever, just the oily reek of

demon cars and the sickly sweetness of flammable gas
. . . and of magic.

Every light in Knollbrook was blazing; its windows
leered like the eyes of blood-maddened fiends; its courtyard was littered with demon cars parked everywhere.
From within came the unnaturally loud voice of someone singing to the strains of a great orchestra: ". . . a
kiss is just a kiss . . ." said the singer.

That very much depended, Tempus knew, on whose
kiss it was: Cime's kiss, the kiss of a winsome witch, a
soul-sucking vampire, a mesmerizer, a devil from the
underworld, or the kiss of Death herself.

In his experience, a kiss was never just a kiss. Nor
had he ever heard a singer sing softly so loud, or an
orchestra play so tenderly at such volume.

Cime was sure that the music they were hearing was
the same sort she could conjure from the demon car's
bumper with the flick of a finger. Mano authoritatively
proclaimed that, inside, no musicians would be found,
but only black boxes which stole music from the air.

And this troubled Tempus, for enchanters who could
steal music from the air and voices from the dead—for
Mano was sure that the singer was a long dead man
whose name he knew—were formidable indeed.

As Cime stopped the demon car and a youth came
trotting out from the shelter of the central portico to
park it, Tempus said, "Do you smell horses, Mano?
Close by?"

Mano wasn't sure.

Cime said, coming up beside them and smoothing
down the glittery red dress under her wrap, "Yes,
brother, there're horses here. Victor keeps eventers—
hunters: horses of great stamina, somewhat like your
own."

"I would see them." He crossed his arms.

She said, "Stop this. We're here to do a thing that
has nothing to do with horses, or with making yourself
comfortable here and now. Have you forgotten? Or has
some spell reached out to snare you?"

She wasn't really concerned for his welfare, he told himself. And showed his teeth in something halfway between grin and snarl. "I don't forget. Let's go clean house, where house has not been cleaned for far too long."

Mano said, "That's a relief. I wasn't sure for a minute if . . ."

"Don't worry about his nerve, fighter," Cime advised. "Keep tabs on your own. And what's between your legs. You've never seen my brother in action. It's not for the faint of heart or the unduly civilized."

Tempus saw what the youth parking Cime's demon car or the folk visible through Knollbrook's windows surely did not: how Mano seemed to straighten his clothes, but really checked his weapons.

Up the stairs of the wizards' lair they went, their footsteps at first muffled by the music, then audible, as they reached the door.

Mano said, "Exterior speakers to prevent eavesdropping," as if that explained something.

When Tempus looked around he saw no guardian orators anywhere outside, and then realized that Mano meant the music, which was loudest down the steps, quieter here.

Cime pushed upon a lighted button by the door and someone came to open it.

Tempus stepped back a pace through long habit, to stand shoulder to shoulder with Mano on his right. His own arsenal was suddenly heavy: his shortsword burdened the callus on his hipbone where its scabbard rode; his weaponsbelt pinched where throwing stars dipped in poison from the tree of Enlil made it stiff and hard. The seeds of destruction he carried all about his person—in his beltpurse, the pockets of the infernal suit he wore, in the raincoat over it, even bound to his calves under the heinous socks—seemed to warm him to his flesh right through the clothing and their pods.

While the door opened so infinitely slowly, and a blank stare softened in a wizard's eyes to be replaced by

a glow of recognition when Cime said, "Hullo, Arnaud.
You remember my bodyguards, Smoke and Fire." Tempus checked in his head and in his heart and in his soul
for the Storm God.

But Enlil was not there. Only emptiness met his
questing; only echoes responded to his wordless call.

Had the god, upon seeing such a citadel of magic,
turned craven? Deserted him? Fled back to ancient
times, faced with modern magic, leaving Tempus to
fare as well as he might, alone?

Yet the weakness of Enlil's desertion was not upon
his limbs. Whenever in the past the god had withdrawn
from him, Tempus's full age had come upon him like a
haystack falling from heaven.

Then Tempus realized that he hadn't heard or sensed
a peep from Enlil since they'd scented the horses. And
he knew where the god was. They had that in common:
a love of noble beast above dishonorable man.

But it was too late to demand to detour to the stable.
With or without Enlil, the battle was about to be joined.

Arnaud, the son of Victor, was holding out a clammy
white hand first to Mano, then to Tempus, saying,
"Hey there, guys. If he's Smoke, you must be Fire," as
he gave Tempus's hand a limp and languid squeeze.

This was a eunuch or a pederast, no doubt. A young
destroyer, without the boldness in his eyes of a man
who loves other men unabashedly. All around this soft
youth was a sick smell like gardenias mixed with rose.

Mano coughed politely when Tempus didn't answer,
or because Arnaud's perfume was too strong.

"Coming in with your mistress, fellas? There's plenty
of food and fun for one and all." Then, to Cime, "That
is, if you want them in, of course. If they're . . ."

"Don't worry. Each is one of us, or close enough.
No, I don't want them out in the servants' quarters
playing cards, in case I need them. In case *we* do, after
what happened yesterday." She brushed past the young
wizard, adding, "Where's your father, Arnaud? I'm here

to help him with a battle plan, devise some strategy, not hold a wake for souls gone straight to Hell."

"Yes, ma'am," Arnaud said, scurrying after her, his pale hair agleam in the sparkling light of a crystal chandelier that dominated the entrance hall.

Mano looked at Tempus, who still had not stepped over the threshold. Cime was disappearing down the hall before him, shimmying out of her dark wrap and handing it to the mageling behind her as she went.

"Well . . . Fire," Mano said, "are we going in, or not?"

"Smoke," Tempus said with more authority, "you go. I've got to look over the stables." And roust the god. Get Enlil back from dreams of straw and stallions.

"Ah . . . I don't think so. Sir." Mano was stiff now. "Look, you gave me . . . special help, I know. I probably don't have the right to complain if you want to duck out now. But I thought we had a deal."

"Deal? We had an understanding. And still do."

"If that's all it is, if you're not going to leave me to my own devices—"

"I'm not." Tempus wasn't used to being questioned this way. Mano, he had to remind himself, had Cime for a role model of how to treat him. "But no foal with two heads lives to lead a band of mares."

"Excuse me?"

"If you're going to argue like a woman when I give you a simple order, or question me like a wife when I decide to go here or there, we're not going to—"

"I'm sorry. Sir. I just—nobody's briefed me the way I'm used to. What do I do? When do we start? How do I know—"

Tempus almost told the fighter from the future to listen to his heart, but then reminded himself that this one heeded only his head. His impulse to visit the stables was nearly overwhelming.

Yet the need of his righthand man for help and reassurance was just as strong, now that Tempus looked closely at Mano. The fighter was white-faced, exhausted, immutably human, uncertain . . . and afraid.

This was no reflection upon the other's bravery or honor. Mano was mortal, a man who'd traveled through time itself on an unknowable journey and now faced the chance of death in a foreign land at the hands of sorcerers.

Tempus should have realized that not even the Storm God's blood drink could blind the fighter from the future to his own mortality. Or should.

Many men, some of the best Tempus had known, were jittery before an engagement. Some lost their stomach's contents. Some sweated. Some were vile with fake bravado. No man went gaily into combat that might cost him his life but those who were courting suicide—those with wasting diseases or diseases of the mind or heart.

"Come on in with me, then, Mano. We'll see the horses later."

Without the god looking through his eyes, even Tempus found the convocation of sorcerers bone-chilling.

Cime, when they rejoined her, was in a room lit with black candles, on whose walls signs of evil were writ in blood or something resembling it. Scribed there were inverted pentagrams, crosses upside down, and some of the most ancient symbols for lords of Evil that even Tempus knew.

In one part of the room, smoke billowed from a hearth, and before it a woman in a trance was being ravaged by men wearing goat's-head masks.

In another corner, a child was being annointed before an altar, and a tall man in red sharpened a long knife on a whetstone.

From that sight, Tempus looked away, pulling Mano roughly along toward Cime, who was sharing a drink with a man in black satin, laughing gaily as if nothing out of the ordinary was taking place.

Behind her and the man in the black robe, a couple was engaging in bestiality with dogs and chickens. Near to that, a person in a white hood with slits for eyes

exhorted similarly-dressed companions to defile a
dark-skinned boy standing on a chair with his neck in a
rope.

And all of this ugliness was taking place in a cloud of
incense so dense that the chickens in the room and the
smell of excrement and the stink of fear were overwhelmed by its perfume.

Enlil? Tempus tested in his head for the god. No
answer.

Mano saw his face and said, "Pretty vile, I agree.
What if we—" Mano's hand slipped inside his coat as he
looked over his shoulder at the child being readied for
the altar.

"Not yet. There are no demons here, no manifested
devils, no fiends from the abyss—only despicable folk."

Was it because Enlil had deserted him that Tempus
couldn't detect a true adept here? He looked from one
practitioner to the next and saw no nimbus of witchery,
nothing to show him who was the archmage, who the
true sorcerer.

Cime caught his eye as he approached and signalled
caution with a frown and an outstretched hand. "And
these, Allegro, are my bodyguards. Smoke and Fire
will do for their names."

True names were seldom given among adepts, for
your name was a path to your soul.

The black-robed man whom Cime called Allegro was
dark and his eyes were bloodshot above a hooked nose.
In his hand he held a glass pipe and offered, "Little hit,
gentlemen? Tune you up for the entertainment?"

"Drugs," Mano whispered, stiffening.

Drugs were no evil on their own, any more than
weapons were. At least, not where Tempus had come
from: those who lost their souls in one drug would lose
it in another, or in strong drink, or in frenzied out-
bursts of maddened temper if nothing more exotic was
available. This Tempus knew for a truth. He'd used
addictive drugs and put them down without ill effects,

and seen others suffer to the death from the same concoction.

Yet to Mano, drugs were an enemy to be feared. So Tempus said, "We're here as protectors. We must keep our wits and our reflexes clear, Allegro. Another time, perhaps . . ." He let his wistfulness show. There was nothing better than an unclouded mind, and yet a taste of whatever drug this was might teach him something about the enemy: his capabilities, his weaknesses.

Even Cime seemed relieved when Tempus refused the pipe, as if she'd forgotten the truth that men use whatever excuse they can to loose their worst selves upon the earth, if that is their intention.

She said, "Gentlemen, Allegro and I can't seem to find our host, Victor, anywhere. Nor can his son, Arnaud, locate him. All three of his lieutenants are late, too. Do you think you could ask around—outside, perhaps in the garages or out at the horsebarns, and see if they're out there? I've got to talk to Victor as soon as I can."

Tempus, understanding that Cime was telling him that the targets of their mission were not yet present, said he and Mano would go take a look, trying not to let her see how his heart leapt, or how proud he was that the god had known where to look before any of them.

Not in the house. Did that mean this Victor knew they were coming?

He couldn't guess, without the god to guide him.

The one called Allegro fingered his satin robe and stroked its collar as he said, "If you find him, tell him for me that the voodoo priest is getting out of hand with these babies and chickens of his. If Victor doesn't show soon, I'm going to begin the summoning without him."

"As you wish," Mano said before Tempus could inquire as to what "summoning" that might be.

They were searching for a door that would lead outside when the mageling, Arnaud, stepped out of a corridor into their path.

"Looking for someone, fellas?"

"Your father," Mano said, stepping in front of Tempus, who had his sword halfway out from under his jacket and was still considering lopping off the mageling's head. He'd always hated being surprised.

"He must be out at the barn, or somewhere. Like, I think, maybe he's worried about something. He's been checking all the wards personally tonight. Expecting trouble." The mageling had curly pale hair and he twisted a long lock in his fingers. "You wouldn't know anything about that, would you? Dad told me specifically to watch out for strangers."

"Then you do that, son," Tempus said, striving to see if a blue and sorcerous nimbus really swathed this snide but pretty boy. "Watch everybody who comes and goes. And meanwhile, tell us how to get to the barn. Our mistress—" That circumlocution came hard to his tongue, but he managed it. "—has told us to find your father and make sure he's not in need of help."

"Also, we got a message from Allegro to deliver," said Mano as he began to edge out from between Tempus and the young magician.

Magician this one was, Tempus was reasonably sure. Though the god was not granting him His sight, the smell of sorcery, like a mouldering thing, clung to this youngster as does the grave to a zombie.

Tempus could take this one now, where he stood in the back hall of this warren called Knollbrook, and none would be the wiser how it happened until the battle was fully joined and Tempus no longer cared who knew what he was, or why he was here.

His sword arm twitched with eagerness. But Cime's caution stayed Tempus's hand: she wanted the leader, and would settle for nothing less. If just to avoid her carping, he'd let this young wizard go until a later time, he decided, lest her wrath be worse than the rousing of the whole household prematurely could ever be.

Mano, however, did not know Cime as well as Tempus did. And Tempus did not know Mano well enough to anticipate the foreign fighter, or to judge how hard the scene in the big room full of evil's supplicants might have hit the other.

So as Mano's hand snaked into his jacket pocket and out again with a small, black box, Tempus hardly paid attention.

Neither did Arnaud remark it: many things in this land were small and square and black—some turned on magic windows, some made sounds come and go, some told the passing of time to those who needed a box to tell it.

Arnaud was saying, ". . . not supposed to take anybody out there . . . at least, I'm not supposed to go out there. Dad said he'd take away my Testarossa if he caught me in the stables tonight. The four of them are doing something . . . sensitive, you know how they talk." The youngster's mouth grew petulant. "So I can't help you . . ."

Tempus said, "Just tell us where to go; we'll make our own way," when a flash of light from somewhere on his right half-blinded him and a shove on his right arm threw him violently to the left, where he hit the wall and recovered, sword out and pointed at Mano.

Mano was holding up a placatory hand, and watching the boy sorcerer, who was blazing silently in an ephemeral fire that threw no heat.

The boy's mouth was open. He was batting at himself as if he could put out the flame. But instead of blackening, he was getting . . . thinner, more ethereal by the moment.

Soon, as Tempus watched, Arnaud's entrails and pumping heart could be seen, his bones, and then those too were gone.

All in silence. All in the space of ten heartbeats. All without a piece of char or bit of bone or a shred of clothing being left behind.

Tempus looked at Mano, then down at the box still in Mano's hand, then back to see a chagrined, uncertain expression on the fighter's face.

"I'm sorry. Nah, I'm not. I had to . . . do something.

I don't know how you could walk away from that little boy back there, from the woman, from the rest . . ."

"I'm biding my time, gaging our chances, doing my best to make sure we don't warn the principals by slaughtering minions. Minions are cheap. Come on, before we find out someone saw what happened and we're knee-deep in local talent wanting a piece of us."

Tempus, this time, shoved Mano roughly down the hall to where a door was—a door that the mageling had eyed when Tempus asked directions to the stables.

He could have found it on his own, by now: just look for Enlil. The god had known what Cime had not, what Mano had not, and what Tempus should have known but hadn't had the sense to guess from the god's absence: the true wizards were convened in one of their outbuildings, most likely the stables.

Those inside were just perverted men and baby enchanters, not worth the Storm God's attention.

Not worth his, either.

But it troubled him that Mano would strike without waiting for Tempus's signal, and strike with a weapon against which a helpless youngster—mage or not—had no defense.

When and if Cime found out about what Mano had done, and how, there'd be hell to pay. At the very least, she'd demand the weapon for herself. And Tempus wasn't sure he'd know how to argue, for, like the poison Cime by now had put in the party punch, Mano's was a woman's weapon.

A man deserved at least enough time before he died to call upon his god, or devil, or whatever power he served.

They went in silence to the stable, unerringly now that Tempus wasn't befuddled by Cime and could give his instinct its head.

For him, finding a horse barn was as easy as finding his feet in the morning. Mano stumbled along in the bushes Tempus easily avoided as if he'd never been on a night hunt through strange territory in his entire life.

"Quiet," Tempus finally had to whisper. "Look where you go, not out into the dark where you can't see anything. If you can't see them, they can't see you. Watch your feet, which must carry you into battle. We need what surprise we can muster, even for weapons like yours."

And Mano whispered back, "That's not necessarily so . . . but let's not argue. You're angry that I took that kid out. Why? It was too good a chance to pass up."

This was no time to discuss the niceties of warmaking etiquette, and Tempus wouldn't have known how to begin. This fighter was from an alien future. He told himself that all was fair when warring against wizards; that he'd broken more rules of fair fighting than Mano had ever learned.

He told his righthand man, "If that thing has more cold fire in it, keep it close to hand. If, that is, it will work on a real mage and not just a mageling."

For answer, Mano pushed something into Tempus's hand. On the small black box, a red eye gleamed dully.

Mano's voice said, "When it's armed, the red light's on. When it's recharging, it goes to yellow. Push on the red button, then let up when you see the beam envelop the adversary. Don't waste its juice. I can't recharge it here."

Tempus handed the black thing back. "You fight with your weapons, I'll fight with mine."

"But you gave me the seeds . . ."

"You'll need them. They work. For all I know, that child of Victor's is reconstituting himself right now where we left him, ready to race around sounding the alarm."

"Shit. That won't happen," Mano mumbled, and then swore more extensively as he went to his knees in a clump of bushes.

"You're sure?" Tempus said. The stable loomed to his dark-accustomed eyes; there was no more time for idle chatter.

"This way," he told Mano softly and, crouched low, started to circle around to the front of the barn.

"What do you—oh, I see it now: barn, right?"

"Ssh," Tempus said, going as soundlessly as he could. This Mano knew nothing about stealth, that was certain.

"Why don't we just raze the barn? I can set the whole thing—"

Tempus stopped short, stood up straight, and Mano bumped right into him. Tempus grabbed the other man by the shoulders. "You can barely see in the dark, so perhaps you can barely think. Mayhap it was the god's drink which was too much for your flesh, so I'll excuse you. There are horses in that barn, fine animals who're not guilty of any wrongdoing. Or don't you make a differentiation between guilty parties and innocents where you come from?" He pushed Mano away from him, not hard, but hard enough to make it clear his patience was exhausted.

"Right," came a sigh from the shadow in the dark. "I should have realized."

Tempus resumed stalking the sorcerers, keeping one ear peeled for the progress of the man behind him. His righthand man, who had no respect for horses and no compunctions about dealing death without warning.

Maybe it was the rush of Enlil into him as he came around to the front of the barn, or the degree to which Mano's behavior troubled him, that made him fail to realize that the sorcerers were expecting an attack.

Or that they were out here summoning forces to meet any enemy, no matter how strong—forces great enough to have drawn Enlil right out of him.

Nor did he consider what ready adepts, prepared and waiting, might mean to Cime, back in Knollbrook all alone against the likes of Allegro and his depredacious minions.

For the god was whole and huge and raving inside of him, surging up into his eyes and down into his hands and feet and loins and demanding that the battle be joined, *Now, slow-witted mortal! Now! What took thee so long? Has that accursed sister of thine leeched what precious little manhood remains from your bones?*

Under Enlil's whiplash tongue, Tempus nearly forgot about Mano, close behind, or what the fighter might do, unguided.

Enlil had a hand upon Tempus's sword and was using his tongue to call the wizards out into the open. *"Hiding in your horses' stall, are you? Women, are you? Come out and meet us or we'll come in to get you,"* bellowed the god through Tempus's mouth, as if the element of surprise meant nothing to Him either.

But then, Tempus reminded himself as he tried to mitigate his body's god-sped rush forward and to shut the mouth that Enlil was using to taunt the sorcerers, the Storm God had little to lose: only an old, much-used avatar out of his depth in modern times.

Behind him, Mano called out in surprise at Tempus's words and actions.

Dimly, he heard his righthand man. Grimly, he told himself that Cime had her rods and the poison from the Storm God's tree, and never pretended to need him in any case.

And then the door to the stable slid back and a great light and heat enveloped him.

From that light came an adversary such as Tempus had only met in dreams.

Mano, still following in his wake, yelled something. Perhaps it was: "I'm coming. I'm right here. Don't worry."

Perhaps that was the voice of the god in Tempus's head.

The thing that reared up out of the light and bore down upon him was a demon horse, or a demon in the shape of a horse. This horse was scaled and it had raking talons where its fetlocks should be. It had snakes for mane and snakes for tail, and its tongue was long and forked.

In the light it seemed molten. From between its eyes grew a long, curved horn as it charged him, squealing.

He knew he couldn't fight such a thing with his sword and yet the equine form made him hesitate: what if it were a horse, a plain and simple horse, ensorceled to look like a demon steed from hell?

The ground was shaking from its rush. He jumped aside and it brushed him with its molten shoulder; the snakes of its tail bit and hissed at him.

It thundered on by. Mano shouted and Tempus heard a thud.

Then there was snorting behind him and a great bellow of laughter from ahead, coming out of the light which was so bright his eyes streamed tears.

In his skull, Enlil was saying, *The seeds, fool, the seeds*, and despite all, he was hesitant to use them.

Then the ground shuddered behind as the demon horse made another pass.

The god's hand, not his own, got the seed from his pocket and out of its pod. The god's hand, not his own, cast the seed not at the horse bearing down on him as he turned to face it, but behind, into the barn of light.

He knew that Mano was down. Tempus could see the shape of his righthand man on the ground; he could see bright blood on the demon horse's scales.

And he knew that he, too, would be tramped in the time it took to take a breath if he didn't do something.

The demon horse had blazing eyes and was headed straight for him.

Another heartbeat, another stride, and it was reaching out with its jaws wide and its snake-mane striking and its forked tongue questing.

He jumped for its neck, and caught hold of the snakes in its mane.

It bellowed fury but couldn't stay its great, galloping strides.

He ran one pace with it, then jumped for its back as its front legs hit the ground.

The snakes were biting him, this he knew. Mano was alive, this he heard: deep, groaning warnings that the horse was headed straight back for the barn.

But the poison of the snakes biting him was so profuse in his blood that not even Enlil could forfend it. It was all Tempus could do to keep his seat, bareback, on the scaled horse from hell as it careened into the barn.

And then the seed of destruction exploded in the barn where he'd thrown it, taking everything, including Tempus, with it.

The roar of the explosion in his ears was partly Enlil's raw-throated rage, partly the death knell of poor dumb animals, partly the keening of sorcerers propelled to their rightful home in hell—and partly Mano, screaming at the top of his lungs, "Tempus! Don't!"

But he had, and the white flame around him licked him clean in an instant, as if he were on a funeral pyre back home and his soldiers were making him a great pyre-day of games and sacrifice.

But pyres turned you to smoke that wafted up to heaven—turned you to ash that sped on a clean wind and roamed the earth; turned you new and clean and sent your spirit back to heaven, where the Storm God's priest awaited with old friends to meet you.

This death was a matter of roiling clouds and a howling god in his ear and a squishing of the beast between his legs and a feeling of being ripped asunder from everything proper and righteous.

For a moment, he was afraid that the sorcerers had won and he was going to Hell.

Then he was afraid he wasn't going anywhere: that he'd been confined to eternal limbo, a disembodied wraith of knowingness that had once been Tempus . . . a ghost made by cursing wizards, to wander eternally, lost between noplace and nothingness.

And then he was afraid that none of the above was true, that something even worse had befallen him.

For now he had eyelids, and they burned like hellfire. And now he had limbs, and each was wracked with pain. His joints ached as if he'd been pulled apart between four strong horses. His throat was full of barbs; his tongue was made of shoeleather; his heart was beginning, however furtively, to beat.

And in his head was an ache and a pounding pain as if Enlil's very pulse sought to burst his skull.

Throughout all that interval, he kept pretending he didn't hear Mano's voice telling him he'd be all right.

And he kept pretending he didn't hear Enlil growling wordlessly. If he admitted he heard Enlil, he'd have to decide whether the god was growling in his inner ear or using his mouth to growl at whatever was out there, beyond his lids, closed so tight that he'd never be able to open them in a hundred years.

And he kept pretending he didn't hear Cime, as if from a farther distance than separates one end of heaven from the other, cursing him eternally for botching things up and leaving her to fight through on her own.

Chapter 14:

A HUNDRED YEARS

"Welcome to twenty-first century America. A hundred years in the future," Mano was telling him softly, "is a very long time in such an age as mine. You mustn't be frightened at what you're going to see."

"If not for the god's drink you swallowed," Tempus grunted hoarsely, pushing himself up straight-armed in the white bed and looking about him at the white room in which he lay, "you wouldn't be alive to caution me, righthand man." And then where would Tempus have been, if Mano's weak flesh had succumbed to the wizards' strike? With the god? With the Slaughter Priest and his Sacred Band in heaven?

Somehow, Tempus didn't think so. Nor could he waste precious time with might-have-beens. He was here, in Mano's world (if the fighter could be believed), by Enlil's grace. And the god was here with him, peering intently through his eyes and as restless in his flesh as a child kept pent up too long indoors.

Mano sighed and rubbed his freshly-shaven jaw. "I keep trying to explain to you: we lucked out, that's all. If it's an explanation you want, and credit to be given, the *deus ex machina* in this case was technology—mine, that is, tech indigenous to my birth era . . . plus a little help from what I picked up in Lemuria about point calibrating timelike loops to avoid paradox effects by phase shifting through parallel dimensions . . ."

Tempus shook his head wearily. "So you still insist that man is responsible for all, good and bad, despite what you've seen and tasted, heard and felt, with me? Then what of fate, and spates of ill and good fortune?"

"Randomicity; probability distribution curves; luck, if you will—augmented by your sorcerers' meddling with the Anthropic Principle . . . The universe doesn't care about mankind, Tempus. It can't tell bad events from good events, because in its terms all events are equally valuable. It likes events, that's all: what we call catastrophe, it calls wave propagation—and all those so-called wizards calling upon the universal mind can bend that propagation to their purposes . . . Quit shaking your head at me. Think of what I'm telling you as the prevalent religion. I've got to get us through the next few days of meetings without my higher-ups deciding you're a dangerous wacko, a schizophrenic with unique symptoms and a prize our academic and scientific communities can't let go unstudied."

"Days?" Tempus swung his bare legs over the side of the white-sheeted bed. The god counseled immediate flight. Tempus wasn't sure that even the god knew how to quit this place, wherever it was.

But Enlil was. Though Tempus clamped his jaws together so that they ached, the god could not let Mano's slights pass. *"Righthand man,"* they said together in a voice that echoed back from slat-covered windows so that the metal slats rattled, one upon the other, *"mortal moron of a god's-bereft future beset by sorcerers,* will you never learn? *If I am come in the person of My avatar to empower you, if you have drunk the fruit of My tree, if you are worthy to be called human, then bow you down before Me on this spot!"*

Tempus, wresting control from Enlil, hung his head and closed his eyes. Never would he forget that moment, when the god asked a proud man to bow to another. Of all things on earth, Tempus hated the demeaning of man by man the most.

In his head he told Enlil, *Get You out of me, then, Pillager. Show Thine Awful Self to this man whose ignorance appalls Thee. Otherwise, he'll bow to me, not Thee. And You surely wouldn't want that.*

But Mano wasn't bowing, Tempus saw when he squinted through watering eyes.

He was staring at Tempus, his face expressionless, his gaze cold and very distant. And he said, "That shit won't play here, soldier."

Upon those words, the god wrenched Tempus to his feet and began stretching and pulling upon his person while wordless noises came out of Tempus's mouth. The room seemed to shrink about him until his hair brushed the ceiling. Mano, too, got smaller, and looked strange to Tempus's eyes.

If those eyes were, at that moment, Tempus's any longer—for of that he was not sure.

In a mirror across the room he caught sight of what had been . . . was . . . still must be . . . himself, and he did not credit what he thought he saw.

For there, in that mirror, was the Storm God's glowing form and the Storm God's supernal majesty. In full panoply and grandiose stature, flaring so bright in this white cubicle that Mano threw his hand up to cover his face and dove to the floor on his belly, Enlil manifested upon the flesh of Tempus, as he had never done in all these hundreds of years.

Inside himself, Tempus's own self keened, *No! Let me fear You, not be You!* and his soul cowered shamefully in the great cavern of the god's heart, begging Enlil to withdraw, to make the manifestation pass.

But Enlil was not yet finished with Tempus's flesh. First he moved one huge foot, ponderously, then the other, until the right foot of the god was beside the face of the man belly-down on the floor.

And the god said, through a mouth which once had

been Tempus's, *"No man has ever bowed lower than this before My Majesty. I will hear a fervent supplication."*

There must have been some such, if silently phrased, from Mano, who still covered his tiny head, for the god chuckled in pleasure and slowly began receding, leaving Tempus, eventually, dizzy on the bed, head in his hands, naked and trembling and hoping that Mano would have the good taste to pretend that nothing at all had happened here.

But Mano, when he sat up, was breathing hard and pale-faced. He pulled himself back to the room's white door without getting up and leaned back against it, legs outstretched, watching Tempus with unblinking eyes.

Tempus stared back at Mano, too exhausted to move.

They sat that way too long for friends. Finally Mano licked his lips, saying, "You realize, we run constant surveillance tapes in rooms like these. If that was some kind of trick, I'll be happier. If it's on the tape . . ."

Tempus said, "The god has shown himself to you, as once He showed himself to me. Be careful, from now on, Mano, what you ask for. And keep in mind that you drank the blood of the flower, and lived when you should have died. That's the way of it when the god chooses an avatar. I'm going back where I belong." He forced himself to his feet and weaved there, his naked skin pimpling in the cold, sterile air. He had no idea how to accomplish any such return, but he was sure now that Enlil knew his way.

It was a piteous thing that the ignorance and the arrogance in Mano's mind prevented him from accepting the reality of the god's visitation. What he'd said about tape meant nothing to Tempus, but what Enlil said to Mano meant nothing to Mano. Tempus was willing to bet that, of the two lapses in comprehension, Mano's was the more significant.

His righthand man scrubbed his face with his hand and levered himself to his feet, subdued and unable now to meet Tempus's stare. "Look, let's get you dressed. We've got a meeting scheduled. Be nice, okay? Polite.

You're real interesting around here, you must know that. Let me lead the discussion, and we'll have you out of this place and back in a jiffy."

"Back to where?" Tempus said as he moved unsteadily to the closet that Mano indicated and slid aside its door. Inside were his own clothes, and others.

"Back to where we left your sister. Where else?"

Among the garments, Tempus did not find any of his weapons, nor a single seed of destruction—not the shortsword of Enlil or even his weaponsbelt.

As calmly as he could, with Enlil so hot and attentive inside him, he dressed, concentrating on not letting Mano see that his hands were trembling with rage and reaction from Enlil's commandeering of his flesh.

"Where else, indeed?" he answered. "You said the sorcerers from here might have chased you to that past of yours, where we met Cime. Now what makes you think that they've not followed you—that they're not here as well?"

"I . . . I don't know. I mean, of course they're here. But here they're too strong . . . I told you. We've got to win this back there, in that time."

"If you could, why did you not?" Logic said this right-hand man of his was fooling himself. "If I am here, and you are, and even the god is here . . . then there is some reason to be here, now," Tempus said slowly, trying to explain matters to Mano as if to a child. "Enlil would not have spared you without good reason; you should have died in the enchanters' onslaught."

"I told you—I had a quick-return panic button; I pushed it. It caught us in the field effect, that's all."

"That's all? Us, and not the demon horse? When you have just seen the god in person, you still doubt there's a reason we're here—that I am here? I have no interest in any man's future." This was not entirely true. He remembered the Shepherd of Sandia with great interest; hers was a future he might be keen to explore. Next to his Tros horse that he'd left in Lemuria, finding her again was the thing he'd like most to do.

And he'd do just that if, when this was over and Enlil was finished warring with wizards, Tempus wasn't so entangled with Cime that he'd never get free of her. Do it, that is, if he could make some accommodation with Enlil, whose increasing liberties with Tempus's flesh—with their shared flesh—were so troubling that one of the reasons he trembled so was the effort he made not to confront that problem, here and now.

Later, he and the god would hash matters out. Now, they needed one another, in a stranger than strange land full of idiot infidels and moral cowards who had spawned battle strategies such as Mano counseled when he'd urged Tempus to destroy the barn without warning those within that a battle was even in the offing.

Mano had even offered to do it *for* Tempus with his . . . technology; as he offered now, with a shake of his head, to help Tempus get back to his own time, without Enlil's help, this very day if that was what Tempus wished.

Tempus had snuck up on enemies during night attacks, had debilitated enemy horse lines, had thrown plague-infested rats over fortress walls in his time. Under orders. Against superior forces of combatants.

But he'd never considered warfare as pure slaughter, as eradication of faceless hordes by trick and proxy. If war was fought without personal risk, then how was the morality of the combatants tested? How did the gods judge who was right and who was wrong if not by deciding a winner—by favoring one side over the other, and giving victory where it was due? And how did this government maintain fitness within its ranks, if its leaders were never tested in the field and thus never learned compassion, the difference between reality and rhetoric, and all the ineffable wisdom a man learns facing death not once in life, but a hundred or a thousand times?

And how, more to the point, could Mano's people hope to triumph over a soulless, sorcerous enemy if they used the same tactics as that enemy, and yet had neither god nor magic upon their side, but only technology?

He said to Mano, "How is it that you have no gods of your own helping in this battle, here and now?" Might as well learn what he could before he was thrust among these people who'd taken his weapons from him. Over his own clothes, he started to put on the suit Cime had bought for him.

Mano said, "No, try the coveralls. Step into the feet and pull it up . . ." Then, when Tempus did, "We've got gods, they just don't . . . come down and walk around and scare the hell out of people. They're sleepy, I guess. Remember what I said to you and Rath: people fear evil, not gods, these days, so gods don't get much more than lip-service since they're not perceived as strong enough to fight with or for a man. But we've got Christians and Jews and Muslims and Sikhs and Buddhists—"

"Christians are the flock of the dying god?"

"That's this country's major . . . let's not talk about this. There's a transcript of everything we say being made as we say it. We don't want to go on record."

"There's a record of everything everyone says and does, which lasts forever," he told his righthand man gently. "Surely some temporary mechanical ear to the door is of no significance, compared to that. Hasn't your travel to the past taught you that much?"

"Look, you've got a good grasp of basic physics, for an ancient, but you don't realize yet that there are mutable pasts and mutable presents and mutable futures: it's a quantum-mechanical model—never mind. Let's go meet the heavies."

"And get my weapons back." Tempus was dressed, all but for bare feet. He eyed the torturous shoes Cime had made him trade for his sandals.

"Try the boots in the closet; they'll fit." Mano had his hand on the doorknob. "About the weapons: don't worry. Our tech boys are just looking them over. You'll get 'em back."

Mano did not sound certain of this, but Tempus let the statement pass unchallenged. Enlil was with him. They would make their way where they must, however they must.

"And my sister? Shall we go collect her before this meeting?" Was she in another room like this one, alone and wondering where he was?

"She . . . she didn't come back with us. I thought you understood that. I told you, you were caught in my return field, that's all."

He found himself at Mano's side, his hand holding the door shut. "Then we must go back to that place and time. Immediately. And find her."

Alone she was, back there with those wizards. He tried to tell himself she could handle whatever fate threw at her. She didn't need him; she was fond of telling him that. But his blood grew cold and his heart beat fast.

Mano said, "That's not so damned simple, getting exactly back there, to the same moment, or however close we can manage it, in the same dimension. You wouldn't want to meet yourself and go bang."

"Myself is here with me, fool. I want to return to the battleplain."

"Battleplain. Jesus, man. Riddler, sir, what if she's not there anymore? Maybe the locus of battle's shifted. Let's just go to the meeting, okay?"

"As you wish. To get my weapons." He wanted the god's sword on his hip. He wanted his weaponsbelt at his waist. He wanted, if truth be known, the Tros horse under him and a wide sky above filled with massing clouds.

But he'd settle for the return of what had been taken from him, and transportation back to Knollbrook, where he had unfinished business.

His mind was so fixed on his own needs that he hardly noticed what lay beyond the arching windows of an elevated corridor through which Mano led him: a city below and around and above, much more dense than the city of New York that he'd left. Great silver birds and insects flew through its skies; tiny people scurried like ants on streets far below.

Normally, the height might have daunted him. Even when he traveled in stormclouds, he never looked down on what lay beneath his feet. But now he was too busy chasing the convoluted logic of the events surrounding his arrival here. And no matter how he tried, he could not shake the feeling that something was wrong with the way Mano was perceiving what had happened and what might happen.

Cime had spoken to him in his dreams, cursed him for mucking things up. He had heard her as clearly as he'd heard Mano, while he was recuperating, before he could open his eyes. Thus either Mano was lying to him, and she was here—at least had been here—or even a hundred years was not enough to separate them, brother and sister.

And that made no sense—unless Askelon was somehow involved; and this Tempus would not credit. He had enough to wonder about, without adding the dream lord. Therefore, he did not wonder about Ash's interference any further, just took it at face value that he'd heard Cime while he was recuperating, and that, because he'd heard her voice, she was not separated from him by anything so vast as the phased dimensions of which Mano spoke.

He said only, "How long was I insensible?" as Mano and he made their way through the corridor to another which gave off it.

Mano said, "A week, our time."

"That long."

"You were half dead, god or no god. Torn to shit. Nobody here can believe how fast you healed."

"How does one disbelieve the evidences of one's senses?"

"Figure of speech. It's amazing, that's all."

"It's the god," Tempus reminded Mano. And then he

couldn't resist it: "The god and I will reunite with Cime, as soon as we can, wherever she is."

"Is that a threat or a warning?"

"Perhaps an invitation, if you still fight this enemy wheresoever he can be found," Tempus said.

"We got other enemies, buddy, the kind your god's never come up against, to deal with first," Mano said through gritted teeth as he stopped before a door marked, "Conference," and pushed it open.

"After you, sir," he said.

Inside were four people, all before little black windowboxes that made the table at which they sat look like a four-eyed frog.

Chapter 15:

A DREAM IS JUST A DREAM

Tempus heard his own voice, and the voice of Enlil, coming from the little windowboxes as Mano shut the door behind them.

Then the recitation, which sounded to Tempus like exactly what he could remember of Enlil's exhortation to Mano, stopped and the silence in its wake was pregnant and cold.

In it, all eyes looked him over as if he were a wonder from a foreign land or a clue in need of interpretation—or a death card turned face-up in a fortuneteller's hand.

One by one they rose, and Mano introduced each to Tempus.

The first was an ambassador, white-haired and plump, and it was she who called the meeting to order once Tempus and Mano had been told to sit at the frog table.

Like the ambassador, none of the others gave their names, but only titles—a sure sign of people in fear of sorcery.

To the left of the ambassador was a general of the armies, a red-nosed man who had the ravaged features of one who liked his wine too much.

On the ambassador's right was a scientist called "Doctor," a balding, thin man with an elongated skull and tiny shoulders hardly broad enough to carry his big head.

To the right of the doctor was another man, this one called "Director," who reminded Tempus of many men he'd known: deep furrows scored his brow and crosshatches of worry screened his quick, piercing eyes.

Across from Director, Mano sat, in a way that made Tempus know that he was Mano's superior officer.

Tempus himself was nearly eye to eye with the ambassador, who welcomed him to her country, and said, "We've never had such a visitor before, and you'll excuse us if our exigency makes us blunt. What is it, Mr. Tempus, you think you can do to help us with our . . . problem?"

Before Tempus could answer, Mano said, "He didn't suggest this trip, Madame Ambassador, remember. But this is the man I traveled to . . . uh . . . Venue Eight . . . to enlist. When we arrived at Venue Three, he proved invaluable to me in locating and infiltrating the enemy."

"Venue Eight, was it?" the big-headed doctor mused. "That's significant. And how did you get to Venue Eight, Mr. Tempus?"

"Commander," Mano said, leaning sideways to murmur in his ear, "Venue Eight's Lemuria."

He had gathered that. He looked at the doctor and said, "In my country, all things are possible with the help of manifest gods, especially when fighting wizard weapons." He watched closely for signs of disbelief. The doctor only scribbled a note on a pad before him.

"Commander, is it?" said Director. "Well, Commander, Mano tells me you've had a lifetime's experience with—"

"More," Tempus said.

"More," amended Director, and cleared his throat, "fighting these . . . uh . . . wizards, as you call them. Do you think, if we could return you and Mano to Venue Three, you'd be willing to continue helping us with your . . . special methods?"

"If the god allows," said Tempus. "But tell me the problem here and now. Maybe we can fight it here as well." Through the window, he saw no signs of sorcerous depredation: the sky was clear, with no dragons or hell's eyes or tornadoes in it; no buildings flared unquenchably with witchfire; nor had any rents in the firmament above or the fundament below been obvious to him earlier, when he'd looked out and down upon the streets.

"Tell you . . ." For the first time, the general spoke up, his red face growing even redder, "You expect us to reveal sensitive information like troop strengths and the locations of our fortifications? You're a stranger. And one the director's people haven't been able to clear to anyone's satisfaction but their own. You must think we're stu—"

"Sir," Mano said quietly, "he didn't mean that. He meant, let him see what the enemy's tactics are like here, that's all: so he knows, better than I can explain, what we're fighting."

"We're fighting," said the ambassador, reaching out to cover the general's gnarly hand with her own, "for our very lives as a nation, Mr.—Commander Tempus."

"Thus it always is, with the wizard enemy," Tempus allowed.

"They're insidious; the very order of things is breaking down," she continued, "day and night, right and wrong, tides and moon phases, the tendency of fissionable materials to behave in predictable ways . . . all are coming unglued. You never know, when you turn on your stove in the evening, whether bolts of lightning aren't going to come shooting out and chase you around the room. Some parts of Florida are in an eternal night. The Texas oil fields are filled with fires we can't fight and there are . . . things coming out of the fires that roam the countryside, preying on the cattle herds . . . We'll have Officer Mano show you news highlights, if you need proof."

"I'm beginning to understand. None of this is so unusual. How big is Florida? How many gates does it have? Are the defenders running short on—"

"It's not a city-state or a fortified castle, Commander, it's a state . . . the size of a country where you're from, with no borders of the sort you mean. It's got swamp and upland, coast and grove . . . it's an area," Mano told him.

"So large? And Texas is large as well?"

"Very large," said Director. And then turned to his peers. "People, as I suggested before, let my staff take this . . . foreign leader . . . in hand and give him the background he needs. If you're satisfied, that is . . . ?"

Director gave Mano a knowing, all-suffering look.

"We're not satisfied," said Doctor. "This man—both of these men—have made historic trips that need to be documented. The commander has recuperative powers the like of which our science has never seen before. At least give me a few days to try unlocking the secrets his body holds, and to give Officer Mano a thorough going-over."

"No," said Tempus; nearly simultaneously, Mano said, "I haven't got time for medical exams, let alone briefings and debriefings. I'm in the middle of a mission— sirs. And lady." He looked imploringly at his director once again.

"Go on, Mano, speak up," said Director.

"Tempus thinks that it might be wise to prepare for an attack . . . close by. At least," Mano shot Tempus a sidelong look, "he thinks they might chase us back here."

The ambassador groaned and put her palms over her eyes theatrically. When she took them down, she turned on Director. "If your gambit leads to an attack on our central command structure, Dick, you're going to regret it for as long as any of us have left to live."

"The god is here with me, Madame," Tempus said to her. "Try not to worry."

"Don't you patronize me, you . . . ancient person," she snapped. "I saw that tape, where you turned yourself into . . . whatever that was. Some trick. But we're not primitives, here."

"I can see that." He was beginning to realize that these folk were as good as deaf and blind in the war they were fighting. Else they'd not be sitting together wondering about Tempus and how he'd done what he did; they'd be readying for a counterattack any fool could anticipate.

Instead, Ambassador was ready to blame one of their number for sorcerers behaving like sorcerers and tit being exchanged for tat. Tempus looked with compassion on Director, whom the ambassador had called "Dick." "I should go with the director and Mano, to learn what I may so that if trouble comes while I'm with you, I'll be of help." He stood up, signalling an end to the audience.

The woman ambassador got to her feet as well, a flush rising in her cheeks, shushing the men on either side of her. "Do that, Commander Tempus. Then have the director schedule you for a private meeting with me."

Tempus intended no such meeting. He wanted only an end to this one. And he wanted his weapons back. "Before I go, I would like the return of the artifacts I brought with me, every one. Right now." He crossed his arms.

"Artifacts?" The ambassador was genuinely puzzled. "Have we items belonging to this person?" she asked generally.

"We do," said the doctor, who was also on his feet. "They're in national security quarantine, Madame Ambassador."

"They're mine," said Tempus.

"They're as good or better than anything we've got," said Mano. "I'd hate to be without them if trouble does come."

"As good or better?" Doctor sniffed. "Ha!"

"Give them back to him, Doctor. They're all going over to the Director's office; surely they'll be safe in that citadel."

"I must officially protest," said Doctor warningly

"And I must agree," said the general, who obviously had a great deal of influence on the ambassador, "with the doctor, here."

"And I must disagree," said Director. "It's my job to decide what's a national security matter and what's not. Keeping this man's special expertise out of our reach by separating him from his electronics isn't in our national interest." He put both hands in the pockets of his suit and glared at the doctor.

"We'll see about that, Dick," Doctor threatened. "We're talking about primitive wea—"

"Ambassador," the director interrupted, "we'll go pick up those items ourselves, on our way. Get a count and have Commander Tempus sign them out. That's enough to satisfy protocol." Then the director waved Tempus and Mano toward the door. "If you'll excuse us, gentlepeople, I'll file a full report with all the appropriate agencies as soon as I'm done appraising the situation."

"It's going to take more than a situation report," the doctor called after him as the director shepherded them through the door, "to save your butt this time, Director, if your people fail again."

Then the director was out in the hall, shutting the door on those inside the conference room.

And Mano was saying, "Great. Thanks, Director. I didn't know what to expect in there."

"Expect the worst," said Director, "then you're never disappointed. Now, let's go get the commander's electronics and get over to my office, just in case our friend is right and there's going to be onshore trouble . . ."

"It's not electronics, sir," said Mano as he and Tempus fell in step with the local leader.

"It's not," said the director, who was not very tall and

had to look up to meet Tempus eye to eye. "What is it, then, Commander? Mano said you were exceedingly effective in the field."

"Seeds of destruction," said Tempus. "And a sword the god has taught to know sorcery when it's drawn against it."

"Oh," said Director. "Well, let's have a look, then. My ride's waiting. Commander, we'll give you a tour of some sights you're not likely to see again."

All this time, the god had been quiet in Tempus. No longer. The god was suddenly restless, anxious to be away. "Now I must tell you," Tempus said, "that when I have my weapons back, it's best for all that Mano and I depart."

"And go where?" the director wanted to know. They were standing beside a door down at the end of that white hallway. The door drew apart, exposing an even narrower hallway, at the end of which someone was waving to them.

Then the someone disappeared. Tempus blinked and looked again, but the wraith was gone as if it had never been.

So Tempus answered the director's question, "Back to the time where we were battling," his feet planted wide where he was, unwilling to take another step until he had the leader's agreement. "We must draw the sorcerers away from here."

Mano said, "He left his sister back there."

"We don't know how to—" the director started.

Tempus interrupted, "Otherwise, the sorcerers from there will find me here. The god knows it. And me they will battle unto the death, for I am their most ancient enemy. You don't want this war to take place here, where so many of your folk live in close quarters. And I do not want it to take place where men destroy undifferentiatingly, rather than seek a real enemy."

"Let's get in the chopper, gentlemen, and we'll talk on the way," said the director, looking around as if he feared being overheard.

"You don't understand," Tempus said. "The danger is fast approaching." The god in him was too restless and too determined that he rearm for him to be mistaken.

"That's why," promised the director, "we'll pick up your weapons on the way."

All Tempus could think of, as he settled into an oily-smelling chariot with no horses and tried not to look down because this chariot rode the air without benefit of wheels or horses, was that he'd heard Cime's voice and that voice had damned him to eternity for leaving her to fight those wizards all alone.

He had to find her. Once he had his weapons back, there was nothing keeping him here, if Enlil really could do as the god promised and deliver him, sword drawn, to Cime's side.

Then the enclosed chariot pulled away from the building as if it were a boat pulling away from a quay, and Tempus tried not to think of the long fall between him and the ground below.

Mano, in the seat beside him, reached over and tugged on two straps. "Belt yourself in. Like this."

Mano demonstrated. Across from him, the director was harnessing himself to his chair.

Tempus couldn't see the logic of it, but did as Mano did, while his righthand man asked his superior, "How bad's it been, Dick, while I was away?"

The director shrugged and said, "Bad enough. We lost American Samoa and Guam—we can't even find them on topo scans. Just gone as if they'd never been. Satellites get nothing, only open water. But if you send out a ship, or try to overfly under twenty-five thousand feet, you loose contact with the ship or plane as well. Whatever goes in, doesn't come out. They're eating the damned planet up alive."

"All things are in their places," Tempus told him. "Destroy the sorcerers, and the wards will disappear: your towns will be returned to you."

"That's all?" the director wanted to know. "Just 'destroy the sorcerers.' " He puffed out his cheeks. "I keep dreaming about Shakespearean witches with cauldrons and magic wands."

"What kind of wands?" Tempus asked, leaning forward.

"Uh . . . " The director's eyelids crinkled. "You know—wands. Magic wands."

"What did the witches look like?" Was it Cime?

Even Mano understood what Tempus wanted to know. "Not a black-haired woman in her prime with diamond-type rods that might remind you of laser-enhancement and targeting—"

"Sometimes," the director admitted.

"And how is she?" Tempus wanted to know.

"Excuse me?"

"Look, Tempus, a dream is just a dream . . ."

"You know better, Mano. How is my sister, whom you see in your dreams? More important, where is she?"

"I don't believe we're having this conversation. She's—in the dreams, that is—someplace I've never been. Not here. But not in any too ancient a past, either."

"Sometimes," Mano sighed, "I worry we shouldn't have let this thing spread into temporal venues. We don't know what we're dealing with."

"They give you no choice," Tempus told his right-hand man softly. "They never desist. And the more dangerous to you, the better for them."

"But maybe we're playing into their hands," Mano muttered, looking out the window where the city was thinning and a waterway gleamed below.

"Tell me more of this dream, Director Dick," Tempus pressed.

The man with the tired eyes looked at his hands in his lap. "I'm not much at remembering dreams. Maybe it was here, but everything looked . . . tilted. Wavy, like a dimensional shift. And, honest to god, there were

these bulls, but made of clouds, pulling a wagon. And a
. . . shiny . . . guy driving it. And the town, the wavy
town . . . was overrun with a bunch of Class Three
enemies."

"Class Three?"

"Nonhuman. What you'd call fiends or devils," Mano
explained.

"Which? Fiends or devils?"

"Green, covered with warts, some with tails; lots of
claws, prognathic jaws . . ."

"Fiends," Tempus declared with satisfaction.

"Well I'm glad you approve," the director said sourly.

"Fiends are easy to fight. They're stupid. Just drop
chunks of meat, raw and bloody, from these flying
chariots of yours, and they'll forget their battleplan.
The smell of blood overwhelms them. They'll sit right
down in the midst of any chaos to eat, and you can have
your archers destroy them from a distance."

"Thanks for the hint but we're short on archers this
season."

"Dick, he knows what he's talking about. Never mind
the archers. Try the airdrop, next time. I'll lay you odds
it'll work."

"If you say so, Mano."

The chariot tilted crazily. Tempus undid his harness
and struggled to his feet, stooped over in the narrow
confines, wishing he had his weapons, suddenly aware
how vulnerable they were to wizardly attack.

"It's just final approach—landing." Mano tugged on
Tempus's sleeve. "Sit down. I'll tell you when to worry."

Director Dick was also unbuckling himself from his
chair. "Tell him now. Does that look anything like my
building to you?"

Mano leaned over, looked down, and swore. Then he
reached into the pockets of his coveralls and held out
two closed fists to Tempus: "Sir. I . . . was holding
some of these back." He dropped two seedpods into
Tempus's eager hands.

Then he reached into his pockets again and held out two more to the director. "Dick, you just think of these like antimaterial grenades. Pull one out of its pod, throw it, and you've got about a minute and a half to duck and cover."

"Thank you, Mano," Tempus said softly.

But Mano was already reaching above their seats and pulling out thunderwands from a locker there.

When he gave one to Tempus, he said, "Like I showed you before: Press the red button, then let up when you see the beam. And don't tell me, 'it's no use, they'll come back.' I just want to get through this, so we can collect your damned sword and get you where you want to go."

The chariot and the ground connected with a heavy bump. The director was still examining the seeds of destruction he held in his hands, and Tempus had to caution him to replace the seeds in their pods until he wanted to use them.

Mano, having shared out the thunderwands and also some thunderclubs that had triggers much like those on crossbows, handed Tempus four more seedpods.

Then he said, "Dick, next time, I'll fly you on manual. And get yourself a full-time pilot. No more fly-by-wire until we've got things under control, okay?"

The director was still looking at the seeds of destruction. He said only, "Just let's make sure we've got a next time. Meanwhile, I'm going to give the servo one recalibration shot. I can't see just walking out into whatever this is . . . but then, I'm not a field player."

Tempus was already at the door, studying the unlatch mechanism and realizing that, in retrospect, the figure that had waved them down the narrow hallway into this chariot was oddly shapeless, faceless, and obviously an enemy.

The god had tried to warn him, but he hadn't listened: he'd mistaken the warning for one to be passed along to these folk who seemed incapable of coming to terms with their enemy. He'd been more interested in Cime, and in the director's dream.

Tempus shoved at the door. It didn't budge. He looked out the window. The place outside was once part of a city. Now, wrenched from whatever land it had known, it was a maze lit by witchfire and hung with lichen, full of eye-twisting parts of buildings canted impossibly and leaning upon one another, half-caved in and half aflicker, as if they inhabited more than a single plane at once.

Askelon would have understood what Tempus was looking at, but Ash wasn't here to explain. And Tempus knew evil when he was about to walk into it. As did Enlil, who was conspicuously absent from his head, if not his heart.

The god would find his own way, Tempus knew. As must they all, for shapes that teased the eye and rocked the mind were hopping and oozing and slithering from the crazily-tilted fragment of city before them, swarming toward the grounded chariot in a multitude.

If they didn't go forth to fight this enemy, they'd be burned alive or buried alive or overwhelmed by attackers where they stood.

But Mano couldn't convince Director Dick of that. Mano's leader had a cabinet open and was fiddling with buttons and playing with lighted bosses on a panel, cursing softly as he did.

Tempus warned, "Don't curse unless you're willing to live by those curses, not here."

Director Dick didn't raise his head, but the monologue stopped.

Tempus asked, "Mano? Are you ready?"

And Mano reached past him, worked the latch with first his fingers and then his palm, and pushed open the door.

A stench like putrefaction and offal and marsh gas surrounded them as they stepped out upon steaming ground.

At least this was familiar. Even without his sword,

even with the god withdrawn for His own reasons, Tempus felt better: this was the kind of battle he understood.

He took the first seed from its pod and, yelling to the fiends to come and get him if they could, started trotting determinedly away from the crippled chariot, with Mano close behind.

When he was a hundred yards from the chariot, he threw the seed with all his strength into the forefront of the horde that followed him like a herd its leader.

Then he stood where he was, one of Mano's thunderclubs in his left hand, a thunderwand in his right, and fired both at once into the mass of evil-doers bearing down on them.

Yellow flame spat out from the weapons he held. Mano whooped and fired as well, slightly behind him.

By now Tempus could see the foremost fiends, and these were normal, warty-headed killers with long yellow teeth and ragged claws.

Some were caught in his beams, and in Mano's. These batted at themselves and howled and called their antagonists foul names. Some flared brighter and began to burn, but kept on running toward Tempus and Mano.

And then the first seed of destruction blossomed in the middle of the pack of them, back where six-legged vipers of gargantuan proportion bore purple demons toward the front lines.

The seeds came up from the ground like great trees sprouting, all white and fiery bright with questing tendrils so hot and fierce even Tempus couldn't look upon them.

Through streaming eyes he squinted at the melee where the seeds exploded. Now there was a huge cloud of flame/tree/flower/fiend/demon/viper. And now there was a merging whiteness that seemed to spread in all directions, before and behind.

The city fragment to the rear of the battle seemed to shudder.

Tempus heard a great groan like the very earth opening its maw and looked up, through the smoke and the white flame of burning fiends and silently screaming demons, toward the tallest spires of the tilted town.

And there he saw Enlil, with a great plow and mighty cloudlike oxen, tilling the soil of the city and turning under each and every lichen-hung, witchfire-lit tower.

The god, too, was silent. This was not a battle for warcries or for taunting enemies.

The very forces of nature were engaged, one against the other, on that piece of uprooted town which didn't belong anywhere but in hell.

The smell of roast fiend and fried demon was pungent; it burned Tempus's nostrils.

Stragglers were beginning to regroup and it was they who broke the eery silence.

As the warts on the fiends popped and the demons' skins crackled, he realized that he could hear Mano's ragged breathing beside him, and that he could hear a more distant whining and keening, from the town Enlil plowed under the earth.

He thought he saw wraiths and shapes there, in the distance.

He thought he heard Mano, hoarsely, from a great distance, telling him, "Fire, man! Throw the rest of the seeds. Don't just stand there!"

But he stood there, trying to make sure of what his streaming eyes thought they saw: Cime, or an effigy of Cime, whose face left its form and flew through the air so that he knew it was none other.

The disembodied face of Cime hung before him, no farther than the nearest remaining fiend. The face said, "Come get me, brother. Don't leave me to die alone." And there were tears on her cheeks.

Then the face spun in on itself and was gone with a pop that made him know he hadn't imagined seeing it.

Mano was yelling now that he'd thrown another seed and Tempus should get down, take cover.

The remains of the army from hell was heading toward them, and toward the grounded chariot.

But so was Enlil. With His great cloud oxen bellowing like the wrath of heaven, with his plowshares glowing with godfire and demon blood, the god came on as if driving a warrior's chariot, right through the fiends, through the second blossoming of a seed of destruction, toward Tempus.

Mano was pulling him back, saying, "Dick's got the autopilot fixed. We can get out of here."

The god, above and descending, was holding out a hand to Tempus.

He hardly heard Mano, hardly felt the fighter pulling him back toward the grounded cart in which the director was.

For a moment, Tempus shook Mano loose and stood there, legs widespread, looking upon his god and upon the fiends, both of whom would reach him at nearly the same moment.

Then Mano tugged again on his arm, nearly dragging him backward. "Don't you want your sword?"

The god would take Tempus out of here, back to Cime, across whatever terrain they had to traverse to get there. But the god would not take Mano now, this Tempus knew because Enlil was telling him so.

These folk did not deserve a Storm God; they had faith in nothing; they were calling this evil up out of their souls and down onto themselves by the like evil in their small and selfish hearts.

Enlil wanted him to come away, now, and fight this war the old way—just the two of them.

He called out and up, hesitating though a fast-running fiend was so close he could see the acid spittle dripping from its open jaws, "I'll get my sword; I'll bring this fighter. Wait for me."

The god didn't answer.

But the choice was made, and Mano was half-dragging him toward the horseless chariot, firing over his shoul-

der as he went, his thunderclub leaving bright trails in
the air.

The foremost fiend was struck by the beam from the
thunderclub. It howled and that howl was as loud as the
crash far behind that made Tempus look that way.

Enlil had brought the final tower of the uprooted
town crashing down, and now was trampling the entire
place with his oxen.

Mano was pushing Tempus into the covered chariot.
His knee hit the sill. He crawled inside, turned, and
cast another seed of destruction at the remainder of the
horde, all of whom were now chanting filth and lies and
taunting Tempus that he'd become a coward.

Mano tumbled in over him and pushed him back,
shutting the door before Tempus could see how many
fiends died next.

Dick was telling them, "It's going to be a rough
takeoff."

The shell of the chariot was rocking; its heart roared;
it came to life.

A fiend, and then another, hit the window, trying to
break through with force of claw, to use their acid
spittle on the glass.

The ground seemed to buck: the chariot was leaving
the earth.

Tempus closed his eyes.

When he opened them, he was face to face with a
grinning fiend who was outside, holding on for dear life;
behind the fiend were clouds.

Tempus watched the fiend and the fiend watched
him until its grip slipped and it fell away.

In his head he saw the face of Cime, and the god
plowing the sorcerer's manifested stronghold into the
earth.

Mano was breathing hard, covered with grime and
muck. He came to collect the thunderwand and thunderclub from Tempus without a word.

The whole trip through the air was devoid of conversation until Dick said, "We're here," with a sigh and began making the chariot descend.

Then Mano said, "Well, Commander, I'd say you've seen our problem."

"Give me my sword and my weaponsbelt and come with me out onto the clean grass, there." He pointed to a field behind the building toward which the chariot flew.

The god would do the rest.

Mano cast a sidelong glance at Dick, who was watching them both through his troubled, weary eyes.

And the director said, "Don't worry, Mano. I saw it too: the bulls made of clouds, the rest. We won't write it up, but I saw it. Just like in my dream."

"Oxen, not bulls. So a dream is not just a dream, is it?" Tempus couldn't help but say.

Both men looked at him and shook their heads, but neither could think of a single thing to say.

Chapter 16:

COUNTERFORCE

"Their counterforce is prescient, Tempus thinks," Mano had told the director, while farewells were being said and Dick returned Tempus's weapons to him. Then he and Mano walked out onto the green, weedless grass to wait for the god.

Tempus was sure Enlil would come. No message had ever been clearer when Enlil was manifesting outside their shared flesh.

Mano was afraid now, in a way Tempus hadn't sensed in the other man before. So he said, "Why do you tremble, righthand man?"

Mano replied, as they sat on the cool green grass which had not a single weed, "You don't realize, do you? Nobody's ever lived through one of those attacks, never mind got back to base to decide whether to talk about it. Dick was some disturbed. And so am I."

"Why?"

"Jesus, Tempus—gods fighting in the sky, chunks of city, like a look into our worst future, manifesting where nothing like that should be . . . We're out of our depth. And it's clear you aren't. I guess I'm just along for the ride, but I feel like I owe you my life, so if I lose it back there, what difference does it make?"

"Life is the only thing that makes any difference, Mano. We'll make a wizard-fighter out of you yet."

181

"You think they're on our track?"

"How could they not be? It's good for your country, that you and I lure their attention elsewhere. The god loves you, Mano. Have courage."

"Then you and the god'll have to give me some. What happens now?" Mano craned his neck to the sky, which was dusky and full of large, long cloud banks like a far horizon, a mountain vista, or a restless sea.

"The god will come and take us where we need to go. There's no purpose in guessing where that is, even if your machines could dependably take us there."

"You know, nobody's ever going to be able to explain any of this . . ."

"You had better try. It's your only hope. If we can destroy the sorcerers, your people will have to understand what it is they did to attract the evil ones, and not do such things in future. And you will have all your human minions of evil left among you: not so powerful, but still perverted. And desperate, without the strength of their demon lords, knowing they'll end in hell when life is done."

"Terrific. I hadn't thought that far ahead. But we'll handle it, if we get that far. The leftover crazies, that is."

"And the credit, due the god?"

"Look, Tempus . . . you can't expect us to revive a religion that was lost to mankind by the time of Athens."

"You must learn to drive evil from men's hearts, or bear the consequences."

"If they're human consequences, we'll manage."

"With these technologies? Is it better to destroy yourselves with the weapons of technology than with the weapons of magic? There are always weapons, Mano, and men capable of using them. It's only ethics and morality, a sense of place and the wonder of heaven, that makes man better than beasts, so that whatever weapon is at hand, it is used to protect the helpless and promote freedom, not to humiliate and enslave."

"Tempus, men just aren't . . . good."

"Nor are they evil. They are lazy, opportunistic, and vain; yet they are also courageous, noble, and generous. Men need their gods, and the fear of their gods, to make them good and keep them good."

"Well, you're right about one thing: I'm beginning to know what 'god-fearing' means." He smiled weakly.

"Then you'll know all the magic you need, and where to find it in your heart, to fight the most evil of enchanters. You say yourself that the universe likes events. Teach it what you want it to show you, Mano. Have your people do the same. Strife is all, this I have long known. But strife is controllable, and the human heart is within your breast for a reason. You have tears, like no animal does, for a reason. Your tears are your link with god. Your dying god came to show you that. You are a part of this universe, you know—the seeing part, the reacting part, the knowing part . . . man is the eye of god, Mano. Never forget that."

"Tempus, I'm just a field officer. I'm not . . . religious. And I'm not a moralist. I don't even pretend to act within some high-flown ethical matrix: I just do my job."

"With pride? With honor? With differentiation between what is appropriate and what is not?"

"Yeah, I guess so."

"I know so. And so do you. Else the god would never have chosen you, sent you to me, let you drink of his flower's blood. Since the battle against the fiends, Enlil has softened his heart unto you. Whatever good we do against these wizards will be because of you, not me. In my world, we fight this fight to lift the darkness. In your world, you must light a fire to beat back a final night."

And for that battle, Tempus could not be with Mano. The god chose his avatars in clear and unequivocal ways, and ever since the battle for the grounded chariot, Tempus had known beyond doubt that Mano was one. This man would fight alone, fight for a lifetime, fight beyond his lifetime: the god had chosen him.

Tempus wanted to ask Enlil why the god did not
make life easier for his chosen ones, but he knew the
answer. He was simply resentful. Part of him wanted to
warn Mano away, but he could not.

This world needed a caretaker, more help than Tempus could ever give it. Tempus understood his folk and
their needs, their failures and their hopes—even their
dreams, though the god had barred the door of dreams
to keep Tempus safe from what lay beyond.

These folk had more personal power than those of
Tempus's era ever dreamed that any but god or wizard
could possess. So it was their dreams themselves, their
wants and petty gratifications, that endangered them.

Their souls would be tested, in this world, as no
souls had been tested before: when a man can have
whatsoever he desires—hot or cold, light or dark, food
or drink, woman or boy, knowledge unending, power
over the beasts of the field and the fields themselves—
then everything depends on the wisdom of that man's
choice.

And these were children playing with gods' toys, who
either would grow up in this final battle with evil, or
take not only their world, but all worlds that preceded
them, down with them if they failed.

So Tempus would fight in his world, and Mano in
his. Eventually, there would be a final victor. But now
Tempus understood why he'd been fighting so long and
yet his enemy kept getting stronger.

The wizards did indeed, as Mano had told him, con-
vene out of time to work their mischief upon it.

So said Enlil, by bringing his plowshare to the future's battlefield.

And so Tempus understood it now, as a chariot from
heaven began rattling down the plains of cloud to take
them where they should be.

Mano shaded his eyes with his hands and looked up
at the swift-footed horses with lightning sparking from
their fetlocks and their manes.

Not many men rode the chariot of the Storm God

while they still had mortal flesh to call their own. Mano's face went white.

Tempus said, "Speak not, not to me, not to the god if he should appear. Keep your eyes upon your feet. Hold to the chariot rail, and to my coat if you must. And trust in me. I have said we will fight together. We will fight together."

Then the Storm God's chariot came racing down the lowering banks of clouds, empty and waiting, and even Tempus looked at the grass between his feet.

To take those reins in his human hands was something he'd never thought to do.

The chariot's bumpers felt real enough; the braces for his feet were solid. Yet the inside of the cart was covered with cloud and he knew if he tried he could put his arm right through it.

So he didn't try. He got his righthand man situated close behind him, and he clucked to the great cloud steeds and snapped his reins in his hands as if they were mere horses of the earth.

Enlil did not appear to him, that whole journey, but was within him: warmth and excitation and battle lust that wracked him and made him sweat although the ride through the clouds was so cold that he could see his breath before his face.

And Mano said not one word, as Tempus had counseled, but merely held on tight, as if he held on for his life.

When the horses of the Storm God began to pick their way down the cumulus in sunrise, Tempus did not recognize the land to which the two of them had come.

And when the chariot disappeared into wisps of morning mist once they'd dismounted from its cart, Tempus was only wistful, not surprised.

The god had brought him here to fight, so here was where he should be.

Only after they had walked the sun above the treetops did he see a barn in the distance, and lights beyond that might be a citadel.

Chapter 17:

HUNTERS FROM THE FUTURE

Something scrambled among the bushes, and Mano
dove after it in the dusk.

Tempus might have let it go, whatever it was: sentry,
craven fiend, guard dog or wart hog. Stealth was of the
essence. As the sun was being buried in the trees for
the night, the citadel was coming to life: its lights lit,
one on a great tower, others down below.

He could smell Cime, even from this distance. And
he fancied he could hear her calling him, taunts and
brash curses in the face of death, all barely out of
earshot, so the tone was there but not the words.

Thus he paid little attention to Mano, crashing around
in the bushes with his prize. If the god's new avatar
couldn't handle one lurker, then that was between Enlil
and Mano, not Tempus's concern.

Cime was. Here where the god had put him, deposited on a rolling plain dotted with stone walls and fruit
trees, he was certain of confrontation, ready for war.
The blood in his veins was like molten iron. The heart
in his breast beat like thunder. The pulse in his ears
was like the drumbeat pounded out to march a rank to
war or keep galley oarsmen rowing together. His skin
seemed too small for him and its every hair seemed to
stir in a sorcerous wind. His eyes tingled, drawing color
from the night.

187

He knew he was locked in the god's time-distortion, girded for battle with all of his attributes about him, and heedless of his righthand man because of that.

Tempus had never been more acute, or more alone, than in that moment while his body and mind adjusted to this arena that Enlil and His sorcerous enemy had chosen.

So he didn't notice Mano coming back, triumphant, a boy locked in a chokehold before him, until Mano wrestled the youngster square into Tempus's path.

"Look what I found." In the light of a rising moon, Mano's face was clearly scratched; his breathing was ragged.

The boy he held before him couldn't utter a word: Mano's elbow was under his chin, locking his jaw shut. Both his arms were pinned by Mano's free one, his spine and neck strained to the breaking point.

The wild-eyed youth struggling for breath and freedom was dressed like a peasant in a rude chiton and sandals. The scabbard on his hip, even in the dark, was homemade to Tempus's practiced eye. The sword that once had been there was lost now, a casualty of the fighting.

"Be still!" Mano lifted his elbow slightly and the boy went up on tiptoes with a sound between an agonized moan and a defiant groan. "Well, Commander, what do we do with him? We can't let him go . . ."

"Kill him," Tempus suggested, to see what the youth would do.

The boy didn't turn into a viper in Mano's grasp, nor ooze acid spittle, nor spin inward and disappear with an audible pop. He struggled feebly once again, then slumped against Mano, peering at Tempus with huge and helpless eyes.

Mano was saying, "Easy, kid. Tempus, I can't do that—he's just a youngster, skulking around in the bushes with a scrap-metal sword."

"In these bushes." Tempus indicated the citadel's lights. "Let him speak. Then we'll decide."

Tempus's body knew the boy was no wizard—not a mageling or even a possessed soul. But he wanted to see what the youth might say, and learn why he'd been here, now, where everything was fated and nothing, surely, could occur by chance.

The sorcerers must be patrolling their grounds. The god had slipped them by the wizards' wards. So how had the boy come here? And why?

In Tempus's head, Enlil only rustled. The god was watching with some interest. Tempus was beginning to have a suspicion of the prisoner's nature. And he didn't like what he suspected.

Here, in this place, neither he nor Mano were native. But the boy was . . . And Enlil was hungry for avatars this season.

Beyond, something whined, keened, and chittered like a scavenger baying at the moon.

The boy shivered. Mano took his elbow away, holding the youth with one hand in his hair and the other round his chest.

"Speak up, kid. What are you doing here?" Mano demanded.

"I . . ." Teeth chattered. "I didn't." Tongue twisted. The young face, barely capable of raising a beard, shone with sweat in a shaft of moonlight. He was trembling all over. "I'm . . . Look—I'm just a kid, like you say. It's just a game, that's all. My character's supposed to find a magic talisman and then go to the castle . . ." Desperation broke the voice. "I don't know who you guys are, or what this is all about. I'm sorry. Let me go, okay? I'll be on my way and I won't tell anybody about this . . ."

"Magic?" Tempus bore down on the youngster. "Castle?"

"Oh, shit." The kid writhed in Mano's grasp.

Over his prisoner's head, Mano looked at Tempus and pulled hard on the hank of hair he held.

Tempus didn't need a weapon to deal with such a youth. He took the boy's chin in his fingers, letting his thumb press painfully into the soft spot there. "Tell us about the magic, and about the castle."

"L-l-look," the youth said when he could. "My name's Jerry, and I just play fantasy games. I thought . . . I mean, your outfits. I thought you were part of the group . . ." His chest began to heave.

Mano kicked the boy's legs and brought him down to the ground so that he could vomit into the grass, instead of all over himself and Mano too.

"Tempus," said his righthand man as the boy heaved and wretched like a drunkard, "what do you think?"

"Bring him," Tempus said, and started off toward the castle.

"Shit is right," he heard Mano mutter, then roughly tell the boy what would happen to him if he made an outcry or tried to run.

When Mano caught up, he had the boy's hands trussed behind his back with the makeshift swordbelt, and his other hand firmly in the youth's hair.

The boy's teeth were chattering as he said, "Honest, it was just a game. It's not really a castle. It's a farmhouse. And I don't understand the lights, either. It was foreclosed last month. It's abandoned. You gotta listen to me—there's no magic, no magicians, no anything. It's just a game, a scenario we made up. Somebody buried something out here, a pretend talisman, for me to find . . ."

"It's no game, Jerry," Mano told him. "Now tell us the truth, or I'll take Tempus's advice and gut you here and now."

Tempus said, "Wrong, Mano. It's the god's game."

He was very angry at Enlil for thrusting this youngster upon him at the worst possible time. The god, however, was unimpressed with Tempus's displeasure. Enlil wanted a third soul for his own, a native of this land. And the god had found one. Tempus deemed the choice unacceptable. To take the first available believer, even were it a down-cheeked youth, was not fair, to Tempus's mind.

The boy was young, innocent perhaps, and frail of spirit. A peasant with a homemade scabbard was not a fighter for this battle. Yet the god was looking fondly upon the boy. Tempus could feel supernal lips being licked and a dour amusement welling up inside him. The god wanted this games-player for his own, because in the youngster was belief and a longing for all the terrible attributes of the god-bound.

Maybe, with Mano on his right, a child was not the worst adherent. But Tempus had no time to test the boy.

Yet he said, "Jerry, there's real magic here. A real battle in the offing." He held out his beltknife to Mano. "Cut him loose. If he runs, so be it. If not, then he's ours."

The boy was saying, "Somebody tell me what's going on?" as Mano cut him free.

He stood still when he could have run, in the silver moonlight, tugging on his chiton. His lips seemed blue in the moonlight, but his head was high.

Tempus said, "The magic you sought has found you. So has the god of storm, of war and rape and pillage. He is the god of the armies, and you think you're a fighter. Are you?"

"I— Whew, if I find out who put you two up to this . . . Okay, I'm in. Take me to the battle, men. I ought to tell you about my character—"

Mano looked at Tempus and Tempus shook his head. "Give the boy my knife." Enlil was adamant. The knife knew sorcery and thirsted for it. It was already glowing pink.

"Damn," said the youngster. "I'm Stinger—"

The boy had a warname. Tempus relaxed a little. Perhaps the god was not wrong. "The knife is yours, if you survive the test. It will find sorcerers and it knows its enemies."

"Test?" said the youth.

"Tempus," said Mano, "let's tie him to a tree and get on with this."

"Give him one seed. Give him the benefit of the doubt. You and I will fight here and depart. This one will stay, and a part of Enlil will stay with him."

"Commander," Mano began to argue, "let's think about this. We don't know this kid. He can't do anything but cause trouble."

"He can die here," Tempus said. "I won't tie him to a tree with sorcery about to be loosed. And Enlil is choosing His avatars, not I. Give him the knife. And one seed," Tempus repeated implacably, his voice so thick with regret that it was hardly more than a growl. Perhaps if Rath had survived, Enlil would not have needed this boychild. But Rath had not survived.

"Your knife. Right. Sir." Full of rebellion and disbelief, Mano handed the knife to the youngster.

The boy said, "Wow!" He held the knife up to catch the moonlight. "No kidding, man? I can keep this if—"

"Man-*o*," Tempus corrected. "And I'm called the Riddler, Stinger. You will lead us as silently and stealthily as you can to the great citadel's tower." He pointed.

"To the barn?" Jerry called Stinger wanted to know.

"Yeah," Mano breathed. "To the barn. Then take your new knife and get the hell out, while you still can. You don't realize it, kid, but you just walked into your worst nightmare."

"Do as your heart dictates," Tempus advised. "Listen to the god speak there, for you will be Lord Storm's eyes and ears in this place, long after we've departed."

Stinger looked up at him and said, "Damn, okay. We're going to save the lady taken prisoner by the magicians, right? That's the game I'm in . . ."

"Now, if you please," Mano prompted.

"That's the game we're all in," Tempus told Stinger, wishing the god would stick to men and leave boys be.

The youth tore his shining eyes from Tempus and, with one last glare at Mano, started walking away. He rubbed his arms. He turned to make sure they were coming. He crept through the bushes, the god's knife in his hand.

And the two of them followed.

Chapter 18:

CITADEL OF CORN

"What is this land called?" Tempus asked Stinger when the boy, crouched low, motioned them to halt behind a great haystack covered with a tarp.

"Land?" Stinger repeated the question.

"State," Mano clarified, from Tempus's right. "We're not in New York . . ."

"Kansas," said the youth wonderingly. "Greenfield, Kansas."

"I should have known," Mano said with a chuckle Tempus didn't understand. "And the year?"

"The year? You guys are carrying this too far. But okay . . ." He gave the date.

Mano nodded and whistled ruefully. "Venue Three."

"The same country we left?" Tempus asked.

"Same. Within a week after we left it. That god of yours is beginning to earn my respect."

"He's your god, after what happened," Tempus reminded Mano. "And give your respect freely, or He'll teach you lessons no man needs to learn."

"Like what?" Mano said, challenge in his tone, and frustration.

They were watching the barn for some sign of activity, waiting for something to come or something to go. Beyond was a house and in it were lights aplenty. It was made of stone and Tempus could feel the cold of that stone even from this distance.

"Lessons, that's all," said Tempus. Mano didn't yet realize what being the god's avatar meant. Tempus was beginning to feel guilty about Mano; the inclusion of Stinger in their party had brought the hungry god to full attention.

And the boy looked between them wordlessly, trembling with adventure and his first taste of manhood.

Tempus said then what he'd hoped not to have to say, would not have said if the youngster wasn't present: "The god took you up, Mano. You slew sorcerers in His name. You've drunk the sap of the tree and flung the seeds of destruction into His enemies. You'll not die with your contemporaries; you'll fight these wizards until they or you are no more. I knew it when the god made you bow before him. You must have known it when the fiends attacked."

"Fiends?" Stinger whispered.

Mano ignored the youth. "Tempus, just because we got lucky—"

"Mano, I am older than your civilization. Do I look decrepit to you? You've fought by my side. Do I seem some maundering oldster? Have I ever told you aught but the truth?"

"No." Mano looked down, at his black thunderwand with its red button.

"You hear me, too, Stinger. You say you play at killing magicians. Thus you've made the god think you long to be a warrior. So warrior you'll be, and if you live till tomorrow, you'll be one until this war is done. What say you, son? Take your leave now, go back to your game, or stay and fight."

"No way I'm leavin'," Stinger breathed.

In Tempus's head, Enlil let out a mighty roar that made his teeth water, furious that Tempus would try to dissuade the newly-chosen representative of His power.

But either Enlil had already gotten to the boy, or the

boy was doomed by fate, for Stinger added, "All my life, I've wished that something like this would happen. And it couldn't. At least I thought it couldn't. But now, whatever this is, it seems like it's real. If your god wants me, Mr. Tempus, and that means I can be a . . . help, then he can have me."

Tempus squeezed his eyes shut. In his head, Enlil laughed uproariously, saying, *See, insolent avatar. Old fool. It is the youth of your breed who sustain Me. Feel your regrets, fool, but know they're for yourself. The young mortal wishes immortality. He wishes power in his right arm and an enemy worth fighting. You wish peace for those who fear only inconsequence. We will put you out to pasture, old warhorse, Me and Mine.*

Tempus remembered his soldiers, every one, in that instant: a parade of eager faces, then bloody faces, then faces swollen in death. There was no lack of lethality in the young, only of understanding.

The fighters he loved had all died, or been lost to him in time and space. He couldn't empathize with a boy who'd seen so few seasons or hope to understand what went through so alien a mind as Stinger's. But he knew young fighters, and he knew that, to the young, anything was better than nothing; war in a cause was better than a life of drudgery. They all wanted something to believe in, a consecrated enemy, a head to lop that would change their lives.

The war was within each soul, but they never learned that until they came face to face with Death and took a life, or lost their own. No words would turn this child back, when Enlil wanted him as a servant. Better to turn Mano away, and with more reason. Tempus wondered at what a poor world this must be, if the best the god could find was a youth just barely shaving.

But it had been that way for thousands of years, and it would be that way forever. Tempus missed his Sacred Band then, all his seasoned fighters, so hard with battle that none had any questions left, or anything to save but pride.

Stinger's eyes met his and the boy was full of excitement. He was honored, he was at Tempus's service.

Hero-worship dripped from lips that had never been split in mortal combat or burned with acid spittle from a demon's mouth. Tempus didn't listen to the youngster's chatter. He said, "Quiet, Stinger. Save it for the enemy."

And Mano said, "Send the kid around the back."

Tempus understood the deeper message. "Stinger, circle the barn. Make sure you're not seen. If you see a woman, or any . . . unusual manifestations . . . come back and tell us. If you're caught, use the knife if you can. The seed makes a great explosion, a hundred heartbeats after it's released from its pod. Don't use it unless you're capable of getting out of its way. Now, go."

Just like that. No more warning. No soldier's honorific, no ritual farewell. This child was not one of his, this was one of the god's. The god must take care of Stinger, whose name was Jerry. Tempus had neither the time nor the heart for another boy.

Mano was more than boy enough.

"Right, Commander," said the quick youth, who'd heard Mano call Tempus that. And he scuttled off, leaving Mano and Tempus alone.

"This sucks," Mano said before Tempus could.

"It's the god, not I. Perhaps we need him."

"He'll be dead by morning."

"I doubt it. Death is a blessing that avatars don't have. Keep in mind, for your soul's sake, that you're not as mortal as you used to be."

That was clear enough.

Mano made a derisive noise, then looked at him very closely. "You're serious, aren't you, about all of this?"

"Would that I weren't. Don't fall alive into the hands of sorcerers, Mano. You know too much of your world's secrets."

"Can I . . . kill myself, if it comes to it?" Mano asked, very low.

"I don't know," Tempus admitted. "You can put it to the god, if the need arises. But I've suffered until He has deigned to remove my flesh from plights where death would have been a blessing."

"Can't you . . . quit?"

"I don't know how," Tempus replied. "Nor do you, so don't pretend. Call for help when you need it. Demand your due from heaven. And eradicate the enemy, wherever you can find him."

"So you're saying, do the job in front of me and let the god take care of my mortal butt?"

"That's exactly what I'm saying."

"Can we lose the kid, leave him behind?"

"He's not ours. He's Enlil's. He'll do for his time what you'll do for yours."

"And you—what will you do, when this is over?"

"Find Sandia." It just slipped out.

"You're a cocky son of a bitch," Mano muttered. "You're that sure you'll come through it."

"My horse is in Lemuria. My heart is there, also. Enlil keeps his bargains. If I don't see you once the battle is done, remember what I've said. You tend your war, Mano, and teach the god's way. Someday, the world won't need sacrifices such as we. Now, it does."

"In order to survive? I don't understand any of this."

"Yes, you do, rightman. You just don't like it."

And that was true enough.

They stayed where they were until the boy came around the barn, scuttling back toward them like a creature born of the night.

Tempus could see the pink and blue glow of magic and antimagic surrounding him. Perhaps Mano saw it too, for the fighter from the future rubbed his eyes.

The boy said, "There's nothing in the barn but corn," as if he knew it for a certainty.

"Then we'll go to the house," Tempus said, and added: "Stinger, you first. Reconnoiter and bring back word to us."

The god in his head was clear on what to do: wait, and let their presence bring the confrontation to them.

He sat on his haunches then, with a sigh, and said to Mano, "If there's corn in the barn, go get some. We'll eat and rest until the time is upon us."

"Jesus, you want to *eat*?"

"I want to violate the sorcerers' place and sup on their sustenance, yes. I want to bring them here, to me, where the god has chosen the battlefield. And I want to sit, and rest, and wait, and consider the way the wind blows and the chill of the night. What else? What do you do before a battle?"

"Ah . . . we don't fight battles like this," said Mano, ducking his head. And then he raised it. "I guess that's not so. I'm always antsy before action. I'll get the corn."

And off he went.

Tempus watched with sadness as Mano skulked toward the barn, then made a second full circuit of it before he found a door and slipped inside. The god wanted both men committed on their own, each alone with his destiny and fully prepared by ritual. Thus, the circuit of the barn, which Enlil had decreed.

The sorcerers would bring the battle to them, this was certain.

Tempus knew the god and knew the way that men were tested and confrontations were begun. And he could smell his sister, still—her musk, her pain, and her acrid sweat were tickling his nostrils. Eating of the sorcerers' bounty was not necessary, but he liked the fitness of it.

What was necessary, was circuiting the barn and the house, crossing the wards and making introductions by those means. When he was ready, he'd go himself.

But he was not ready, yet. He wanted the sun to rise. He wanted the one called Stinger to find time to make peace with himself and be alone with the god. And he wanted Mano to learn to listen to his heart.

But Tempus knew that seldom in life does a man get what he wants.

No sooner had Mano opened the door to the barn and slipped inside than a bright light began to glow through the door's cracks.

The light was so bright and so unholy that Tempus shaded his eyes and looked away.

He knew the fighter from the future would use the seed he carried, as he knew that the god was inside with the fighter, among the corn and the magic there.

It was like being bicorporal: he could see through Mano's eyes as all the corn became whorls of fire and that fire attacked the righthand man, who had only the god's seed and his thunderwand to protect him.

But it was between Mano and Enlil on the one hand, and the sorcerers on the other.

Enlil held Tempus back with all the power that the Storm God could command.

The barn flared with light, and Tempus could no longer see what Mano saw, if Mano still saw anything at all.

The light burst around the boards of the barn and ate them. It crawled up the citadel's tower and spurted out its top. It consumed the corn and a great wave of superheated air hit Tempus broadside, throwing him through the air.

When he landed, the place where the barn had been was a raging conflagration that no man could have survived.

And Stinger was running toward him, yelling unintelligibly. Behind the youngster, the stone house was illuminated as bright as day, every crack and chunk of mortar showing.

Within it, lights were ablaze and shapes peered out the windows.

"Where's Mano?" Stinger yelled. "What's happening?"

"The fight's begun," Tempus yelled back, over the

roaring of the inferno behind him, drawing his blade as he trotted toward the youth.

"But Mano—"

"Back there," Tempus said, grabbing the boy, who seemed about to hurtle past him. His grip on Stinger's shoulder brought the youth to a halt and nearly jerked him off his feet.

"Back there?" Stinger shouted, squinting into Tempus's face. "Nothing could live through that . . ."

"This is the game, Jerry called Stinger. Play for your life, and don't worry about a man the god has called."

"But what if he's hurt in there—"

"We can't help him. We help ourselves. Now, how many did you count in the house?" As he asked the question, Tempus pushed the boy roughly away from the barn, toward the house where the sorcerers had manifested.

"Ah—maybe, five guys, a woman, and a bunch of . . . things. It seemed like they were coming out of the woodwork . . ."

"Once the barn went up, yes. They had to get out fast."

Stinger was pacing him, but reluctantly. The firelight danced on his face, giving it a masklike, frozen look. His eyes were round with fear and excitement.

He stumbled, trying to jog backward, still fascinated by the blaze. Then he looked around, at where they were headed.

"We're going in there? Just the two of us?"

"Perhaps. Perhaps they'll come out, who knows?"

"What about *Mano*?" This time, the question was a hoarse and tortured yell ripping from the youth's throat.

"You don't know Mano. You don't know me. You know only yourself and your fear. Cut and run, if you can. Otherwise, come along."

Tempus picked up his pace, leaving the boy to fight it through on his own.

Cime was waiting, and the first round had gone to Tempus's little force.

Wherever Mano was, Tempus hoped the god would let him know that he'd won his part of the battle.

As for the youth called Stinger, only the god knew what the boy was for. Tempus headed straight for the front door, where raised steps led to a porch.

In the front windows of the house, he could see black shapes watching him come. And some of those shapes weren't even vaguely human.

From behind, he heard Stinger calling breathlessly, "Wait up, damn it. Wait for me!"

Chapter 19:

GOOD VS. EVIL

The last thing Tempus expected was that one of the sorcerers would come sauntering out to greet him.

He stopped the youth with an outflung arm that struck Stinger in the midsection.

The boy gasped, swore, and halted in his tracks.

"Don't swear," Tempus advised the pale youth, whose eyes were so huge in a soot-grimed face. "Not unless you'll abide by the results. Stay here. If I don't come out, use your seed upon the house."

"Okay, if you're sure. But 'don't come out' for how long?"

Tempus didn't bother to answer. Enlil was guiding the boy. His own attention was focused on the man who stood now on the bottommost step, beckoning.

Tempus had no choice but to go to meet his adversary. Behind, the barn was blazing still, but the fire dying down. Something crashed and exploded amid the fire. Tempus neither flinched nor looked back.

The sorcerer waiting to meet him had a face like all the beauty that corruption ever devised. His eyes were wide and guileless, pale like Askelon's, and red flecks of reflected firelight shone from them.

His body was fine and in proportion to the leonine head on it shoulders. He wore clothes of the time, cut to make his shoulders broader and his waist slimmer than they were. Under the dark clothes, a white tunic gleamed against his firelit skin as if it had a light of its own.

When Tempus was two horses' lengths away from the man on the step, he stopped.

And the man said, "They call me Allegro. You must be Tempus." His eyes flickered to the barn and back to Tempus's face. "Your sister said you'd come. But I didn't think it would be such an expensive visit. Shall we talk a treaty?"

So the barn was crucial; its loss, costly. Only Enlil had understood its value. To Tempus, it was a matter of following orders, listening to the god in his head.

But in the face of the sorcerer's words, the god was silent. Tempus had never treated with evil—well, almost never. There had been a witch, once, with whom he'd made a deal. And there had been an adept, the archmage who'd loosed the curse upon him and his sister both.

And these were different times. Without Mano, he was short on understanding of just how different.

He said, "Let's talk."

"Good," smiled Allegro, coming down the last step so that the two men were eye to eye.

Tempus could smell the sorcery on the other, and feel his sword heating on his hip. But he needed to know more, before he started flailing away at a single enemy.

"How is my sister?" he asked, following the other's lead. They walked away from the house and the barn, toward the shadows and the night.

"Corporeal," said the wizard. "How did you destroy the citadel?"

"The god used a man to do it." It hurt to say so, even in such a way.

The sorcerer nodded. "And you have the boy."

"The god has the boy. What have you?"

"The usual: fiends and demons, various minions."

"How many men?"

"In the house? Myself. Victor, my executive assistant." He smiled and showed perfect teeth. "Three more magelings, like your boy. That's not the point, is it?"

"What's the point?" As they got farther from the house and the burning barn, it became easier to talk. Here he could hear his own breathing, and Allegro's. So the sorcerer was not undead, or at least, not undead enough to have given up using lungs.

"The point, dear Tempus, Riddler, Commander by a dozen other names, is a treaty. We don't want to destroy mankind. We need them. We don't want to destroy you—in fact, we're not sure we can. We think you know we're capable of the former, if not the latter. How if we could come to terms? You and your sister could walk away from this, into a different . . . dimension, that's the word you'd like . . . and leave this one to us. And the folk here to their just desserts."

"Why would I agree to such a thing?"

"To save yourself."

"Myself, like yourself, became the struggle long ago."

"You're saying," said Allegro carefully, "that you have no existence beyond that of this war? Surely you jest. Even I have saved something out."

"I'm saying that in a treaty, both sides save something. I'm representing this place, by default. I have a boy who's indigenous, back there, to remind me should I forget." In his mind, Lemuria's lessons spun. He saw the dead seas of Sandia; he saw the windows into futures no one wanted; he saw the face of Mano, and of the boy from this place. "And I have my sister to consider, who cannot leave well enough alone. If you've hurt her . . ." He let the sentence trail off.

"She's done more damage than even your destruction of the barn, which I admit was considerable. How did you find us?"

"The god found you, not me. Have you harmed her?"

"She harms herself. We're doing our best not to damage her, but she's difficult to confine."

Tempus stopped where he was. "Let me see her. Let me talk to her. And think about what you'd offer me for this treaty—what concessions your side will make."

"Concessions? We are winning." With those words, Allegro's sorcerous eyes glowed so brightly that Tempus was certain this was a true power, an archmage of potency, who could make his word good.

Tempus's hand was on his swordhilt, and it ached and burned with the tightness of his grip, so much did he crave confrontation then and there. But Cime was within the house; the boy, Stinger, was behind him, somewhere; and at that moment he could hear even the Storm God counseling caution.

All the world's fate could not be decided by lopping the head from one malefic soul's body. If it could have been, Tempus would have done it long ago.

"You are not winning, Allegro," he heard himself growl at the god's prompt. "Not with your storehouse destroyed." Had Mano been too much to sacrifice to be able to say that? Tempus thought yes; the god thought no. "If you were, you'd offer no treaty. Now that the fight is fairer, you're afraid for your soul."

"And you aren't? We've all paid the same price."

The sorcerer would go to eternal unrest. Tempus knew his own end, and he wanted to shout at Allegro that it wasn't the same. For him, who had labored so long in the god's service, there was a place in heaven. But what heaven might be, not even Tempus knew. And when the Slaughter Priest guided his slain fighters up to heaven, the ghost never looked happy; there were always tears on the priest's face.

"Not the same price," Tempus disagreed. "Let me see my sister. And come up with a better offer."

"Then come inside with me, Riddler. If you dare."

There was nothing for it but to accept Allegro's invitation.

As they walked back to the house like any two men of

an evening, Tempus caught sight of Stinger, kneeling in the grass, backlit by the low-blazing barn, and waved a signal.

Then he remembered that the youngster didn't know the ways of a warrior, and wouldn't have understood the cautionary handsign.

Well, the god would have to tell the boy what the god wanted him to know.

As for Tempus, he needed to see Cime, and then perhaps he'd understand what he was supposed to do.

For in his head was an emptiness. The god was not speaking to him. Enlil had made no response to Allegro's proposal, unless that response was the utter repugnance that Tempus felt as he paced the sorcerer up the stairs into the stone house of his enemies.

He fancied he could feel the wards slide against his flesh as he crossed the portal. And he found himself thinking that the place was much roomier inside than out.

And he asked, then demanded, a sign from Enlil, but got nothing. Not a rustle or a cough or a murmur came from the god in his head. It was as if Enlil had deserted him utterly, as if merely entertaining the concept of a treaty with a timeless enemy had caused the god to withdraw in disgust.

If Enlil was really gone, then Tempus was lost, on his own, to make do with his own sense of right and wrong, good and evil, time and space.

And in the sorcerer's stone house, time and space were very different than outside.

But then, inside, Tempus was feeling different: he felt empty, cavernous, deserted and alone. And he felt weak, tired, helplessly adrift.

He called out for the Pillager, and got no response. He baited the god, as he stepped onto a carpet of rose and mauve and peered around at fiends seated by the huge hearth and demons hanging from the rafters and four men in robes clustered in the carpet's center.

Enlil ignored him.

So be it, Tempus thought. If the gods and the devils stayed out of man's business, then man could solve his problems—would have solved them, longsince.

"My sister," he reminded Allegro, whose face was beginning to shiver and to change.

The thing that was the archmage said, "As you wish, mortal," from a mouth that seemed too wide for his face. "But first, meet my adherents."

The touch of Allegro's hand on Tempus's arm sent numbness to his shoulder as the sorcerer led him toward the men in the center of the room.

Chapter 20:

IN THE STONE HOUSE

Demons rustled on their perches overhead and Tempus's hackles rose. The stink of them, like amoniac urine and fearful sweat, turned his stomach. The mass of them, above his head like a canopy of giant bats, made it hard for him to look away.

But before him were the archmage's minions, all four. And these were staring at him as if in disbelief as the shape-changing Allegro said, "This is the representative of our adversary, brother of our prisoner. Call him Tempus, it's close enough."

The face of Allegro was as wide as a field of wheat now; it blocked everything out of Tempus's peripheral vision, obscuring everything else on his right side. Allegro's visage was shimmering with landscapes and tableaus of war from all times: chariots mired in muck with foundering, squealing horses trying to free their fragile legs; armies at close quarters, fighting hand to hand, stumbling over the bodies of the slain; mountains spewing molten rock over whole towns suffocating in demon-headed clouds of black and acrid smoke; great javelins with tails of fire slitting the night sky; and explosions rending the very earth with a force Tempus couldn't look upon, so blinding was the blaze in the adept's eye.

Instead he looked at the first of the men in the room, and that one said, "Victor, call me. For it's the truth:

I'm born to win this. I'm the one that penned your sister." He stepped forward, chest puffed out under a black robe worked with serpents. His hair was slicked back and his skin had an unhealthy, olive cast. His eyes were different colors: the left was brown; the right was gray, within a blood-red eyeball.

Tempus realized immediately that he was looking at Cime's handiwork: she'd gotten the point of one of her diamond rods into that eye, and not all the powers of hell would ever heal it.

The mage called Victor was no immortal; this was clear the way he sidled up to Tempus, looking at him out of his good eye: an adept of power could have found a way to restore his own sight.

This foremost of Allegro's adherents held out his right hand, expecting Tempus to shake it like a gentleperson of this era.

But Tempus's right arm was heavy yet, and felt as if his sleeve were full of pins: the archmage Allegro's doing. He couldn't let on that the mage's touch had hurt him, so he spat on the hand that Victor held out.

And he said, "My sister's marked you for eternity, I see. Ready for the grave, fool called Victor? Once she's sucked on a wizard, the ghouls and the demons get hungry for him." Tempus risked a look above, though it chilled him. His heart beat faster, sending blood through his arm that hurt like fire.

One of the upside-down demons opened an eye, then both, stared straight at Tempus, and yawned.

Meanwhile, the mortal sorcerer called Victor was drying his hand elaborately on his robe. "Your spittle lacks venom, Tempus. We're told you're from another time. It must be true: spit doesn't carry much weight with me." His face was drained of blood. His single seeing eye glared, belying his words. "We're here for pleasantries and negotiations, so be pleasant. Or I'll forget myself and your slut—excuse me—your sister will suffer for it."

"Temper, temper, Victor," hissed the voice from the

great face on Tempus's right. He didn't want to look that way again, but he did, and glimpsed a fine-looking man with rosy cheeks and a frown upon his brow.

"You'll suffer eternally in any case, Victor," Tempus said from deep in his chest. "You have my word of that. Now step back, and let me greet these other pawns of evil. Then your master and I have something to discuss."

Victor flushed and nearly stamped his foot, and flounced back with a tittering laugh on his lips.

But Tempus had marked the worst in him: a human who'd given himself totally to depradation was worse than a nonhuman power such as the archmage, Allegro. Allegro had once been a man, and become something that fed on men. Thus, he valued life as a herdsman values his sheep. Victor, on the other hand, was consumed by the process of evil. And such an adept knew in his soul that he had exchanged his afterlife for arcane pleasures.

All those who served archmages such as Allegro were the same: frightened fools who'd gotten in too deep because of fashion and rebellion and bitterness, because of errors in their makeup; men who found horror titillating, like sex; who found death exciting and power its own reward. Such men were the natural prey of beings like Allegro.

Behind Victor, the other three clustered close, hanging back. They whispered together like women. They minced forward in a group. These were tittering insults and slights and making lewd suggestions to keep their courage up.

One was blond and one was black all over, with skin like an eggplant; the third was freckled and carrot-topped, and each was dressed in a robe much like Victor's.

Not one spoke to him, or gave his name. Of the three, not one dared extend a hand. All together they said, "We're glad to have you, warrior. We'll make good use of your manna; we'll make cocktails of your soul." Then they laughed together, having given their rote speech in the fashion of singers.

And they stepped back together, so that Tempus realized that these were possessed by Allegro, only bodies now, not men at all. The blond had a painted mouth. The black wore a necklace of chicken bones. The carrot-top wore a shirt of many colors and a billed cap on his head. But none of them had anymore soul left than a zombie.

They were mere containers.

It was this that Allegro had wanted him to see. So Tempus, to make sure Allegro knew he understood, turned and said, "Get your servants to fix a meal. I'm hungry. Destroying a storehouse full of slime from hell whets the appetite."

Victor's silky voice protested, "Allegro, we needn't pander to his fool. We're strong enough—"

The three zombies hissed in unison, drowning Victor out.

And Allegro, whose head was bowed from the sheer effort of will required to keep everything in the storehouse as he chose to have it, said, "Tempus, don't strain my hospitality."

Just then, above, a demon unfurled its wings.

Tempus nearly leaped out from under the rafters. His hand found his swordhilt and he expelled a sigh of relief that the numbness was wearing off.

Now he was closer to the fiends by the hearth, who were somnolent in the heat, but still dangerous if he should wander into their midst.

One raised its warty head from its fist, and lifted a heavy eyelid, and sniffed the air. "Man," it said. "Yum. Hungry."

And the others stirred then, fully a dozen as they untangled from a heap like dogs before a more normal hearth, all chanting "Hun-gry; hun-gry; hun-gry."

Retreating from them, flexing the fingers of his sword hand, Tempus made straight for Allegro, whose human shape, whenever it was not directly in Tempus's sight, seemed to thin and blur and widen and stretch.

It coalesced with his approach, and Tempus said,

"Let me see my sister, magician. Otherwise, there's no chance of a bargain."

Before Allegro could reply, Victor scoffed, "Magician? Bargain? Surely you're not falling for that old ruse, Tempie. We just lured you in here. You'll never get out, if there is an out. You're here; here you'll stay. Until there's no more nights or days." And he giggled.

"Allegro, get this 'Victor,' who once was a man, out of here. Have him supervise the zombies in the kitchen. He might still be smart enough to serve the wine. But since he's given up his birthright, he has no business in a discussion among men."

It was risky: Allegro was no longer any sort of man, but probably remembered when he once had been. Or wanted to be.

Behind the archmage, the walls of the place were beginning to shimmer and undulate, as if the very stone were alive. And so it might be: for all Tempus knew, each stone could be a demon's egg, and not stone at all. A hatchery must exist somewhere, and the demons hanging upside-down could well be gravid.

He said to the god in his head, *Pillager, make this place extinct, if you can. Vain and foolish god, don't hesitate. Use me or whatever, but this hole goes straight to hell, and must be plugged.*

And the god said back, as if from a great distance, *Just find your sister, fool. And leave Me to make My Will known in My own time.*

Enlil had a craven streak, this Tempus had always known. If He'd retreated to His heaven to watch the battle from afar, to see what might be seen through Stinger's eyes or the eyes of a bird or beast or supernal manifestation, then Tempus was truly on his own.

Yet the god had spoken. They'd been together so long that even the rebuke was a relief.

Allegro rippled into view, his pretty mouth back to the size of a man's mouth, saying, "I apologize for my minions, for my assistant: Victor takes everything person-

ally. It comes, I am afraid, from the name he's chosen.
He's a terrible loser."

"I'm *not*," huffed Victor, amid his clutch of rainbow
zombies.

"Then feed those fiends, and make us something too.
Take the others, and get to it."

The fiends, who had been murmuring among themselves, now started chorusing, "Feed us! Feed us! Feed
us, Victor! Feed us men! Feed us . . ."

"Tempus, come this way," said Allegro and reached
for the Riddler's swordarm again.

Tempus slid away from it, and away from the demons
overhead, but paced the archmage as the handsome
one led him toward a door, and then into a hallway.

The hallway was narrow and their shoulders brushed.
This time, the tingling was not numbing. It felt like a
kiss of lightning; it made his body hair tickle. It left a
stinging sensation behind.

At the end of the hall was a single doorway. The hall
itself was long and poorly lit, or purposefully ill-lit.
Behind, the door by which they'd entered closed with a
thud.

"Don't be afraid, Tempus," said Allegro, on his left.
"I said you'd see your sister."

"And you said you wish a bargain."

"From you? I do."

Tempus turned his head to look the archmage in the
face, and saw nothing but a wraith, a dark cloud wafting
by his side.

He looked ahead again, toward the far door, and a
whole man was clear to his peripheral vision, in suit
and shirt, with pleasant features.

"We've hurt you badly, destroying the citadel of corn,"
Tempus ventured. "I've fought enough of your kind to
know what it means when manifestations waver. You
haven't got power enough to control all your fiends and
demons, minions and dominions, and keep your visage
stable while you do."

"So? And what have you lost? Only everything: your

place in time and space, your sister, your Sacred Band, your beloved fighters, every one. Even your horse."

"But I have my soul."

"Do you? Or is it the god who has it, a master little different from my own?"

"We split hairs. I can't cede this place, or any place where the sons of man will live, to you and yours."

"And we can't live without those very sons of man, who define evil in its place and give value to differentiation. Without consciousness, there is no evil. Without mankind, there are no devils and no gods. So let's divide the turf between our sides. That's the bargain I offer you."

"You and I? What makes you think I can commit the gods? Or even one god? I'm merely looking for my sister."

"You're dreaming all the time, that's why you don't sleep," said Allegro mysteriously.

And that made Tempus uneasy. "Where are we going? How much farther?"

"Not far. Just through that door. You want to see her, don't you? See what, if anything, Victor's done to her."

"I saw what she did to Victor. Not even you could heal the damage."

"You assume I want him healed. He suffers; it's a joy to any rational being that the guilty suffer."

Tempus moved closer to the righthand wall, away from this shape-shifting entity. "Why aren't you a hungry maw of mindless evil?"

"Why aren't you back there laying about you with your sword, beheading my fiends and gutting my demons?"

Tempus chuckled. "A waste of energy. You'd just make that many more, or import them or whatever you do."

"Just so. And mindless evil comes only from the ruined minds of mortals. I told you, we're all part of the minded matrix. You can't obliterate us and not your own race. Only men can banish evil, and they'll never do it. They like it too much. What is forbidden is always prized."

"Not so. Work your mindgames on minds you control, not on me. I'm too old to be swayed and too tired to be frightened. I haven't slept for as long as you've been alive."

"The dream lord, yes? Your sister's lover, whom she despises. Ash is your last good hope, but your jealousy blinds you. So you're like any other man: doomed by self and greed and pride."

Tempus's hand was caressing his swordhilt. He was sweating in the neverending hallway. The door, he was certain now, was no closer than it had been when they started walking toward it. He looked back the way they'd come. That door had totally disappeared. The hallway ended in a merging of perspective.

Under his fingers, the swordhilt itself was growing warm. He didn't need Enlil in his head to tell him what to do. He was sweating and the bile that Allegro's words had put into his stomach was coming up into his throat.

Just as he decided what he'd do, and started to sweep Enlil's antimagical sword from its scabbard and kill the archmage, if he could, then and there in that hallway, a resounding thunder came from behind them.

The archmage flickered, or the hallway lights did. Allegro fell back against the wall, his hands spread upon it as if he were grasping it for support. His face turned white, then became a skull with staring, wide and glowing eyes.

Then the whole man was back and the face of that man was livid with fury.

From the end of the hallway, back the way they'd come, issued more thunder, and a wailing like the damned in hell.

Tempus glanced back over for his shoulder to see a fiery point at the place where the hallway seemed to begin. The point of light was so bright and so awful that he knew exactly what it was, and looked back to his adversary.

Allegro smoothed his hair with a translucent hand. He smiled a broad smile with only half the teeth in his head manifest. He said, "Well, that's it for the stone house. You should have played me fair, Tempus. Instead, you left your boy behind to destroy the house. With you and me inside, I must assume. I'm impressed that you'd sacrifice yourself to destroy me, but not happy. Not happy at all."

Stinger had used his seed of destruction, as he'd been instructed. For a moment, Tempus wondered whether the god had known he was safe and away, or simply hadn't cared.

Allegro was growing huge, glowing bright and horrid. His clothes and then his skin were melting away. And what was revealed filled up the whole hallway so that Tempus backed toward the door at the nether end, away from the archmage and the explosion, his sword between him and the evil one.

With this he'd thought to treat? Even for an instant?

Something unhuman called Allegro said, "Go see your sister, mortal! See what you can do. Think your thoughts and talk to your god. Pray if you like. Now that this has become a personal matter, not your god nor the dream lord nor all the might of heaven can shield you from my wrath."

The words issued from the walls or from the brightness, and they hung in air suddenly stinking of stomach acid and illness and putrefaction and death, long after the image of a corporeal archmage was gone.

Tempus stood there, his sword naked and flaring from pink to red as the wisps of sorcery touched it. He didn't remember drawing the sword. He didn't remember just what had occurred.

He remembered Cime, though, and the door toward which he'd been walking so long. He walked that way, backwards, his sword at ready, for what seemed like forever.

He walked a thousand years along that hallway. He walked until pink clouds were under his feet and then hot rock was beneath the clouds. He walked through a place so arid that it sucked the spit from his mouth and the water from his eyes. He walked ever backwards, always with the sword before him. Now the sword flared blood red and bright; now electric blue and sparkling yellow. Where, for all of his fighting life, it had warmed when it sensed sorcery, now it was blazing hot.

His hand on its hilt blistered and bled. His legs grew tired and his muscles ached from striding backward through eternity.

Wherever Cime was, she wasn't close. And she wasn't happy. He could hear her, now and again, cursing like a soldier and sobbing an occasional, heartrending sob.

He hoped Stinger was safe. He was sure that the stone house and all it held was destroyed. He told himself that the god was with him, or the sword would not be behaving as it was.

And he told himself that he'd reach the door at the end of this hallway eventually—the door behind which Cime was a prisoner.

He was sure that was the situation. He was sure it was a matter of perseverence. He walked on, backwards through eternity, until he was sure of nothing whatsoever, not of how he'd gotten here, or where "here" might be—not of anything at all.

He kept watching the brilliant tip of the sword the god had given him. And he kept remembering what he was: he was a soldier, he was a sojourner, he was a brother, he was a man.

What a man could do, he would do. If more was needed, the god would have to take a hand.

Some of what Allegro had said came back to haunt him: it rang true to him that evil was man's creation, or else why would the Storm God have picked him up, changed him through and through, and cast him again and again like a favorite die into this wager or that?

Yet he would not accept that evil was a preferred state, or a necessary concommitant of good, or that harm and horror were necessary to make men better than the beasts of the field.

For there was justice, and it was man's creation, as well. And there was love, shelter in the burning night. And there was honor, which he and so many of his had risked themselves for, time and again. So there was more to man than to the beast of the field; there was more to life than mere survival; there was more to right than a parallel with wrong; and there was more to good than the backside of evil.

He could not give up any of his conceits, if conceits they were. And that, he finally understood, was what Enlil needed in Tempus. Tempus was a man who'd found a god like unto his image of the universe.

In that hallway which went on forever, for the first time squarely, Tempus faced the possibility that the god and he were one. If he died, then Enlil might die as well.

Else Tempus would have died a thousand times by now, on a thousand battlefields, for a thousand lesser causes.

The clues had been before him all the time. The enormity still scared him, as nothing less ever could.

He thought that if he saw his sister, and she was well enough, perhaps they'd hash it out together. Tempus had been born of woman, a mortal child. He'd lived a youth no better than many others had. All that followed had come to him unbidden.

Or so he told himself, alone with his thoughts in a hallway that led only to Cime, with no god in his head to argue, or to upbraid, or to blame for all his sins in heaven's name.

Chapter 21:

THE BACKSIDE OF EVIL

Cime still had her diamond rods. Allegro had not been able to get them away from her, Tempus realized as he stepped through the door and hesitated before what he saw there.

At the end of everything—through eternity's final portal—there she was. The door he'd thrown open with his left shoulder as he'd charged in, sword ready in his right hand, slammed shut behind his back.

Cime sat within a circle, her dark hair disheveled, her cheek bruised, a wild look in her eye. Her rods were crossed in her hands, their tips pointing straight at him.

He gave her a moment to realize who he was. If his sister sent a bolt of hate at him through those diamond rods, or cast one or both his way, he wasn't sure he was quick enough to avoid them.

He knew that face; he knew her all too well. He was stock-still where he stood, waiting for her to recognize him as more than an intruding magician, a torturer, a keeper of her cell.

And what a cell it was: no wonder she was tethered here. The woman who slew enchanters was in the center of a circle; the circle was barred with shimmering green spokes. The spokes were set into a blasted sur-

face underfoot and crossed each other repeatedly as
they wound their way toward a ceiling of lowering
cloud.

On every side was a void broken only by the drifting
weight of the ceiling above and the single door behind
Tempus's back.

It was a nasty place to spend eternity. No other living
thing was anywhere nearby. It was as if she sat in the
innards of a tornado, or a cloud conveyance of the gods.

For a moment, his heart wrenched, seeing the defi-
ance on her face, and the hatred there for whomever
might venture next through this door, whence all her
tormenters came.

Then he wondered if she recognized him at all, if
what was there was his sister any longer, or only the
husk of her, with nothing left but enough instinct to
survive.

The rods in her hands stayed crossed at their tips,
sighting on him like a crossbow as he took a step
forward, then another.

The ground beneath his feet, if ground it was, gave
like a heath or a moor, but held. It sucked slightly at
his boots with each step he took, and a superstitious
fear of sinking into wizard's mire overswept him.

Allegro wasn't about to make this easy.

Tempus said, "Cime? It's me," as he took another
step.

The woman in the circle cocked her head just slightly,
blinked once, and kept following his progress with her
diamond rods.

He told himself he couldn't assume she saw what he
saw. He told himself he couldn't imagine what she'd
been through. And he told himself that the red-hot
sword in his hand might defeat even a bolt from those
rods, what with his battle-speed and the sword's own
hatred of the supernatural.

He wasn't sure of anything, as he moved slowly
through the muck toward her, and with each step, as if

his boots kicked it up, a fog or mist began to eddy along
the surface underfoot.

"Cime," he said again in a gentle voice he'd forgotten
that he had. "It's Tempus. Don't be afraid."

The woman he'd once known would have railed at
him for suggesting such a thing. This Cime merely
blinked once more, and shifted, following his every
move.

Perhaps he was farther from her than he thought.
Perhaps she couldn't see him as he could see her. He
realized he didn't know the rules here, and anger began
to wrack him.

Allegro and his ilk made no differentiation between
fighting men or fighting women, children, ancient folk
or helpless babies. Souls were what they wanted. Souls
were what they caught.

This soul who sat in Cime's body was very tired,
more tired than Tempus could remember ever having
been. He could feel the exhaustion coming out of her.
He could see the dullness in her eyes.

He started moving faster, straight toward her through
the rising fog which was crawling up the spokes now
and lacing itself around them in long strands.

If he didn't get to her before the fog made the cage
opaque, he might never get to her at all.

"Cime," he called again, and this time, he saw a line
appear between her brows. He saw her squint and cock
her head a third time.

The fog, he noticed, was climbing up his legs as well.
He shook one foot to free it, and the fog slipped down
like stockings to pool around his ankles.

He was liking this less and less. He looked over his
shoulder: behind, the door through which he'd come
was far away, half-obscured by all the fog he'd kicked
up. Ahead, Cime was hardly any closer.

Or was she?

He called her name again, and he saw her come up
on her knees.

The rods she held were beginning to glow, and he

thought once more that if she struck him with them, he'd probably hear firsthand what heaven had to say concerning Allegro's proclamations about its nature. And his.

"Tempus?" came a whisper in his ear, as if she were right beside him. "Tempus?"

"It's me," he called hoarsely, feeling impotent and ashamed that he'd let her come to this. "I'm coming."

It was all he could think of to say.

But with every step, up came the fog to wind around her prison. The whole bottom half was now enmeshed, as if she was on a ceremonial meadow in a virgin's circle wrapped with gauze, waiting for her first lover.

He blinked away memories of a simpler age and when he'd done that, his vision was swimming.

"Tempus?" Her questioning call was weak and trembling, hesitant to believe in him.

But they'd always been hesitant to believe in one another. They'd vied for everything, lost it all, and made do with what they had. Now that all their time seemed spent, he was mournfully sorry he'd never let them have their day.

It had been he, not she, who'd brought the curse upon them and put pride and hate between them. She'd only wanted what women want, and to be given her well-earned due.

The rods she held quivered in hands he saw were scratched and black and blue.

Whatever they'd done to her, he couldn't undo. If one man and one woman could ever look at each other clearly, seeing all the right and all the wrong, then strife might cease throughout the heavens.

But strife was bred into Tempus to the bone. And wiles were bred into Cime, to make the battle fair. And nothing would change that but a loss of human form, which he feared above all things.

Faced with her, battered and imprisoned, he was nearly paralyzed with fear. What if she died? What if he couldn't save her? What if he lost her? What if life lost her? It was inconceivable to him that Cime, with all her heart and all her fury and all her hungers, could cease to be.

So he called on Enlil with more fervor than he'd been able to summon in a hundred years. And he said to the god, *Do what you must, Pillager, but help me save her. All she is, We made her. If she dies, then evil triumphs, for I will not fight on alone. And if I die, what of You? Bargains with evil are one thing; with You, another.*

He could fall on his sword; not even Enlil could keep him from it. If he'd brought her to this pass, then the least he could do was trade her soul for his . . . give a bargain to the underworld it could not bear to refuse.

The god didn't speak. The god didn't rustle in him. Tempus's will was strong. His mind was set upon his goal: either he reached her, and freed her, or died trying. Not even Enlil could make him live, or take another breath, if he would not have it so.

Even a horse can lie down and hold its breath until it's dead, if what you ask of it is too much for it to understand.

He was as much alive as any beast of the field. He loved life beyond any choice but this: he would not let his sister die and face the wrath of hell, all because of him.

Yet and still, she stared his way. The rods were blue-white in her hands and he saw how they tracked his progress.

So he said, "Slay me and you'll go free." He couldn't know it, but it was a likely story. And he needed to wake her, somehow.

The fog was nearly as high as the rods' tips. He couldn't see her knees, or her hips, only her waist and her arms and what remained above.

Nor could he see his own legs, for that matter: nothing below the knees.

With everything at stake, with complete destruction less daunting than living on, unendingly, this final guilt upon his conscience and her death heavy on his heart, he might have made Allegro's bargain, if the archmage had been here to cut the deal.

But he was alone in his head, and alone in his heart, with all the unresolved conflicts of his life before him in the person of his sister.

"Cime," he called out hoarsely, one more time. "Don't die. Don't give up. I love you . . ."

He clamped his mouth shut. He'd never said that, in all these years. He'd never dared to say it. Those he loved died of his curse, of time itself, or because all things die.

He couldn't look at her. He couldn't look up to see what, if any, effect his words had had. He just slogged forward, watching the fog crawl up his legs like living creeper vines.

Those vines blurred into a fabric that sucked at him, and with his sword, in a sudden rage he hardly understood, he struck downward, determined to hack them away.

He struck himself along the calf, a long searing slash with his god-given weapon. That sword had felled a thousand enemies. It had brought sorcerers to their ends. It had slain broken-legged horses and neutered slaves and vampires and demons and snakes.

It had fought all of his enemies, faithfully over the years, and never once failed him.

It cut to the bone, and blood spurted. He went to his knees in the fog, and found he couldn't get up. The fog was deep and warm and soft as a featherbed. The surface under him was more than welcoming; it caressed him and slithered over him. He could feel the blood running out of him, but that was not anything to worry about . . .

"Tempus, get up!"

He brushed covers from his face and realized they were not covers at all, but hideous, clinging fog with a mouldy smell about it. Still, he was sleepy and cold. He hadn't slept for year upon endless year.

"Tempus, you dolt. You melancholy fool, get up!"

The voice was an irritant. It was stern and haughty and familiar in his ears.

"Tempus, get up right now or you'll be sitting in the god's lap for eternity, with nothing to do but relive this foolish, ignominious death!"

"Ash, go away," he heard himself mutter. His eyes were closed. The covers were back over his head. He was tired, so tired, drifting into sleep.

Then came Askelon's voice again, so startling that his entire body jerked and twitched.

"Get up, and lay the side of your blade against that wound. Go open the door to Cime's prison, and let her out. Then, if you want to die—die. But don't take her with you."

"Go away, Ash."

But there was the dream lord, a stern face staring at him from the underside of his eyelids. "Go back to Meridian."

"If I go, Riddler, I'll take you with me. Die in your sleep, and you're mine if I want you. I'll make you rue this moment of weakness forever!"

"She doesn't even know me, Ash. She doesn't know herself. She's better off . . ." Now he could see the dream lord's face clearly, hovering before his closed eyes.

Askelon of Meridian looked as if his heart would break; then he looked as if his stern, compassionate face was about to break into a derisive smile.

"Better off dead? You too? What of all your newfound knowledge? What of your god, who'll fade away to a shadow without you? What of these mortals you think you love? What of your honor, soldier?"

That got his eyes open. With open eyes, he saw only mist. Tempus pawed at his face with his left hand, then with his right. In his right was the god's sword, still, and it cut the fog with a hiss and a spatter.

The hot strands of fog, like melted wax, dropped on his face and stung him.

He struggled to his knees, and saw the blood on his leg. He remembered Askelon's words, and laid the red-hot sword against the wound.

The pain chased sleep from him. The smell made him want to wretch: burning hair and seared skin and human meat wrought a sickly smoke like pig over a fire.

He lurched upright, afraid that if he didn't then, while the pain was wracking him alert, he never would.

He was covered with the sticky fog like a mummy, or a corpse pulled from the earth. He sluiced it from his arms with his sword's edge, unmindful of the hot blade against his flesh.

Then he stood there, breathing hard, rubbing goo from his eyes and trying to make some sense of what he saw.

There was Cime, and there was the cage, and he was only an arm's length from it.

She still held the rods upon him, but her hands were wavering: the fog was crawling up her torso. It had nearly reached her neck. The rods were free of it, but her hands and arms and her fine body were all enmeshed.

The least that the god could do was let them both die in honest battle. The least that Askelon could do was not come lurking around, trying to steal his soul just because he'd had a waking dream.

"Cime, wake up!" he snarled, and lurched forward, nearly falling flat when he put his weight upon his wounded leg.

To steady himself, he reached out for the green spokes, and his hand went right through one. He tried his sword on the spokes, and it was as if they weren't there.

The prison was locked from the inside only, but the woman inside was nearly wrapped in fog and hardly knew that he was there.

He pulled back and said once more, "Cime!"

She didn't move.

Tempus reached again through the bars with his sword, and began cutting the fog away from her. Carefully,

carefully, trying not to wound her as he did, he cut and cut, always keeping his feet outside her prison.

If he should step inside, whatever the ward was, it would imprison him too.

When he had her torso free, he began fearing that her mind was gone forever, so little attention had she paid to him the entire time.

But she'd spoken before. He knew she had. So he crouched down in front of her, on the far side of the green and glowing spokes, and said quite conversationally, "I'm going to sheathe my sword and lift you out of there. I'd like you to help me. I want you to hold on tight to your rods, and think of freedom. Or revenge, if you must. Don't be afraid, and know that I . . . love you."

There, he'd said it twice. The world hadn't stopped in its tracks. It was easier the second time. But he knew he owed his life, and her own if he could save her, to Askelon. And he knew he'd never say those words again.

He did as he'd told her he would. He sheathed his sword. He reached through the bars, carefully; he kept his balance and both feet firmly planted beyond the perimeter's circle.

And he prayed she wouldn't wake up or half-awake and stab him with those rods because suddenly she was frightened.

When his hands reached for her, she shuddered. He saw her come alert and saw the murder in her eyes.

She didn't know who he was, he told himself, as he grabbed her wrists in his hands and pulled with all his might, jerking her through the circle and out of it.

She landed atop him, her rods pressing against his chest.

He felt the burning, and the puncture and the weird sensation of being drained.

He yelled as loud as he could in the ear of the woman struggling on top of him: "Cime, for Enlil's sake: it's me, Tempus!"

And then he fell back, in the fog, too exhausted to do more.

So they'd die here, both of them, and Askelon would get a chance to claim their souls, he thought.

She'd always been determined to bring him to heel, he thought.

And then his eyes were closing, and as they did, she struggled up on her elbows and brushed hair out of her eyes.

"Tempus? Oh, no . . ."

There was a scrabbling and a scrambling and a touch of the butts of her rods on his chest.

He felt strength flow into him, and fury and fire course his veins.

And he felt hands all over him, brushing away the fog like cobwebs.

And then someone was urging him up, cursing him and wizardry and demanding to know, ". . . how you thought to do anything but get yourself killed, you wonderful fool? Now come with me, and watch your step. This fog'll make you forget what an overweening boor you are, and we wouldn't want that, Commander . . . would we?"

He leaned on Cime and limped from that inconceivably horrid battleplain without a single thought to how it would be, in later years, to listen to her tell the story of it. He leaned on her gratefully, because he was weak, because he was tired beyond measure, and because he was so relieved that she was there for him to lean on that he couldn't let her get a glimpse of his face.

"Don't fall, Clumsy. We just need to get to that door there, and I can do the rest with my rods . . . It's lucky you happened by, however you blundered in here."

"Lucky," he agreed.

"Without me, Tempus, I don't know what you'd do. You and your little-boy god with your outmoded ideas of right and wrong are going to lose this battle for us yet. Gods teeth, you're heavy. Can you walk on your own, do you think?"

"I . . . A little while longer, then I will," he said, just wanting the feel of her against him, not ready yet to face the possibility of being separated in the fog. Or by the lives they'd led.

She walked him all the way to the door, and there she took her arm out from under his, and said, "Well, where's Mano? Do we have to go rescue him?"

"I . . . Dead, or lost. He blew the sorcerer's barn."

"Another casualty of your vendetta? I should have known. Well, he's gone to your voracious god, then, or to some place better or worse than this. Where would you like to go, Tempus?"

"Back to the place we left," he said. "What's left of it. But, if you're granting favors, not inside any building." The stone house was no place to wander into, whatever was left of it. "In the field between the house and the barn."

"Not up to finishing it with Allegro, eh? Your wish is my command, Lord Tempus," said Cime, and looked up at him from under her disheveled hair. The bruise on her cheek did nothing to mar her beauty. Her eyes were full of spark and vigor once more. Her smile was taunting as she said, "Then we're even, yes? We've saved each other and there's nothing owing."

"Even," he said with a sigh, feeling the complaint of his seared leg wound and the complaint of his heart.

"Good," she said. "Let's go then. Stand back while my rods pick the lock . . ."

"Wait. One thing."

"*One* thing, Riddler. But a short thing, if you please. I've been in this place too long already."

"Do you remember anything I said to you back there, when you were in the green cage?"

"Anything? Things, brother. I remember things. Why?"

The smile that tugged at the corners of her mouth was almost girlish, but her eyes were disingenuous and bold. "You were saying something about revenge, I remember. Upon our joint enemies."

"Open the door, sister," he suggested, standing free and stepping a little away from her. His heart's words were forgotten; just as well. She was a slut and a shrew who lived for vengeance, scores settled and justice done.

So be it. Women, he'd never understood.

When she'd opened the door, she thrust it wide and then she waved him through, almost shyly. "After you, Favorite of the Storm God, the Hero, my protector." And there was no taunt in her words, this time, no derision, no grating edge to her tone.

So maybe she did remember more than she was saying, after all.

Chapter 22:

BACK FROM HELL

"Tempus!" Stinger cried joyfully as they came upon him in the meadow. They'd come out of the dawn, and the boy was shivering with cold and dew, sitting on the rubble of the stone house.

"Where did you come from?" Stinger wanted to know, scrambling to his feet. "Who's that? What's going on? How'd I do?"

"Slow down, Stinger," said Tempus. "One question at a time. And none of them here. This is the Lady Cime, and this is—"

"One of your adherents, no doubt," she sniffed. "Come on, child, if you're coming."

"Coming where?" Stinger wanted to know as Tempus and Cime strode past him, headed east.

"To the road. To civilization. To our destiny, sonny," Cime said before Tempus could explain about the boy or warn her off. "You think carefully about this, young man. We don't need another soul to care for."

The boy looked at Tempus accusingly, faltered, fell behind.

Tempus didn't look back until the boy called after them, tremulously, "Is that true, Commander? You don't want me?"

"Tempus," Cime warned. "Let him be."

"Come on if you choose, Stinger," he called to the boy gruffly. "Or stay. You've done well enough already."

"How could you?" said his sister, drenched in the ruddy rays of morning light and striding ahead angrily. "We don't need a child."

"We need a guide, now that Mano's not here."

"Now that Mano's dead, you mean." Cime stopped. "Let the boy hear the truth, before you feed him to your god as well."

He pushed her, not roughly, just a little shove to get her moving so the boy chasing after them wouldn't hear her. "I don't know he's dead. The barn went up. He was inside. He's Enlil's avatar. The god—"

"—'decides.' When *will* you get this god and yourself sorted out?"

"Sometimes I think Ash is right about you," Tempus muttered, as Stinger came puffing up asking too many questions that neither of them could answer.

"But where are we going, Commander?" the boy persisted. "There's nothing over this way . . ."

"There's something everywhere, child," Cime said.

"Who's that?" Stinger hissed and tugged on Tempus's arm.

"My sister," he said.

"*Oh*," said Stinger, with a commiserating shake of his head. "I've got one, too."

Cime heard that, and turned in her tracks. "Why don't you lead us, Stinger, to a road where we can find a ride, some help, whatever is available?"

"Yeah, okay," said the youth, brightening with his new responsibility. "You wanna come this way . . ."

They trekked until the sun was above the distant line of trees, and by then Cime was making Tempus regret he'd ever found her, ever said . . . what he'd said . . . ever thought that she was worth risking his life to save.

When they came to the road, she whispered to Tempus, "Don't interfere," and beckoned the boy close.

"What?" said the youngster suspiciously.

"Stinger, you have a home and family, a life of your

own to live. If the god wants you, the god will teach you. Hope that He does not. Go find your life, don't risk it fighting battles that aren't yours, but are ours. My brother is through seeking rightmen and avatars and all of that. He just doesn't know it yet."

Stinger thrust himself past her and stood before Tempus, hands on his young hips, his lower lip trembling, his eyes very bright. "Is that true? After all you said, and Mano, and the stone house and . . . everything, I've got to *go home*?"

"Did you not destroy the enemy's citadel?" said Tempus, more sternly than he intended.

"Aw—Yeah, I guess."

"Did we not rescue the . . . lady?"

Stinger glanced at Cime, in her party clothes much the worse for wear. "I suppose."

"So your game is done, and you won."

"Yeah, but . . . Mano . . . *died*. And the farmhouse blew up . . . What am I supposed to say if anyone asks me what happened?"

"That you don't know. You don't know, do you?"

"Well, I know what I did. I threw the seed when the voice told me to . . ."

"If you were to tell anyone that, they wouldn't believe you. But listen to the god's voice, and you'll be fine."

"What about the evil—?" Stinger bit his lip and bowed his head.

"Here." Tempus reached under his coveralls, under his chiton, and unfastened a thong from around his neck. From it, a tiny amulet of the Storm God swung. "Take this. It's your talisman, the final prize in the game you were playing before we came. Don't lose it. All your questions about evil and good and right and wrong will be answered in your lifetime. On your last day, you'll understand everything. Until then, understand that life is about learning, not knowing. And heed the god when he speaks."

"Wow! For Me?"

The eager young hands took the amulet and Cime swore in a language that Stinger, mercifully, didn't comprehend.

The boy put the amulet around his neck and Tempus said, "Stinger, you choose what way you'll go, and we'll go another." He wasn't sure that he'd done the right thing, only sure that he hadn't done the wrong thing. The god was high in the sky, now, massing thunderheads and eating up the light. He wanted the boy safe and away if Enlil was going to manifest a cloud conveyance.

Lights shone, down the road: a pair. The roar of a demon chariot accompanied them.

"A car's coming," Cime said. "We'll be going our own way. You hitch a ride, Stinger."

And she pulled Tempus into a hollow.

The boy looked deserted, destitute, standing there alone. But Tempus wasn't going to argue with Cime. Anyway, the god didn't need Tempus to recruit avatars.

Enlil was doing quite well enough on his own.

When the car came, and the boy got in without a backward wave, Tempus and Cime were out of sight in the bushes, and the clouds above were lowering.

He told himself he regretted nothing, not even losing Mano, certainly not setting Stinger free.

He didn't need a boy to worry about in this battle with Allegro, which wasn't over yet.

Chapter 23:

REUNION

"I'm not getting in that thing," said Cime, hands on her sequined hips.

The cloud conveyance was bending down toward them, looking very much like a tornado on its side or a snake slithering from branch to ground. Its maw was open. Inside, green lightning quested and jumped.

The god didn't like the idea of conveying his sister any more than Cime did.

Tempus crossed his arms and said, "Would you rather walk, Cime? And to where? Only Enlil knows where Allegro has gone to lick his wounds."

"Tempus, are you really so dim-witted as you pretend?" Cime nearly shouted, stepping backwards in high heels as the cloud-conveyance switched toward them out of the sky. "First and foremost: I'm not your sister. Get used to the thought. Ash has proved to me beyond doubt that we have no blood in common. So what is between us . . . is apocryphal, for the most part, and our own doing, for the rest. Second: I'll get us to Allegro without the fanfare your foolish god will flaunt. Now banish that thing, immediately." She had her hand on her forehead to keep the god-spawned wind from lashing her eyes with her hair.

The gale trust her evening dress against her so that nothing remained to the imagination.

He couldn't trust her. She'd been trying to get him to lie with her for eons. It must not happen: that prohibition was as ingrained in him as was his allegiance to the god, or his hatred of magic, or his unwillingness to bring down onto the innocent and the unsuspecting the ancient curse that had followed him forever.

Not that she was either of those. The curse was done and gone, so all wisdom said. Yet men who fought with him still died in their multitude, and loneliness was his only companion in the night. He squinted at his sister, better than naked in the gale, and at the cloud conveyance that Enlil had chosen.

The tornado was winding toward them, like a great python upon the ground, sucking up grass and leaves and small animals of every sort. Its roaring made it hard to be heard.

Still, he called to Cime, "You'll find another way, then?"

And she said, "I promise, brother. Let's fight this battle fair, for once."

So he said, to the god in his head, *Pillager, leave off. Take Thine awful cyclone and depart. If You had wanted her to ride with us, a chariot or fleecy cart would have served us better.*

And Enlil said, all hot blood in his veins and pulsebeats in his head, *We could have her forever in those clouds. My Majesty would humble her. The roar of My might would teach her a woman's place.*

Once and for all time, Enlil, I will not inflict Thy supernal lust upon my sister. Now take Thine overweening Self and Thine overdone conveyance and get Thee hence.

Whap. Whoosh. Ssshup!

The tornado seeking Cime like a blind snake was gone. The silence in its wake was pure enough that he could hear her breathing.

Then she said, "Well, that's that. Now we hitch a ride." Hands above her head, she scooped her wind-blown hair and wound it round, fastening it with her diamond rods.

And Tempus had to look away from that body so displayed, all the seductiveness there, flouted boldly like a challenge.

"Hitch a ride?" He'd given the god's amulet to a child, because of her. He'd let Mano walk into a mael-strom, because of her. He'd left Lemuria behind, with his Tros horse and all chances of finding Sandia, be-cause of her. "You'd better have a plan, resources, and something better than a cloud conveyance at hand, woman," he growled.

He found his fists were balled, and his right one, where the archmage had hurt him, ached like a broken tooth.

He uncurled his fingers and turned away from her, walking blindly up the embankment, toward the weird slagged roadside with its yellow line.

This was truly an accursed world, he thought as his booted feet jarred on the black slag. The perfect place for Allegro and his kind to build a bastion. He remem-bered the empty husks of the adept's underlings, and Victor, all of whom had gone up with the house.

He hoped. The god's seeds of destruction were po-tent. If Stinger had done his job, only Allegro, who was with Tempus, had escaped to rise again. The others would be easy to replace, but hard to reconstitute, taken down by the god's own force of lightning.

He barely heard Cime coming up behind him, until the *tap*, *tap*, *tap*, *tap*, of her stilt-heeled shoes came hurrying after his heavy tread.

He hardly saw her. His eyes were blind with fury and unconnsumated longing. Not only had she rejected him, but his god's helping hand as well. So why did he care? She'd proclaimed them unrelated, and all their long lives a sham where one another were concerned.

So he should leave it. Leave her to her own devices. Find his way back to the door by which he'd come here, and go back through to Lemuria. He could nearly feel the velvet of his Tros' muzzle snuffling in his palm. He could nearly smell the sweet hair of Sandia's shepherd, almost hear her throaty invitation.

"Wait, Tempus," Cime called. "Slow down. What are you running from, yourself?"

That turned him in his tracks. "Keep a civil tongue in your head, sis—woman, or you'll fight this through upon your own."

It must have been his tone that made her stop, and blink, and cock her head at him. For a moment he thought that Allegro's magic had reached across time and space to catch her soul again, but then he realized she was merely mulling what he'd said.

"Testy, aren't we, Riddler? You've left this part to me, now bear with me. A car will come for us." She pulled her rods free and her dark hair tumbled around her shoulders.

He shifted slightly, looking over her shoulder because it always hurt to look at her when she was like this: full of contest, making all their strife a game with sex at the bottom of it and taunts laced throughout it.

While he watched, she touched her rods' tips and put their points to her forehead. She closed her eyes. He'd never seen her do such a thing and he stiffened, expecting he knew not what: self-immolation, explosion, discorporation. The rods were deadly.

But she didn't disappear, and on her face a tiny smile grew, full of mischief and guile.

When she took down the rods, he'd nearly decided that she was right: they were unrelated; the god was sulking, withdrawn from his flesh. Now was the time to settle what lay between them for eternity.

No woman could be what he'd made her. It was only that she was forbidden that caused her touch and form and voice to be so much more desirable than any other's.

He'd had enough women to populate the fields around

him with a village or two of strapping boys. He'd had
enough violence in his lifetime to win a dozen wars.
He'd commanded armies and freed countries and suppressed revolts. But he'd never won out over his own
feelings, where Cime was concerned.

He took a step toward her, then another. She swung
around, presenting her round buttocks and slim waist,
one hand shading her eyes as she looked off into the
distance where the road twisted out of sight.

He could come up behind her and banish all their
doubts and all their unrequited craving. He was bound
to do it, here and now, where he could consider it his
choice, not hers, not Enlil's, not a trick of fate.

He was just about to put his hands on her when a
second pair of lights came round the bend, and with it,
the roar of a demon car and its oily stink blown down-
wind by the same gusts that touched her before he
could.

For an instant, he considered wrestling her into the
bushes and letting the car go by, or lifting her skirt with
a hand around her neck and doing the deed there and
then. He could accomplish the task before the car arrived, he told himself.

But he hesitated, and then the car was upon them.
She backed a step, then another, and collided with
him, so close was he. Heat flared up his trunk where
she bumped him. She turned around. "Our ride, dear.
As I promised."

The car was black and as it slowed, Tempus had an
awful premonition of who might be inside, driving it
with such abandon.

Stones skittered from under its wheels and smoke
issued up from them as the demon car squealed to a
halt. The rear door opened on its own, and the door on
the far side as well. The glass of the car was blackened.
It rolled down far enough for a hand to beckon and a
voice to call, "Come on. Get inside."

Cime, hiking up her skirt, crossed before the car and
got in the far side.

Tempus had no choice but to enter the door to the rear.

He knew, by then, whose car it was he climbed into, whose door he shut with a thud.

Regretting he hadn't taken Cime while he could, he settled upon the rearward bench and said, "Ash, I told you, go away."

"But Cime invited me," said the dream lord. "Seems you need a little help, Riddler, in this strange, forsaken land."

"Not your sort of help, Ash," Tempus said, but the demon car's roar drowned out his words. Then he was pushed against the benchback as Askelon's demon car sped away in a squeal of tires and a skitter of stones.

Cime was saying, ". . . Allegro, and finish this. Then we'll see about these avatars his god keeps planting everywhere—if you'll oblige us."

"It's good to see you, Cime," said her ex-husband, the dream lord. "And you, Tempus: life to you, and everlasting glory."

Tempus considered strangling Askelon from behind, an appropriate response to being saluted in the fashion of the armies by such an entity.

The entelechy of the seventh sphere read his silence and said, "Come now, Tempus. All old debts are being forgiven today. Once we've finished this, we'll all know where we stand."

"What are you getting out of this, Ash? Not Cime, she's made that clear."

"Safety for dreaming in its place. An end to supernal meddling in mortal affairs—oh, don't worry, your god won't die of anything I can do. But the wizards are out of balance, even you can see that. Strife, as you once said, is all and king of all—but only when there are two sides. Man has his two sides, and the universe has its: waking and sleeping, life and death, hot and cold, light and dark—"

"Boring and simplistic," Tempus finished for him. "A

fighter of mine named Mano said the universe likes events, and doesn't care what kind."

"Ah, Tempus, I keep forgetting how primitive your age was," Ash said, and did something to the bumper of the demon car so that soft music welled up and Cime sat back, her head against the seat, staring up at the ceiling with a dreamy smile playing about her lips.

"Sophisticated enough to keep you and your dreamlife at bay," Tempus growled. Cime's breasts were rising and falling as if she were nearly asleep. The soothing music crested and swelled with a beauty no musicians of Tempus's age could have emulated.

"An event, dear Tempus—*friend* Tempus, is predicated on a change from one state to the other: before and after, then and now, here and gone. An event implies duration, a complex set of conditions altering space in time. And that friend of yours was right: the universe is impelled toward change. And those of us who are its guardians must change with it. Do you understand me?"

"Are you offering a truce, Ash? After all these—"

"Don't count the years. We'll finish these sorcerers who are begging to have their imbalances corrected." The dream lord smiled a dream smile that made Tempus look away. Cime was already asleep. He could hear her measured breathing.

The music was making his head swim. He reached for the doorhandle: he could thrust open the door of the demon chariot, throw himself out, roll when he hit the road, and survive the worst of that. Better than letting Ash lull him into a netherworld of inconsequence and instability, where nothing was real and everything mutable.

"Say to me," Tempus demanded with all the strength he could muster in his voice, "that you're not on magic's side in this battle."

"I'm never on the side of excess. I'm on the side of humanity. Remember, Tempus, I'm the keeper of their dreams. And they are young, dreaming dreams of power they're not mature enough to wield."

"And may never be," Tempus said sleepily, his eyelids starting to close.

But he couldn't sleep. He wouldn't. Ash would get inside his head and there, the dream lord couldn't be controlled. Fear flushed the tiredness from him, and the god came rushing back into the void of supernal sulkiness that He'd left. And Enlil said, *See, fool? You need Me.*

Tempus couldn't argue with that. He sat up straight. He rubbed his eyes. The car in which they'd been traveling down a winding, pastoral road was parked against a wall.

There was no one in the driver's seat. Cime was softly snuffling in her sleep.

And on the wall, a yellow sign said, "Compact only."

Tempus had made no deal with Askelon, no compact of any kind with the dream lord. But the letters taunted him as he woke Cime.

He'd rather fight through upon his own and lose than think he'd won because he'd let Askelon lend a hand.

So he said to her, when she'd knuckled her eyes and pulled down her dress over her knees, "Let's quit this place. We've won enough. The god is willing, if you are."

"And leave Allegro free to start things up again? After what his slimy minions did to me? Or had you forgotten that?"

He'd forgotten how Cime thought and what she was: she could never let anything go, forgive a slight, or leave an insult unavenged.

"A matter of honor is it? With you?" She was the least honorable of creatures, full of tricks and bound to no standard except victory.

"A matter of honor, Riddler." She was angry still, to call him that. As she rifled a secret pocket in the front bumper of the car, her face was flushed with passion. "Even you can understand honor."

So they got out of the car, not knowing where they were, in their disheveled state, and started looking for an exit or a stairway to get them out of this place, which Cime was sure was an "Underground garage, ninny. Nothing to worry about."

But she hadn't been with his party when one of the demon cars exploded in such a place, taking Rath with it to hell.

Chapter 24:

RETURN TO NEW YORK

Either they were back in New York City, where Tempus had arrived upon this plane, or Askelon had turned Meridian into a simulacrum of New York to trap them.

Tempus was not entirely sure which was the case.

Cime was certain, though, of where they were, and led him hither and yon, her head high, her mouth a thin line. She'd taken a wallet from the compartment in the car, and put it in her little purse. So between the two she seemed to have whatever she needed: scrip for hiring yellow demon cars, a square packet that secured them lodging in an inn of unparalleled splendor, outside of which horses stamped in their traces before spindly carts.

Tempus had stopped to look over the horses, and pet the eldest of them, who'd finished munching in his feedbag. A horse so old, half dray, with great feathers on his feet and booted hooves, should be out to pasture. But the horse didn't seem to mind the light work he was doing, and Tempus was comforted by the line of carthorses.

"Ride in the park, sir?" a girl in odd costume asked him: this was her cart, a carriage with a canvas top and velvet seats and laprobes lying about inside.

The old horse cocked an eye at him, and whuffled softly.

He looked beyond, to the park across the way where green trees abounded, and thought he'd been this way before. Perhaps it was the same park where he'd seen the cavalryman and taken his mount.

"No," he said, to the lady driver, "I'm waiting for someone."

Then Cime was back, flying down granite steps in low boots and leathers. "We're all settled, dear. Our room. Some clothes . . . I had some things sent up for—Oh."

Something changed in her pale eyes as she looked at him and the horse, who'd stuck his head forward so that Tempus could scratch under his jowls. "A ride in the park, is it?"

She and the carriage woman conferred, and off they went, seated in the cart, though Tempus longed to drive.

He could nearly feel the slick long reins in his hands. He could nearly sense the horse's mouth at the end of them, and all the everyday wonder of communication between man and honest beast.

Amid the demon cars, he was worried for the horse at first, but then realized the horse knew his way, and was not afraid.

If the horse was not afraid of the demon cars, or of this place with its piles of rock like dwelling caves stacked one upon the other, why should Tempus be? He'd been to stranger citadels than this, and more malefic.

Cime cuddled up beneath the lap robe and stroked the moth-eaten fur of it. Beneath, her other hand brushed his thigh. "This is something I never thought we'd do. I told them you were in a play, dress rehearsal—that's why no one remarked the sword. But you'll need to . . ."

"Stop the cart," Tempus said, throwing the robe off their laps. "Cime, get out. Driver, get this horse out of here."

He knew what he'd seen: a rustling in bushes, a blur out of the corner of his eye.

"What?" Cime wanted to know. "Why? Gods, you spoil everything—"

"You think this is a tryst? That Askelon brought us here for a romantic idyll? Get out and look about you, sister, or go back with the horse and cart."

He vaulted to the ground.

Cime hurried to the driver's side and told the woman something, giving her a piece of paper, then another, and telling her to hurry on her way.

And then she was following Tempus into the meadow. He knew what he'd seen. He was accustomed to the weather here, to the gray and seamless dusks that lasted far too long, to the slide into night that had none of the clarity of sunsets where he'd been born.

He'd seen a blur of many colors, a place where the grass and air were . . . not right.

Such a place was the mark of a portal through which a mage could come and go.

While they were seeking Allegro, Allegro had been seeking them. He didn't need the god to tell him, although the god did tell him, *Take care, mortal servant. Take care.*

Enlil only thought of Tempus when the danger was severe. Still, he headed toward the spot he'd seen, through the nearly deserted meadow.

A dog barked, somewhere. Beyond that, what he heard was useless, masked by the dull roar of demon cars and all the city's bustle.

Cime's curses were clear enough, though. And all her complaints that they were "Walking into this on someone else's terms. Let's pick the time and the place, not let them do it."

He had to remind himself that she'd been Allegro's prisoner: cowardice was exusable when it came from memory.

"Damn you, don't do this now." She tugged on his arm.

This time he stopped, looked down at her, and said, "Why not now?"

"I'm not ready."

"Then get ready."

She stared into his eyes and, very slowly, took the rods down from her hair. "Let's do it, then," she said at last. "Damn Ash to all he's due, and both of us as well."

"I'll live with that," Tempus said, and let his own hand curl on his swordhilt, to judge the danger by its heat.

They walked toward the blurry spot. And walked. And walked. And walked some more.

The meadow grew before them, and all around, the city receded. Clouds came down and nestled on the tree tops, so that there was no city at all after a time, only an arena of autumn meadow and grass and trees, ceilinged by a tent of cloud.

Their breath went noisily into their lungs. Their body movements were loud and, as he drew his sword, the grate of the blade against its scabbard nearly made him shiver.

"Are we really still in New York?" Cime wanted to know.

He turned to answer that it didn't matter, and realized that she was beside him, on his right, and it had seemed so natural that he'd not thought a thing about it. All this time, and they'd never gone into an engagement with her on his right like any other fighter.

He hesitated. Would she make him slow, there? Would she distract him, dull his edge, because he'd spent so long protecting her?

Her eyes were rebellious. "Don't you say a word. Let's find the scabby sorcerer, dispatch him, and get out of here."

"As you wish," he said, because she deserved to hear it, and because he probably should have let this happen long ago.

There was no taunt in her face now, no contention in her manner—at least, not where he was concerned.

They walked forward, together, toward the blur where magic waited.

And it felt good to him to have her there. He dug in his beltpouch and found the one seed he'd been saving out.

"If you need it," he said. He didn't have to tell her what the seed was for.

An honorable death in the service of the god was preferable to eternity in the clutches of an archmage such as Allegro. She said, "My thanks," and slipped it into a pocket. Then she began tapping one rod's tip upon the other.

She tapped a cadence with the rods, and every time their tips touched, a spark flew. The sparks rose above their heads, and stayed there, like personal stars.

Then the stars began to spin, and to stream out behind them as they made their way toward the growing blur.

The turf beneath Tempus's feet was different now: spongier, with longer grass. And above, the constellation Cime was manufacturing spread out, defying the featureless tent above.

She said, after they'd been walking far too long without closing the distance between them and the blur, "I've got to get us closer. Will you strike the next spark with your sword and bat it toward the portal?"

"My pleasure," he said. "I'm glad you have a plan in mind." Out of the corner of his eye, he'd begun to see things moving among the trees: dark things and slimy things and things with unformed shapes that nevertheless had eyes that glowed.

"On my mark," she suggested.

Tap.

He swung wide and hard at the spark that flew from the rods, as it floated upwards to join the others above their heads.

When the spark connected with the tip of his sword he felt a shock that ran through him like fire. And a concussion jolted him as if he'd tried to bat the bedrock of the very earth.

But the spark flew straight and true, and in its wake,

all the other stars from Cime's wand followed in a stream like a comet's tail.

The spark he'd struck was growing bright as it streamed through the air toward the portal. Streamers spewed from it, and the streamers seemed to ignite the tops of the trees at the clearing's edge and even the clouds above their heads.

Fire was everywhere but where they trod, and in the fire, Tempus could hear unholy screaming.

"Don't look. Don't let yourself be distracted," she warned.

He paced her, determined not to question, but only to fight through to the blur that was closer now, as if tethered by the shooting spark.

The spark was huge and round and from it to them, all the star-sparks had lined up, making a constellation above their heads that was a net of stars that seemed to keep the fire at bay.

On either side, the fire raged, and things howled there. Tempus didn't look away from the portal, but his peripheral vision saw shapes writhing in the flames.

He told himself that if he got out of this with body and soul, he was going to let Ash know that sending them into a battle such as this without fair warning wasn't Tempus's idea of help.

He was beginning to sweat from the fire's heat. Its roar was deep and full-throated and augmented by the screams of whatever magical foes it had caught inside.

And the line of bright stars leading to the portal was sure and straight over their heads, so that the blazing clouds above could not fall upon them, but only rained flame on either side.

"When we get there," Cime said, "how will you have it?"

"This sword or your rods in Allegro, and I'll be content."

He thought he saw her nod, but there was smoke everywhere. Not even her net of stars could keep away so much smoke.

The whole forested ring was ablaze, and things were hurling out of it on either side, and slithering out of it, and rolling out of it, all afire.

Great snakes with darting tongues; six-legged beasts with burning fur; hump-backed fiends whose warts were popping; demons with flaming wings who seemed to fall from the clouds and crash. Everywhere, but under their net of stars, evil burned.

And Cime kept tapping her rods together, so that the net of sparks about them grew wider, and began to drape down on either side.

Just when he could see the portal clearly, he heard someone call his name.

"Don't turn," she warned. "It might be a trick."

But Tempus knew Mano's voice. He called out, "Here, come here with us."

Relief flooded him such as he didn't think he still could feel, to know that Mano had survived.

"Want a little help, Commander?" Mano said, ducking under the net of stars as if he were accustomed to this kind of fight.

"You're welcome, Mano, to whatever piece of this you wish."

"And my friend, here?"

That made Tempus look away, to his left. Mano had Stinger, wide-eyed and open-mouthed, in tow.

"Oh no," Cime said. "Mano, how could you?"

"Ah—well, we're here. Seemed like a good idea at the time. He's got some amulet of yours, Commander. And weapons of mine."

Stinger grinned broadly and held up a thunderwand.

Cime, for the first time since she'd begun, stopped tapping her rods. "Those things won't kill a—never mind. You two take the rearguard: face backwards. Don't come through the portal."

"Commander?" Mano wanted to know.

"Keep moving, all of you. Cime, your rods . . ."

"Certainly, sir."

"Mano, with Stinger on your right, you'll have all the fight you need, back here."

The god wanted what the god wanted. Tempus was making it clear that he didn't want these others in his care. "You got here on your own, you two. You'll get home the same way."

"Tempus, you're not mad?" said the boy as he and Mano fell in behind Tempus and Cime.

"It's Mano you must worry about, Stinger." Tempus knew the signs. "You two have this place to keep, and we have ours."

Cime was muttering to herself that Tempus's meddling god was a worse problem than all the sorcerers in a dozen hells.

At that moment, he wouldn't have argued.

He fastened his eyes on the portal and his mind on the task ahead, and listened to Cime's rods tapping out a battle rhythm, and nearly forgot about the two moderns until the star net fell between them.

Mano, backlit by fire and accompanied by Stinger, looked through the net at him. "So?"

"So you'll fight your war, and we'll fight ours. Life to you, Mano, and everlasting glory. And to you, Stinger."

It was absolutely necessary to say those words to these men—one hardly more than a boy—whom the god had chosen.

"And to you, Riddler," said Mano with a shy smile, as if he'd always known enough to do it.

Stinger's young face was transported with excitement. In his hand, he held one of Mano's thunderwands. The god's amulet dangled around his neck. "Tempus, the god's been telling me— "

"—everything you need to know. That's the way of it, Stinger."

Tempus turned away, not wanting to look through the net at them any longer. The god was telling him in no uncertain terms where his duty lay.

And the portal he then faced was open to accept them, wide-flung and full of whirling colors.

He looked to his right. "Ready?" he said.

"I thought you'd never ask," Cime replied, and picked up the cadence of her rods.

Three more steps they took, and then she stopped her tapping.

Everything around but the portal and the net of stars disappeared.

Her rods began glowing in her hands and his sword shone brighter.

She said, "I'll clear the way," and from the rods issued a bolt of searing light so bright it made his eyes water.

From somewhere in the portal, a scream resounded.

"Now," she suggested.

But he was already moving. His speed was upon him. The god was in him, riding high on his shoulders, it almost seemed.

One more time, he charged into an unknowable situation. This time, on his right, was the most precious companion he'd ever fought beside. If he'd joined forces with her sooner, what might he have avoided?

But the risk was so great, even now, with the god there in him, it rankled.

And yet she was fighting right beside him, keeping pace with wide and nimble strides, as they leaped across the portal's threshold.

Into emptiness.

Into the abyss.

Into nothingness.

And out.

Onto a harder ground, a darker battleplain, a colder wind.

And there, finally, was Allegro, girded for battle with his true adherents all about him. A wall of serpents rose behind the archmage. A flight of demons circled overhead, phosphorescent in the dim light.

And the archmage himself came forward, thrice the height and width of a man, with all the carnage he'd ever instigated writ upon his flesh.

It was Cime who parried his first blow with her rods, who thrust aside a bolt of plasma from a pointing fingertip.

And that brought Tempus to the fore. He couldn't let Cime be hurt.

The archmage was calling her, coming forward on ponderous feet, saying, "Come, come, woman, and find your destiny." All over his huge wide face, horrid scenes of depradation and degradation played out: there was a vision of Cime in her grave, with long white hair and wizened face and ravaged flesh, her curly fingernails clutching her cheek in horror. And there was a vision of Cime undead, among the damned, which even Tempus couldn't face.

So horrible was Allegro to look upon, and so much did Tempus need to spare Cime what he could, that he leaped with all his strength and all his speed, as high as he could into the air.

Then the god lifted him up, it seemed. Or fate took a hand. He could dimly hear Enlil screaming a battlecry through his throat. He could barely sort out the features of the mass of flesh toward which he hurtled.

He knew only that he must shut the eyes of the archmage Allegro forever, and then the visions of Cime's fate would fade.

He remembered hitting something soft. He remembered bouncing off and grabbing a hank of hair with his right hand, then dangling there, hacking away at the great orbs in Allegro's face.

He hacked, screaming wordlessly, until he was showered with blood and fluid, and white stuff like the albumin of an egg.

And he hacked more, while something inside him raged and something else, outside him, taunted him that he couldn't banish all evil by destroying one archmage.

But it had been an archmage who'd cursed him and Cime long ago, an archmage who'd made his life a living hell, lost him any sense of humanity, made him a caretaker and a weary servant.

So he stabbed and he fought and he hardly felt it when something brushed him from the face of Allegro and he fell, because Allegro fell with him, toppling to the ground atop him, crushing him beneath.

In utter darkness, Tempus could barely move. Yet his sword was in his hand and that sword was hot, still, and angry.

And the god was in his head and that god was bold still, and untiring.

He struggled for breath, for the weight on him was too great for his chest to rise and fall.

He struggled to slide out, to slither out, to hack his way out from under Allegro.

He struggled with all his might. And when that was gone and he was spent, he called upon the god for aid.

Allegro's flesh was dead weight. He was caught under a dead thing in some nameless place. Alone.

His lungs were burning. Flecks danced before his eyes.

He couldn't get a breath.

In his head, he told the god, *I hope You're happy, and have spent me in a good cause. Take care of my sister, if You love me.*

And he prepared, as best he could, for whatever would happen next.

He'd never thought to come to his body's end and still be conscious; he'd always healed from every wound. He was not afraid, or even tired, neither regretful nor demanding of some afterlife.

He was merely cold.

Chapter 25:

A TASTE OF ETERNITY

There were clouds, now, and these were white and fleecy, with pink and golden nap. And there was a person closer to hand, or at least it seemed to Tempus that there was.

This person was picking him up, lifting him from the bed of clouds in strong, dark arms. A face looked down at him, eyes as compassionate as forever and as clear as pure water.

The beautiful face of the Slaughter Priest, Abarsis, smiled down on him and Abarsis said, "Dear Tempus, have you come to let me show you your place in heaven? Or are you just a visitor?"

"Stepson," Tempus said, though he could not hear his own voice, "I don't know. I don't understand . . ."

"Don't be confused. Don't be frightened," said Abarsis in his velvet voice. "All things change, but nothing ends. You have given all of us so much, fought so long and so hard . . . the god, and all who love you, welcome you. But it's up to you. You have the choice."

Tears were running down Abarsis' cheeks, along his glowing skin.

Tempus knew he lay in the arms of the Slaughter Priest like a baby. He remembered taking Abarsis up in his arms when the Stepson had died.

Nothing had ever frightened him more than death. At the end of everything, this moment waited. And he'd known life for so long . . .

"Ssh, Tempus. Don't be afraid. It's only life that you'll leave behind, not yourself. Yourself is what you built in life. All the best of you is here with me, for safekeeping. So make a choice."

"I still don't understand." But he was growing uneasy, in another man's arms, held like a babe. Over Abarsis's shoulders he could see faces he'd known, and a great high gate, and an expanse of . . . *place* . . . he couldn't comprehend.

"Heaven isn't a resthome for fighters, my lord Tempus. It's not a memory of what once was. It's a new beginning, another chance at a greater prize. All of us who've come here today love you better than any other. What you've taught us and what we know now is a gift of the god."

Abarsis's tears were flowing freely and Tempus wanted suddenly to stand alone, to stand upright, like a man. If he still was one.

"Put me down, Stepson," Tempus said although he was sure he had no mouth to speak with.

"Not yet, Commander. Not until you're sure you'll stay."

"A choice," he heard himself say.

"If you're too tired. If you're too lonely. If the sacrifices are too great—come with us. The world will get along without you. But the god loves you, and if you still love us . . . it's not written for you to die until you've given all you have to give."

"So what is this?"

"The god tests no man beyond his measure. And you hold the god better than any other vessel. This is your place, that you and the god have made. You can come here anytime. But the god wants you on His earth, to testify and be alive."

The Slaughter Priest leaned down and kissed Tempus

on the forehead. "Riddler, let the god be in you without qualm, and let the children learn their lessons. And take what life has to give you without holding back. Or walk with me, another way, forever."

He knew what Abarsis was saying now, and he felt the gentle sadness of the Slaughter Priest overwhelm him. Behind Abarsis, so many of his fighters stood, and on none of those faces was anything but welcome. Yet none reached out a hand to him.

Everyone waited to see what he would do.

A choice.

A life lived without regret rolled out before his mind's eye, and he knew what he must do.

"It's the god's choice, not mine," he said.

"Then we'll see you when the time is right, and mount a celebration in all the heavens," said Abarsis, and let him go.

He fell free, through the clouds and elsewhere. He fell for a long while, with the sights of heaven in his head.

He fell until he found his body, and therein he was cold and full of pain, gasping for breath and covered with ichor that steamed as the corpse of Allegro decomposed around him.

And over him was Cime, pushing pieces of Allegro away and cleaning goo from his face and weeping freely.

"Gods' rot," she sniffed, running the back of her hand under her nose, "I thought you were actually dead, you bastard. You scared me. Don't ever do that again."

She fell on top of him, hugging him, telling him what she'd threatened to do to Enlil if Tempus was truly dead.

He pushed her away and struggled up on his elbows, staring around him. "Don't threaten the god, Cime. Don't tempt fate." He could still see Abarsis's face, and all his fighters in heaven. And if it were a dream, then it was the first dream he'd had in eons.

Everyone knew that men were given signs in their dreams.

He looked around him, and suddenly he recognized the place where he lay. Before him was the door to Lemuria. Behind him was the New York night.

He said, "Get up. Let's go. Through that door. As far as I'm concerned, this battle's done and we won it."

"What of your students, Mano and Stinger?"

"They're the god's, not mine. And I don't think we could find them if we tried. I've never found this place before but once. I don't want to lose it."

"Through that door?" Cime looked at it critically.

"Right now. Here, help me up. Give me a hand."

She checked the rods in her hair first, to make sure they were both secure. Then she reached down and helped him to his feet and, arms around each other, they limped over to the heavy door.

"You're not hurt?" he thought to ask.

"Nothing I can't survive. Which is more, until just now, than I thought of you. Here, let me help you with that latch. You're weak as a baby."

He wasn't, but he let her help.

Iron hinges creaked, and the door slid open just enough. "Don't bother with the rest. Come, slide through," he said, suddenly frightened that somehow he'd lose her again in this last moment when they could be separated by caprice or evil.

Then they were beyond the door. Cime slipped free of him as he leaned back upon it, closing it with his weight.

"Where are we?" Cime asked breathlessly, looking around.

"You don't know? Lemuria," he said, and slid down the door, all the strength he'd mustered gone.

In his head, the god said, *See, fey mortal? Safe and sound, with your sister. Just as I promised.*

Tempus didn't point out that the god had promised

no such thing; Tempus had only asked Enlil to take care of her.

He watched her, moving about, touching the beautiful things in the room that was still as he'd left it, and he thanked the god shamelessly.

Without Enlil, this was one battle he'd never have won.

Chapter 26:

LEMURIAN SUNSET

All was as Tempus remembered it: Pinnacle House was ashimmer. A thousand candles burned in man-high chandeliers; mirrors played tricks on the eye. Indoor plants stretched skyward, where balconies crisscrossed above a tall man's head. Banners wafted there, brightly colored flags and tattered standards, barely more than streamers from forgotten wars.

And yet, all was subtly changed, and Tempus couldn't help wondering if this were so because, on New Year's Eve in Lemuria, the Storm God and Chiara, the Evening Star, had lain together.

And then he recalled something that the Evening Star had said to him, when explaining the room of many windows that Cime hadn't yet seen: *"For Sandia's Shepherd, it's a chance to change the present by finding a key in the past. For Mano, and I think for Rath, it's the present that has brought them—the present where they struggle to make futures right. For Ash, it's a dispensation from those he serves, a chance to make an error right."*

Had Ash done it? Was the presence of Tempus and Cime, here and now, part and parcel of some remedy? Or all of it?

The thought leached the triumph from his bones as if

he lay on a bed of lime, not upon the Evening Star's
fine feather bed, watching Cime realize they were in
another woman's empty boudoir, wrinkling her nose at
a hundred pillows drenched with Chiara's perfume.

Things were different in Lemuria, he could feel it in
his bones. The room where he'd lain with the Evening
Star was awash in sunset, not swathed in the shadows of
New Year's Eve. But it was more than that. The place
felt . . . quiet.

Chiara, the Evening Star, must know the answer.
She must be somewhere about. She'd offered him
Lemuria and all its power once. He hadn't thought
until now how he might be welcomed back with Cime
in tow.

But he'd fought the archmage of archmages and won.
He'd handle the women, somehow.

Or so he told himself, until Cime sniffed again and
came to the bed, grabbing his hand to drag him off it.

"Come on, lazy oaf. On your feet. I want to see this
place and find some food, its master, another bedroom—"

"Mistress," he said, getting up with a grunt.

"Mistress, is it?" Her brow arched. Behind her,
through the window she'd thrown open, sunset colors
flooded, backlighting her in red and gold and purple,
turning her skin ruddy and warm.

In that light of rose and amber, she looked almost
like the girl he'd loved, so long ago, when love was
reason enough to challenge an archmage.

"Mistress," he affirmed. "This place is all spoken for,
Cime. Don't get too comfortable. Or covetous. Surely
you've heard stories of Lemuria—"

"More than I can credit, brother."

They'd had parents, futures, hopes and dreams like
all young lovers. They'd had the rocky shore and the
mountainous coast and no inkling of what their love
would cost. He'd burned his sacrifice before the god
and asked for strength to fight the archmage and pre-
vail, to keep Cime from a marriage bed she'd abhorred.

And they'd lain once together, thinking that if she

wasn't a virgin, then that might break the troth her parents had made with an adept whose power children couldn't know.

And from that, all this had sprung. Lemuria was a magic place, a place of new beginnings. Ash had come on New Year's to undo an error. Not even the Evening Star had known why Tempus came.

"What *is* the matter, Tempus? You look like you've seen a herd of ghosts."

"Our own," he growled, and moved away from her, past Chiara's chamber of wind and rain, toward the door that once led toward the common rooms, and once led to his destiny—to America, to New York, to Allegro.

His hand hesitated on the knob.

"Now what?" Cime wanted to know, right behind him.

The smell of her was different from Chiara. Perhaps the clash of scents was what made him dizzy, made his ears ring.

"You do it," he muttered, and stepped back.

"Do what? Open the door?" She turned from it, to him, took his face in her hands and made him look her in the eye. "Are you ill? Some aftereffect of the battle? Riddler, say something."

"I . . ." How could he explain to her what he didn't understand himself? Perhaps his trip to heaven had sucked the spine from him; perhaps he should have stayed with Abarsis after all. In an infinitely weary voice, he said, "Sometimes that door goes one place, sometimes another. Try your luck."

"Fine," she said. "You just stand behind me, and we'll get you to the kitchen without mishap."

She was angry, he finally realized, that he hadn't lured her to the bed, or thrown her there, or put his arm around her to watch the sunset transform the sea with its glory.

But that sea led to Meridian, and to Sandia, and to the sort of place he'd just been.

Suddenly, he wanted to leave her to find out Lemuria's

secrets on her own, get his horse, and ride out of here alone. Right now, before whatever strangeness he sensed here got hold of him and Lemuria bound him in its web.

Lemuria, before the fall, or after? he'd asked the sentry at the gate, how long ago?

Cime, good as her word, took hold of the doorknob fearlessly and turned it, pulling the door inward. "See?" she said. "A hallway. A corridor, nicer than some, with a marble floor and plastered walls and . . ." She stuck her head out with exaggerated stealth, "absolutely no one, human or inhuman, to be seen. Come on now, Riddler, let's get you fed and some drink in you to give you some courage. We really must find our hosts; otherwise, I'll feel like we're intruding. "

And out she went, one hand reaching back to grab him by the collar and pull him in her wake.

Well, it wasn't a sorcerer's den; it wasn't a confuting city street with demon cars abounding; it wasn't a meadow ringed in fire or a fleecy heaven where all his solemn ghosts were there to greet him.

But it was as quiet as the grave.

Down the hall they went, past room after room: his bedchamber, that he'd been given here before; the room where Faun, Shepherd of Sandia, had stayed; Mano's room, and Rath's . . .

Tempus closed his eyes, finally realizing what was oppressing him. Always, in the past, he'd found time to mourn for his dead. He'd had his fighters with him. They'd made biers and played funerary games and said the words a god demands over their dead.

There had been honors given to the dead, in those days. There had been respect for lives spent, and lives saved. And there had been time, after a battle, to readjust: the long trek home, on which you healed, and talked things through, or not. But always, he'd had his cadre, his horses, his ritual and his sense that what was sacrificed was worth the price.

This time, he'd fought on alien turf in a battle he

barely understood, for principle only. And principle was not enough. Rath had given his life for a future he could never live to see, no matter if he'd survived. Men shouldn't go blindly into battle: going blindly into death was bad enough.

The warrior in Tempus demanded a reason for fighting, one that was worth the cost. And the reason he'd fought the archmage was . . . Cime.

Or so he'd told himself, because no man who understood the world was fool enough to risk himself for words, or images in a Lemurian magic window, or a future he'd never live to enjoy.

Yet, back here in Pinnacle House, he wanted to go straightaway to the scrying room, to the pillars with their magic windows, and see if Rath's death and Mano's sacrifice and Stinger's initiation had changed anything.

All of which made him seem more a fool than he could bear.

If Faun's Sandian seas were still dead, then that was what the god decreed. He hadn't fought Allegro for ideals, for promises of paradise, or for freedom itself. He'd fought to save a loved one, to save his pride, because he'd been fighting that battle for so many years.

It occurred to him now, in the empty halls of Lemuria, that if men could wake up one morning and not be in the midst of old and bitter wars, then the fighting might stop. If no one was counting slights unavenged from time immemorial, if no one was lying in wait to even a score, then who would start a war?

And who would fight one?

In his head, the god grumbled, *You're getting old, mortal servant. Apes fight over territory; ants fight battles to the death; the beasts of the field fight over females; scavengers fight over scraps of meat. And you fight yourself, which is Myself, because you're afraid to have a moment that you are not at war. There's peace in death, avatar; there's you in Me; there's life ripping out from womankind and screaming its way into the*

world in a sac of blood and mother's anguish. Stop this
maundering, and take the woman before you. That's all
that's wrong with you, and all that's wrong with Me.

He felt the god settle in him, closer than Enlil had
ever meshed with him before. He felt the melancholy
lift, and in its place came Their customary hungers:

Life was a gift from heaven. How you lived it was
your worship. What you learned was your catechism.
What you taught was your ritual. What you took was
your blessing. What you gave was your sacrifice.

And in the end, it was all the god's favor, that you
lived in the world and looked through eyes that could
marvel at the wonders under heaven. The gods made
the earth so that they could roam upon it in the minds
of men and the bodies of the beasts of the field and the
bellies of volcanoes and the eagles in the air. As long as
the earth was fecund, there would be life and death and
birth and species would come and go, giving a manifold
god in all his different guises access to every experience
under heaven.

It was no less fit that Tempus live with Enlil in him,
and rout stupidity and evil and guide the world in war,
than it was that Cime should stalk Lemuria's halls demanding someone to fix her food and make her bed and
talk to her of gossip from all the ages.

Following her around Pinnacle House, Tempus began to count the dogs. The dogs had been there before.
They had great brown eyes like Chiara's, and athletic
bodies like Chiara's, and soon they were following Cime
and butting their heads up under her hand so that she
could scratch their ears.

When they finally found the door to the common
rooms, where the hearth had once blazed on New
Year's, the dogs disappeared.

Good. They were making him nervous. Worse, they
were making Enlil nervous. The god was up in his eyes,
looking around with a sharper vision than his own,
cataloging everything Lemurian as if He were an estate
executor taking inventory.

Here was fruit and wine in golden flagons, and the soft settees on which the quorum had convened.

"Sit, Tempus," said Cime, "have some grapes. I've eaten a handful and I'm not feeling any ill effects." She patted the settee before her.

This place was so beautiful, Tempus didn't even mind that it was out of time. It belonged nowhere. It was equally far from everywhere. It had, the god was sure, the best of every age of man, safe and saved for its own sake.

Before the fall, or after? Tempus asked Enlil straight out, alone with the god and Cime and the dogs in a deserted Pinnacle House.

But the god wouldn't answer.

Tempus ate a grape, to please her. He tasted the wine, because she insisted. Wine had never been his pleasure: he loved his body's skills too much to dull them, his mind's thoughts too much to blur them; his very nature was one of being, fully, and wine attenuated that.

Then, loosened from his self-control, he stood up and bawled at the top of his lungs, "Chiara! It's Tempus! Chiara, come here!"

A dog came trotting, a huge brindle mastiff in fine condition, with glowing eyes and shining fur and long, athletic legs. Dogs were called unclean in his youth, in the temples of his student days. Yet this dog smelled sweet and he let her put her muzzle against his thigh.

An awful suspicion was rising in him. Or perhaps it was just the wine.

He stroked the dog behind the ears and Cime said, "Now, isn't this nice? If we could live so well, even you might settle in, and find yourself more man than wargod. If only we could find this Chiara . . ."

"The Evening Star," he said, rubbing the dog's ears again, "will show herself to you when she's ready."

The more he looked at the mastiff, the more he thought the bitch was pregnant. Well, there was no harm in that.

He said, "Let me show you something, Cime."

"At last, you're coming out of it." Her face was bright as she got up to follow him, wineglass in one hand. "Do you think anyone would mind if I changed into clean clothes, should I find some?"

Before the god could even rumble in his head, Tempus said, "Treat this place as your own. No one will mind."

He led his sister into the room where the wisdom of Lemuria really was.

Here were the black pillars with their wondrous eyes, looking out onto different lands. All were dark, and he was disappointed.

He went to stand by the one where Faun had stood and stared upon her world's lifeless seas, and done what she could.

He'd sent her back bearing the god's seed and she'd been bold and brave and ready to depart. He'd hoped to see those seas, in the magic window, teeming, full of life.

But all the windows were black. Beyond, where the true windows looked out on Lemuria itself, night was falling.

Tempus had been afraid there might not be anyone living in Lemuria at all, just dogs; but beyond, down on the shore, he saw lights begin to shine.

"It's beautiful." Cime came up behind him. "I'm glad we came." She put an arm around him. "Let's find a room and settle in; whoever's here will surely be back soon."

And he couldn't think of a single reason not to do so. Enlil was up against his skin, but not demanding anything. Something in his heart said that for once, in this place suspended beyond time, all things were in their places.

All but he and Cime, and he'd come to terms with that.

He found the room that Chiara had given him, and it was as if he'd never left it, commodious and warm and clean. There was a robe in the closet and Cime said, "Oh good. I'll just put this on."

He knew where this was leading. There wasn't a single reason he could think of, not to let things go that way. They'd given so much for one another, so often, that denying their feelings was worse than a lie—it was denying life itself.

She stepped out of her tattered gown and flipped the white robe about her in an instant.

She was not the only one who turned coy.

He went to the bed and sat there, feeling clumsy, dirty, and suddenly cold. What if Enlil arose in him, all ravening and rough, and made of this one more pitched battle? He leaned back on the bed and watched his hand as he ran his fingers along its spread.

Before the fall, or after?

After, mortal. Long after. On the night We come here to take the helm. And my gift to Thee, unflagging servant, is a night alone with her. You and I are now and forever one, but I will withdraw My Majesty, since your woman cannot survive the sight of Me, and you may have her on your own.

Tempus didn't argue. He didn't ask, what about tomorrow? He merely unbuckled his swordbelt from his waist and took his boots from his feet and pulled off the coveralls Mano's people had given him, and then his own chiton underneath.

They looked at each other wordlessly, unashamed. They were not the children they had been, when all this started. Their years showed on them in strength and stance and caution, if not in wrinkle and in line.

She said, "God, I never thought we'd . . ."

"Nor I. Don't be afraid. It's only me."

And not the god, he meant.

She blinked back tears and rubbed her eyes. "We're going to disappoint each other," she quavered, taking one step and then another toward him. "I'm not sure I even recall how to do this . . . without a prize, without a plan, for its own sake . . ."

She crushed the robe around her and ran to the bed, sitting down beside him there, nearly doubled over as if her stomach hurt.

He said, "Then let's go at this another way. No time has passed. Nothing ever went wrong. We have no enemies. We have a night, free from care and war and magic . . ."

She leaned back against him and he made room for her.

When she lay under him, looking up into his eyes, she said with a little frown, "Didn't you say to me, in my prison, that you loved me?"

"I . . . may have said some such thing, in the heat of battle. But then again, it may have been the god. You know how long Enlil has wanted to be where I am now . . ."

"Well, say it again, then."

"I think that's too risky."

"Say it."

"As you recall, I said it once." Twice, but there was no need to argue.

She called him by a name not even she had used for a clutch of years, and he rolled them over, then looked up. "You first," he suggested.

So she said the words, and he said the words, and something left undone for eons was finished and united, there and then. And even though Enlil kept his bargain and stayed far from him, and the night held itself like a tent over them, still Tempus knew that this was an irrevocable thing that they did.

She, too, knew that love between them was a sacrifice, a union of forces, a consecration and an affirmation of life which would never happen in such a way again.

When it was done, he said, "I'm going to the Day's End Inn, to see my horse."

She said, "I'll come with you."

He said, "Are you sure?"

She rolled herself up in the covers and said, "Come on, out with it. What are you hiding?"

"The god thinks this is our place."

"What? You jest. What of . . . the Evening Star?"

"A title. Yours, if you want it. Be nice to the dogs, though, especially the pregnant one. I imagine you'll find servants about, now. And a few counsellors who'll be helpful."

"What's the catch?"

"Once every so often we throw a party and change some fates."

She nodded. "But, we're alone here?"

"I said, servants and such folk will be around. We had our privacy, as Enlil promised. You ought to know that's the truth, since there's not a mark on you after lying with me."

She lowered her eyelids. "I always knew you could be gentle, if you chose."

He wasn't going to argue. "I'm going to see about my horse." After the fall, there was no reason not to install her here, or to worry for her here. "Askelon's our closest neighbor, keep that in mind."

"You're leaving, aren't you?" She was up now, pulling the bedclothes with her.

"I'm going to get my horse, and bring him up here, if there are facilities. If not, we'll have to build some."

The Sandian situation could wait, until he'd learned to control the Lemurian windows and the gates into other realms.

He was content enough to see what the god wanted, and see Cime right, and bide his time. In Lemuria, he had all the time he wanted.

When he finally got free of her, and through the house, and outside into the town, he was surprised to see that night was done. They'd spent it all, and now the sun was rising.

With the sun came Enlil, filling him up and rustling around in his skull.

So, how was she, vassal?

Better than any woman We've ever had, Tempus told Enlil, to make the god jealous.

There were women in the streets, and men as well. There were some children, even, batting balls with sticks against whitewashed walls.

The Day's End Inn was as he'd left it, and his horse heard his footsteps and nickered loud enough to shake the rafters.

He took the Tros horse out of his stall and curried him for a long while, with brush and finishing cloth as well. Then he soaped and oiled all his tack and saddled up, bedroll behind his saddle.

When he swung up on the stallion's back, the Tros trumpeted his joy to be away, and pawed the ground. Tempus headed the horse out through the same gate he'd entered.

It might have been the same guard who was there, who waved and wished him well.

He was well enough. The horse under him was ready to run; the sun was blazing over the city's walls, and the sea was as blue as the eye of heaven.

Even the god could not have made a better day, after the fall in Lemuria. When he looked back over his shoulder, he could see Pinnacle House glittering.

Cime surely could be happy there, if anywhere. The horse under him was glad to see him and snorting with pleasure in the surf, striking the waves playfully with one forefoot as he ran.

Enlil and he were finished fighting over who was whom. They had brought all things into balance, within and without. From Pinnacle House, everywhere was accessible, and good and evil could be viewed as ebb tides and storm tides.

The danger of being overwhelmed was past. As for new storm tides, the windows of Lemuria monitored all things in their places.

All the strife of all the worlds was as close as Pinnacle House, and as far as Sandia. From here, he could go anywhere he must, do whatever he needed to do, keep his vigil. He could visit with his past, expand his present, mold his future. He could find his Sacred Band,

and bring them to a better place than anyplace but heaven.

From here, if it were needful, he could field an army, or stop one in its tracks. He could visit Meridian, if he chose, and deal as an equal with the dream lord. He could invite Mano, and even Stinger, for New Years. He could sortie even to the city at the edge of time, if he wished.

Anything was possible. Cime and he had made their peace. He had his favorite horse under him, and a truce with the god in his head. And since that god was Enlil, Lord Storm, god of war and part of him, eternally, he was content that this was so.